Cover design by Red Cape Graphic Design

Edited by P.J. Blakey-Novis, Red Cape Publishing

First Edition Published 2021 by Red Cape Publishing

To Alison Greene, the lady with a knack for titles.
Thank you for always being so supportive.

Where Shadows Move

Caroline Angel

Chapter One

"There are way too many people here," Kelli yawned. "What is everyone doing up so early on a Sunday?"

"Same as we are, stupid, they're all looking for a bargain." Sarah dropped her gold coin into the Rotary Club volunteer's cup and watched Kelli search her pockets for a coin. "Hey, I got you, don't stress."

Kelli blew her a kiss as she dropped the second coin and they stepped into the first aisle of the large open-air market, a rack of clothes was poking out too far meaning Sarah had to duck to get past. Kelli had found a dog and was already patting it before the owner dragged it away, the poor animal straining on its leash. Sarah turned to look at the clothes on the rack, a quick flick through and a cursory glance assured her they were not what she was looking for.

"Hey, Sezzy, look at these shoes!" Kelli held up a bright purple pair of stilettos, shiny yellow sequins adorning the heels. "Perfect for the office?"

Sarah laughed and shook her head as she walked to the next stall. Kelli went to the following stall and started to look through the bric-a-brac before moving on. The girls walked down the first aisle to the end, looking through promising stalls, avoiding the ones that looked expensive, or filled with things they had no interest in.

"I can see why you like coming here," Kelli said, trying on a hat before putting it back on a table. "This place is mad. I think Camberwell market is my new go-to on a Sunday when I don't want to sleep in."

"Hey, this would look good for work, yeah?" Sarah held up a black tailored jacket.

Kelli looked at it, her head tipped to one side. "I think you'll have to try it on, it's hard to say just looking at it like that."

Sarah pulled the hanger out of the jacket and slipped it on over her casual T-shirt. "Well?"

"Here, lemme take a picture on my mobile, you can see what you look like." Kelli snapped the pic and handed her phone to Sarah.

"I think it's good, I can wear it with heaps of things, you know, make them look more business suitable." Sarah left the jacket on and looked at the seller's other items, finding a couple of things that interested her. Kelli found a bag she liked and managed to haggle with the lady selling the items down to a very reasonable total.

The girls shoved their items into Sarah's tote bag and moved along, enjoying the atmosphere, finding bargains, things to laugh at, and a really good coffee and donut van to take a break at.

"You've got some real bargains there, some designer clothes and shit," Kelli sipped her cappuccino. "And I got heaps of stuff! I love that bracelet I got from that funny old bloke, it's super cool."

"We've only got a half hour left, the market closes soon," Sarah laughed as the announcement came over the loudspeakers, advising patrons to finalise their purchases as the market would soon be closing.

"You must be psychic, girl!" Kelli threw her empty coffee cup in the rubbish bin. "C'mon, I wanna look down the last aisle, see if I can find something to wear to Hannah's engagement party next Saturday."

"You going to that? I thought you had to work?"

"Nah, I swapped with Rita so I could get the night off. She needs the next weekend for a wedding or some shit."

Sarah stood up from the plastic chair and tossed her cup in the bin before following Kelli along the last aisle. They didn't find anything else to wear, but Kelli grabbed a couple of vintage books from a stall to use as props in her Instagram posts.

Sarah looked through the bric-a brac, not really seeing much that she liked, until she picked up a small pendant. It had a tiny stone, and as she turned it in her hands, she could see the light reflecting from the faceted cut, something cute and a little bit different.

The lady that owned the stall was already packing up, her little hatchback parked in the space behind her tables that overflowed with odds and ends. Knowing they were out of time, Kelli quickly looked through a box of things on the ground as

Sarah lifted up an old velvet handbag. She decided it wasn't her style, but as she went to put it back noticed a smaller leather bag, a little black one with tiny silver skulls all over it.

"This is so me!" She showed it to Kelli and her friend nodded her head.

"You have to get that, it's cool as."

"How much for the two?" Sarah asked the lady as she held out the bag and the pendant.

"Look, I don't really care, these were my sister's things. Just take them, I'm all packed up now, pretty much."

"No, really, I have to pay you something?"

"They're yours, hun, enjoy," The woman tipped her plastic trestle table on one side and started to fold the legs in. "You can have those books, too. There's a couple more in that box if you want."

"You sure?" Kelli asked.

"It's going to the tip if you don't take it." Smiling, the woman lifted another box and sat it in Sarah's hands. "You can have this one. If you don't want anything in there just throw it away."

"Wow, thanks heaps, I really appreciate this," Sarah smiled back at the woman as she hefted the small box under her arm.

"Let's get out of here. I'm hungry, that coffee didn't fill me up and I didn't eat dinner last night."

"You wanna get lunch?" Sarah shifted the box to her other arm, her tote over a shoulder as she searched her pocket for her car keys. "We can go to that dumpling cafe near my place."

"Nah, I want all day breakfast. Feel like avocado and eggs and bacon, and another huge coffee."

"We can go to Alfredo's; they do all day breakfast. It's on the way back." Sarah sat the box on the roof of her car as she opened the door.

"Are you ever going to clean this out?" Kelli screwed up her nose. "You are a real pig when it comes to your car."

"Yeah, I know, but it's too hard carting all the shit up to my apartment. I have to carry it all in from the carpark, then take the lift to the seventh floor, and my apartment is all the way at the back."

"You need one of those little shopping trollies like the old ladies use."

Sarah shoved things onto the floor of the car and put her bag and the box on the back seat. "My mum gave me one, I use it to take my clothes to the laundromat."

"Why didn't you bring it today?"

"Because it's full of dirty clothes." Sarah hopped in the car and put her seatbelt on. "You should come back to mine after we eat and we can go through all our bargains, see what's in the boxes, too."

"Sounds like a plan. Now let's drive, I am so hungry I'm about to eat whatever that is in the paper bag on the dashboard."

"Probably not a good idea, Kells. It's been there for like a month."

Chapter Two

“I’m not sure why I bought this,” Sarah hitched the dress up a little as she looked in the mirror. Kelli stood beside her, desperately trying to do the zipper up on the jeans she’d bought.

“I think it looks good. Try it on with that black jacket you got.”

Sarah pulled the jacket out of the bag and put it on over the dress and smiled. “Yeah, this looks heaps better. I might wear this tomorrow.”

“How’s the new job going?” Kelli finally got the zipper up and turned to look at her bum in the mirror. “I like these, but they are super tight.”

“You just had lunch, and I’m not surprised they’re tight, you ate so much!” Sarah pulled on a pair of heels and looked in the mirror. “Job’s okay so far. They seem nice, and they like that I already know all the systems. Got heaps of open houses tomorrow, and I’ve booked inspections for every day this week. These ones or the red ones?”

“Either, both look good. Actually, I think the black. I might do my real estate licence later this year. Anyway, I gotta go, I haven’t finished half my shit for tomorrow.”

“You do this every week, Kells. And I don’t think you’d like property management; you’d do better in sales.” Sarah took off her heels and jacket, changing back into her jeans and T-shirt. “Do you need me to come down with you?”

Kelli pulled her jeans off and shoved them in her bag before she pulled her leggings back on. "Nah, I'll be okay. I'll give you a call during the week, maybe we can go to Hannah's together?"

"Good, I hate walking in on my own. Love you."

"Love you more Sezzy," Kelli let the door close behind her and Sarah grabbed some hangers for her new clothes. After she put them away, she grabbed the box and sat on the couch, turning on the TV with the remote. The box wasn't very big, but it was crammed to the top with stuff. Sarah took out some old handkerchiefs that were delicately embroidered, putting them to one side. They weren't to her style but would be a nice gift for her aunty. She found some old toys, small ones, they looked like they may have come from a cereal box.

There was a can opener, and doilies, and several very ugly napkin rings. She pulled out a small pot for a plant, so far the only thing Sarah liked, and sat that to the other side. There were a couple of brooches and an old mirror, and several other bits and pieces that didn't interest her at all.

Her hand closed on the last item, a small wooden box, about a third of the size of a shoe box. It was intricately carved, the patterns looking tribal, maybe Celtic, and it was dark with age. She looked it over, trying to find an opening, before slipping her fingers up one side and finding a clasp underneath.

Inside the box was a set of cards wrapped in a silk cloth, and Sarah lifted them out. Unwrapping the cards, Sarah could smell them; they had an ancient odour, slightly musty but dry, like an old book. She turned them over, fascinated with the colours and designs. She pushed the stuff from the cardboard box onto the floor and laid the cards out so she could see them better.

The pictures were very different from anything she had ever seen, and it didn't take her long to figure out they weren’t playing cards. Maybe fortune telling cards, tarot, or something like that?

She turned them over to look at the drawings on the back, then turned them back again. There were no instructions, just the cards. The pictures were absolutely beautiful, enchanting, and very mystical. Huge beasts swirled around intricate patterns, doe eyed, dark skinned maidens looked off into bright sunsets, and exotic birds and flora danced about on the borders. Sarah noticed there were some Australian animals in the pictures, though she could find no maker’s mark or artist signature.

Sarah pulled out her mobile phone and started to search for fortune telling cards to see if she could figure out what set they were but didn't realise there were so many different varieties. She searched for a while but couldn’t find any that matched. Deciding she’d search later, she gathered up the cards and wrapped them in the silk before putting them back into the wooden box.

She put the rest of the things into the cardboard box and placed it near her front door, so she’d remember to take it down in the morning. There was a set of shelves in the foyer of the apartment building where residents could put stuff they wanted to give away. Sarah was sure someone would find the stuff fascinating, and if they didn't, she could throw it in the rubbish bin when she got home from work.

Deciding to have a shower and wash her hair before settling into a serious session of reality television, Sarah flicked the thermostat a little higher and stripped her clothes off, throwing them on the floor. She made sure she had a clean towel, not making that mistake again, thank you, and took a long, hot shower, shampooing and rinsing her hair as her music played on her waterproof speaker.

She wrapped her hair in the towel and dressed in a robe and fleecy pants before pouring an extra-large glass of pink Moscato and flopping down on the couch. She gasped as she sat on something, reaching behind herself to find the wooden card box. Sarah flicked through the channels, settling on a rerun of her favourite reality show.

As she watched, she fiddled with the box, flicking it open and closed, playing with the silk cloth before searching for the cards again on the internet using her phone. She still could not find the exact set though did see a few that were similar and thought perhaps this was just different artwork for the same set. Reading the instructions for a similar set, Sarah touched each card, pulling over her coffee table so she could lay them out and really have a good look at them.

She was fascinated with the cards, they were not only beautiful, but she felt like they had a warmth about them, almost like a connection to her. Every time Sarah picked up a card it felt special, a strange feeling, and she rearranged them on the table, setting them in an order that seemed right.

She got a pen and paper and started to write down the meaning of each card as best she could, trying to match them with the similar set from her internet search. When she was satisfied that the descriptions were right, she wrote down the instructions, and put her phone down. She looked at the cards again, not realising a slow smile had spread across her face when she looked at them. She moved them again, admiring the beautiful illustrations, then gathered them all up and sat the pile of cards to one side.

The card that ended up on top held the image of a man, he was naked, but his back was turned, and the illustrator used plants to cover the lower half of the man's torso. Sarah picked up the card to admire the strong back, broad shoulders, and the dark skin. His face was turned away, so she couldn't see what he looked like, but that back was enough to make her smile.

"You're pretty yummy, Mr. Card-Man." Sarah looked at her phone to see the time and gasped. Somehow, five hours had passed. She double checked the time, frowning as she did so. How could she possibly have spent five hours looking at the cards? Her stomach rumbled, but it was getting too late to cook a meal, so Sarah microwaved something from the freezer and ate as she watched the late news.

As much as she tried to avoid looking at the cards, her gaze kept drifting back to the top card, the one with the strong man, until she turned the card to stop obsessing over it. She unwrapped the towel from her hair, annoyed that it was still damp. Her hair was a constant irritation, it was fine, limp, and there was not much of it. To add insult to injury, it grew so slowly she permanently had short hair. She gave it a bit of a blow with her hairdryer before brushing her teeth, then made sure her alarm, and her two backup alarms, were set before she went to bed.

Chapter Three

Sarah sipped her cappuccino and reached for the sugar. She liked her coffee sweet, adding two sugars before stirring it as she looked out the window of the little Brunswick Street cafe. She was sitting on a high stool, the counter that held her coffee was set into the window of the cafe and looked out onto the side street. The sun was bright, and there were birds walking around outside, pigeons, maybe, she wasn't sure and didn't really care to know what they were.

She looked down at her coffee, stirring it slowly, when a shadow fell across her. There was someone leaning against the window, blocking the pleasant warmth of the sun. She looked up and instead of complaining, or banging the window to ask them to move, she felt a smile tug at the corner of her mouth.

There was a man leaning against the window, he was tall, very tall, and he had broad shoulders that tapered into a narrow waist. She couldn't see any further than the table as it blocked her view, and the bright sun in front of the man made seeing any details impossible. She couldn't tell if he wore a hat or had long hair, or any hair, for that matter.

He moved a little, his shirt tight, outlining his torso perfectly. He turned just as someone bumped into Sarah's stool and she looked behind her as the old lady apologised, her generous hips wider than the narrow space between the shop counter and Sarah's stool. When she looked back out the window the man was gone, and she felt a stab of disappointment.

The door to the cafe opened, and Sarah felt a warmth of pleasure as the tall, dark man pushed the door open, stepping inside. A large pot plant blocked his face, and Sarah leaned back on her stool to catch a glimpse of his face as he stepped inside.

The fire alarm chose that moment to sound its loud alert, and the man paused, not sure if he should enter. The noise grew louder, and Sarah picked up her phone, stuffing it into her pocket as she slipped off her stool, the alarm insistent, loud, an incessant noise that was so loud that it...

...woke her up.

She rolled onto her back, disappointed to be ripped from such a great dream. She yawned, stretched, and rolled out of bed, before hitting the alarm stop button on her phone. Sarah took a quick shower before straightening her hair and dressing in the new dress and jacket from yesterday, teaming her outfit with the black heels and the new briefcase her mother had given her to celebrate landing the job.

The day was a little chilly, summer was still a few weeks off, but the sky was bright blue and there wasn't a cloud in the sky. She hurried across the road when there was a break in the traffic and stopped into the cafe that was directly across from her apartment block. As she entered, Sarah couldn't help but glance at the seat by the side window, the one she had sat at in her dream, but there was no broad-shouldered man at the window.

"Cappuccino to take away, thanks," she told the cute barista as she checked her phone for messages. There was one from Kelli, a picture with her posing in her new outfit from the market, and one from her boss confirming her appointment with the new services guy. It was going to be a busy day, Mondays were always busy in the property market, and being the manager of the whole rental department meant she probably wouldn't stop until closing time.

She accepted her coffee with a smile and walked the block and a half to work. She was so lucky to land this job, being able to walk to work was a bonus, and added to that was a good increase in her pay, a generous car allowance and a weekly bonus to cover after hours inspections. She liked everyone that she worked with, for a change, and that in itself was enough for her to be happy.

Sarah couldn't remember a single position she held in the last seven years where she'd actually like everyone she worked with, usually her temper with some incompetent or nasty individual either lost her the job, or she left because she could no longer tolerate working with morons.

The day passed quickly, everything going smoothly, meetings starting on time, and, more importantly, finishing the same way. It wasn't until the last meeting of the day when Sarah had to tell Noel, the maintenance man they were using, that they no longer would be booking his services. The guy didn't take it well. Not well at all. He slammed his hands on Sarah's desk as his face turned bright red, and he called her every name that no man should use in polite company. His spittle was flying out, and he stood over Sarah, threatening her, his hands gripped tight in fists as he screamed at her.

Matthew, the general manager of the agency, came running from his office to confront the nasty little man and throw him out, threatening him with the police should he be stupid enough to return. Five-thirty couldn't come quick enough after that incident and Sarah grabbed her bag as Joan, one of the receptionists, locked the front door.

"Hellava day, Sarah," Paul, the sales team manager, threw the comment at her as he walked to the back door. He stopped and turned back to Sarah, an apologetic smile on his face. "Seriously, you held your cool well under that barrage of shit he threw at you. Well done. If it were me, I'd probably have punched him in the face."

"Trust me, I felt like it. He's a lot bigger than me, though," Sarah laughed, still feeling shaken and a little crushed after the dressing down. She felt her lip quiver and bit it so no one would notice. The thought of the man yelling into her face, his spittle actually flying out and hitting her in her eye, made her start to well up.

Paul walked back to her and put an arm around her shoulders. "Cheer up, kiddo. Days like that are rare. And the boss noticed how professionally you handled things. Let me tell you, he was very impressed."

Sarah relaxed into the embrace for a moment. "Thanks Paul, that means a lot."

"You need a bubble bath and a chardonnay, girl." Paul held the door for her as they left the office.

"I don't have a bath, so a hot shower and a milo will have to do me."

Paul laughed and waved as he climbed into his car. Sarah waved back as she headed home, her spirits lifted a little, but she wasn't back to her easy mood of the morning. She waited forever to cross the road, the traffic was hell and some homeless guy kept yelling obscenities out to her. Normally this wouldn't get to her, but she was feeling rather sensitive, and just couldn't cope with anything else at the moment.

She was beyond grateful when the lift at her apartment block was empty and waiting for her, and when she stopped at the seventh floor there was no-one around, not the crazy cat lady that kept asking her in for a drink, nor the loud pregnant junkie, or the idiots in the apartment across from hers. She threw her shoes off as soon as her apartment door closed behind her, and even though she had her own rule not to drink on a weeknight she poured herself a water glass full of Moscato and pulled her dressing gown over her clothes.

She didn't feel like cooking, and Sarah was glad she lived so close to dozens of different restaurants that were all happy to deliver. Being only Monday, at least half of the eateries were closed, but she found a nice Thai place that would have her a meal in under a half hour. While she waited, she turned up the thermostat so the place would be nice and warm for when she showered, and she flicked the television on.

Her food arrived early, and she ate while she watched TV, trying to get her thoughts away from the angry face that had shouted at her. Every time she blinked, she could see his red face and angry, violent eyes. Searching for a distraction, Sarah picked up the ornate box that she'd scored from the market and flicked it open.

The cards felt good in her hands.

They felt right.

She already felt better just by holding them, and as she sipped her wine, she flicked through them, laying them out on the table and arranging them in a random pattern, moving them around and touching them. The dark man card showed next and Sarah stopped and looked at it more closely. She could have sworn the card was different to yesterday.

Last night when she'd looked at the card, she was sure she couldn't see the man, that his back was turned and his face was hidden. Today she could see a little of his profile, just a little, and the foliage that covered him from the waist down wasn't as high as it was before. Yesterday the shrubs had covered his narrow waist and the small of his back, today she could see the dimple above his butt cheeks, just on one side, and his hip bone as his torso twisted to the left.

She sat the card down. Maybe she'd had too much to drink last night and got it all mixed up with her strange dream. That must be it, she was half cut and just remembered things a little askew. Lifting the card closer, Sarah studied the man. The illustration was extraordinary, very lifelike, even the foliage was hard to differentiate from an actual photograph or a painting.

She traced her finger down the picture, imagining what it would be like to run her finger down his actual body and feel the warmth of his flesh, the taut muscles underneath that perfect black skin, taste the sweat on his body…

The ringtone on her phone broke her reverie and she answered, Kelli's cheery voice bringing her back to earth. The girls chatted for a while, breaking down their day and Sarah told Kelli about her run-in with the property manager, but didn't mention the cards. She didn't know why she kept them secret but did occasionally reach over to touch the card that held the man. Her dinner arrived but didn't interrupt the conversation, both girls happy to talk as Sarah ate. They talked until it was quite late, and Sarah went to bed after she said goodnight to her friend.

Chapter Four

Sarah was standing outside her building, her takeaway coffee cup in her hands. The morning seemed strange, there was almost an otherworldly feeling about it. It may have been summer, but the morning was very cool, almost freezing, and foggy. She could barely see up the street, the fog was thick, and the headlights of the cars in the peak hour traffic created golden glowing orbs in the white, thick mist. She needed to cross the road but worried she would run out in front of a car; the cloud-like covering was so thick she couldn't really see anyone until they were right on her.

People were busy, huddled in their coats and jackets against the chilly morning, bustling past without a glance in her direction. Sarah decided to walk down and cross at the corner lights- dashing into traffic was not an option this morning. She hurried along, wanting to be out of the cold and into the comfort of her warm office. She looked down at her coffee, a little confused. There were no coffee shops on her side of the street for a few blocks, she didn't know where she got the coffee from. Looking up she caught a glimpse of someone standing there, just up ahead, the fog obscuring them.

There were only indistinct shapes in the mist, distant shadows of objects that she couldn't identify. She moved faster, looking back over to the other side of the street where the shadows moved. A passing car furled the fog and it cleared a little, allowing her to catch a glimpse of someone tall and dark, just as they turned away from her.

"Hey, bitch!" a voice called out, and she ignored it at first, as she didn't think it was for her. Sadly, the area had a few council flats further down, and the streets often saw drug addicts and unsavoury characters hanging around.

"Don't ignore me, you filthy cunt. I know you hear me, Sarah the real estate slut."

She felt her stomach churn at the sound of her name but decided to keep her head down and hurry to the traffic lights.

"Look over here, cunt. Over the road. Don't think you're getting away from me, you piece of shit."

Sarah glanced over, the fog limiting her view, but she was sure it was the maintenance guy from yesterday. She felt a cold sweat break out under her arms as she started to panic. The guy was clearly angry, violent, even, and she didn't want to come face to face with him. She glanced ahead and saw the pharmacy open. She could duck in there, get them to call the police. There was no way Sarah was going to cut across the road and run straight into Mr. Foul-mouth.

"Fuck you, bitch! You can't fire me; you've cost me thousands of dollars. I'm going to make you pay, cunt!"

Sarah's heart was hammering out of her chest, and she ran as fast as her stilettos would let her.

Her coffee was sloshing about and she threw it into the rubbish bin she was passing, her panic starting to take over her.

"You can't run from me, you fucking idiot! I can outrun you any day, and today isn't your day!"

Sarah could feel hot tears start to well in her eyes as she ran, and she chanced a glance over to see if he was gaining on her. This was a mistake, she missed an uneven part of the footpath and fell, her hands out in front of her, the rough bitumen cutting into her palms and her knees. It was the opportunity the man needed. Sarah could see him step out onto the road, his face red and contorted with anger. She pushed herself up onto her ravaged knees and then shakily stood, not taking her eyes off him as he began to run over to her side of the road.

Without warning, a fire engine with lights flashing took him out, slamming into him at speed and throwing his body into the air, only for it to come down in front of her, blood splattering as he fell.

Sarah drew breath to scream as his lifeless eyes stared at her, a piece of intestine hanging out of his mouth, the force of the impact so hard it pushed his stomach through his oesophagus.

She woke with a scream dying on her lips, sweat soaking her sheets and her heart pounding out of her chest. She wasn't one for nightmares, not usually, but this was a doozy. She looked over at her phone, it was about a half hour until she was due to get up, but her hair was soaked with sweat and she was still a little freaked out. Crawling out of bed, Sarah pulled the sheets off so she wouldn't forget that they needed changing when she got home.

The half hour wasn't quite enough time to get her hair dried and straightened, so Sarah ended up putting it in a high ponytail and hurried out the door. She couldn't shake the feeling that she would need her winter coat, the effects of the dream still lingering as she walked out onto the street.

She half expected to see fog and was relieved that the day was as bright and clear as yesterday had been. She hurried across the road, the traffic at a standstill, and even though she knew it was irrational she still couldn't shake the feeling that the maintenance guy would come running around the corner to abuse her.

Joan was opening the door as Sarah walked up, turning and giving her a warm smile.

"Sarah! Good morning. Gee, I hope you have a better day than yesterday, honey. That guy was an absolute creep."

Sarah followed her into the office. "You're not kidding. I even had a bad dream about him. But you know, Joan, I'm not gonna let him spoil my day. I've got stacks of appointments lined up and he is not what I want to think about."

"Hey, you'll get to meet Elyse, the rental girl that's been on leave. You'll like her," Joan smiled at Sarah. "She's your age, too. I think you'll get on famously."

Sarah walked to the kitchen and put on the kettle; she hadn't stopped for a coffee on the way as there was not enough time. She filled it and was checking her phone for any messages while she waited for it to boil.

Paul walked in and grabbed a cup from the cupboard and touched Sarah's hair. "It looks good up, I like it," he said. "Have you met Elyse yet?"

"No, Joan said she was coming in today, though."

"Hiya! She was right, I'm here!" Elyse walked into the kitchen.

Paul grabbed her in a hug and kissed her cheek. "Mary says hi, and she'll send that recipe over in a day or so."

"Thank your wife, Paul. I love her, she's just gorgeous."

Paul turned to Sarah. "This is your new boss, Elyse. Meet Sarah, I'm sure you'll get along well together." Paul picked up his coffee and left the two girls alone.

Elyse was the exact opposite of Sarah; where Sarah was dark, olive skinned, dark haired and had thick eyelashes, Elyse was blonde, slight, her blue eyes bright against her pale cheeks.

Sarah was fairly short, not overweight, but she had curves, a tiny waist accentuated by full hips and a generous cleavage. Where Elyse was tall and supermodel slim, Sarah was voluptuous. They regarded each other for a few seconds and Sarah smiled. "Joan said you were stunning, but I think she left out just how gorgeous you are!"

Elyse giggled. "Look who's talking! I know you; I follow you on Instagram!"

"Oh my god, really? That's hilarious!"

"I have to say, I was really worried that you were going to be like a super bitch. Especially because I was on leave when you started, I'm like, what if I hate her, I just found a job I love, I don't wanna leave!"

"I really like it here, too! Everyone is so nice, so far it's the best real estate agency I've worked at. And every day has been great, well, except for yesterday."

"What happened yesterday?" Elyse asked as she followed Sarah back into the main office.

"Sarah was almost attacked by Noel," Matthew grabbed Elyse in a hug. "Welcome back! We missed you! Yesterday, right, Sarah had to have a bit of a talk to Noel. We've been getting heaps of complaints about him and she had to let him go. He lost his shit."

"He absolutely lost his shit! I couldn't believe it, he had spit flying out of his mouth and he was slamming into the desk," the other rental agent, Mark, told Elyse. "Sarah just sat there, she didn't lose her cool. Matt showed him the door."

"It completely freaked me out. I even had a nightmare about him!" Sarah pulled her chair out and sat down. "He had to go, though, he was charging us way too much, and I think he was stealing stuff as well. You'll like Steve, the new guy, I used him when I was at Mitchells and Ruse. Honest and really quick."

"Hey guys, look at this!" Joan walked into the main office carrying the morning newspaper. "You are absolutely not going to believe this!" Joan put the paper down on Sarah's desk as the entire sales and rental staff gathered around. Joan turned the paper so Sarah could see what it said.

"Shit, really?" Paul was standing behind Sarah, leaning over her shoulder.

"What happened?" Matthew asked as he walked to Sarah's desk.

"Noel, the creepy maintenance guy we fired yesterday, was hit by a fire engine last night! Walked right out in front of it, says he never had a chance. They were on their way to a call out, a false alarm, apparently."

Sarah felt ice cold, her stomach curdling. She had dreamed this. Well, not it happening at night, but definitely being hit by a fire engine. She felt like she would vomit.

"You okay, Sarah?" Elyse frowned. "You look like you're gonna hurl."

"It's just, you know, after yesterday…"

"Hey, he was a douche, and he was probably drunk. Who walks in front of a fire engine with sirens going and lights flashing?" Matthew sat down on the edge of Sarah's desk. "Says here he had a long record, was a convicted drug dealer and a person of interest in a couple of child disappearances. I think you helped us dodge a bullet yesterday Sarah, we don't want the agency connected with someone like that!"

"What?" Sarah couldn't manage more than the one word.

"He was an arsehole, and it sounds like he got what he deserved. I'm betting we hear a bit more about what a scumbag he was." Matthew turned to look at Sarah. "I think maybe you should take the rest of the day off, maybe go home and chill. With pay, of course."

"Thanks heaps, that really means a lot, but I think I'll stay," Sarah smiled at the encouraging faces around her. "I'd be alone at home, but here I have you guys to look after me. I think keeping busy is the best thing for me today."

"Well the offer is there," Matthew assured her. "If you change your mind at all, or feel like you're not coping, just sing out, okay."

"Hey, maybe I should take Sarah for a coffee? Give us a chance to debrief, catch me up on things, and get to know each other," Elyse suggested. "And if Sarah thinks she wants to go home after that, I can walk her to her door?"

"That's a great plan. Grab a twenty from petty cash." Matthew stood up from Sarah's desk. "Take an hour, that's an order."

"Aye aye, captain," Elyse joked and offered a hand to Sarah.

"Thanks everyone, you're all awesome." Sarah took Elyse's hand as she stood, following her out onto the street.

"Any particular coffee shop you prefer?" Elyse asked, and Sarah stopped as they drew close to the cafe from her dream.

"Not this one," Sarah said.

"Oh, okay. I like it here, but whatever you want."

"Yeah, I like it too, it's just, well, I'd rather go somewhere else, if that's okay?"

“Sure thing, chicky, there’s no shortage of coffee shops on Brunswick street, that’s for sure!”

Elyse turned and walked in the opposite direction, opening the door of Sugar Surprise, a cute little pink themed cafe with more cakes than Sarah’s waistline needed.

They found a quiet booth in a corner and Sarah slid in as Elyse ordered the coffee and looked out the window. She knew it was coincidence, that Noel’s death was purely an accident but she had no idea how she could have dreamt such a thing. How could she possibly have known that Noel would die, let alone how he would meet his demise?

Elyse was just the panacea she needed, her enthusiasm, bubbly personality and bright outlook lifted Sarah’s mood, and before long she was laughing along with the willowy blonde, ordering a second coffee and a slice of chocolate brownie to share.

Their hour up, they walked arm in arm back to the office. The day passed quickly, with Elyse accompanying Sarah to most of her appointments and helping fill in the property inspection reports. Matthew kept checking in with her, making sure Sarah was okay and that she was coping with the shocking news from the morning.

Stopping at the supermarket on the corner of her block, Sarah bought enough ingredients to make herself a nice dinner, and hopefully enough to take leftovers for lunch. She turned the TV on when she got home and prepared her meal, then ate it in front of the television as she flicked through her mobile to find the latest on her social media feeds, answered a text from her mum and her older brother, before popping her feet up on the coffee table and sipping her hot cup of tea.

She realised the bump annoying her back was the card box, and she decided she didn't want to look through the cards tonight. She'd leave them in the box, safely wrapped in the purple silk cloth.

The apartments were very well soundproofed, the noise from traffic and trams barely heard, and as she was right up one end of the building, she had no passing foot traffic in the plushly carpeted halls to disturb her. The doors were the only thing not really soundproof, and every now and then the new neighbour across the hall would play her music too loud, and if she got pissed with her occasional stay-over boyfriend the slurry arguments could be louder than Sarah would like.

Tonight seemed to be one of those nights, the sound of some thumping eighties disco classic making Sarah's door rattle with its beat. Sarah turned up her television, hoping to drown out the disco music, but it didn't really help much. It wasn't late yet, so she decided to let it go, not to worry, and not to get upset about it.

She resolved to have her shower early, the warm water would make her forget her worries from the day and hopefully drown out the dreadful noise from across the hall. Sarah had a Bluetooth speaker in her bathroom and she cranked up her own music, singing along to it as she shaved her legs, under her arms and shampooed her hair.

She didn't want to lose the good mood Elyse had spent the whole day giving her, but as soon as she was out of the shower she could hear the full force of the music. Her hair dryer only masked it for the half hour it took to dry her hair, and when she turned off the noisy appliance she groaned at the sound of loud shouting from her inconsiderate neighbour.

She wrapped her fluffy robe around herself and sat back at the TV, but the music was too loud to enjoy any viewing. Her hand rested on the wooden card box and she picked it up, absentmindedly pulling them out and shuffling through the deck. The yelling was louder, angrier, and Sarah glanced at her phone, feeling distraught when she saw the time. If they continued with that noise she'd never get to sleep, and she needed to go to bed soon or she'd be a mess for work the next day.

She flicked through the cards, this time looking at the women in the deck. There were some beautiful women, all naked, all different nationalities. One caught her eye. With a very sad face, the woman looked lost, distraught, her heavy breasts barely covered by one arm across the chest, the other hanging by her side. Sarah admired the woman's hair, it was long, the black waves tumbling behind her shoulder and down over the curve of her hips. She wished she had hair like that.

Sarah had never been able to grow her hair long, it was always a wispy, flyaway short bob, thin and straight. Her mother and brother had thick wavy hair, but that particular gene had skipped her, and she was left with her straggly locks.

Her fingers brushed against the card and she flicked it over. Behind the sad woman was the card she always returned to, that of the dark man. Sarah frowned. She was sure that he was turned more than she remembered, and while she couldn’t see his face she could now see the lobe of one ear, and the jutting edge of a strong jaw. She knew there was no possible way the image on the card could have moved, but she was sure she couldn’t see the top of his buttocks before.

She touched the card, always surprised that it felt warm, almost like it was alive, and again, it felt so right in her hand. The arguing neighbours were very loud, they must have moved their argument out into the hall, and when one of them banged against the door Sarah dropped the cards in surprise. She crept up to the door, checking it was locked before she peered out of the peephole.

She gasped as she saw someone trying to look in, the eye looking weird with the fisheye glass distortion. She heard the person laugh and they banged on her door, but there was no way she was going to open it, not to these druggie pieces of shit.

They were yelling louder, and Sarah realised they were yelling at her, for her to open her door and share any pills or booze she had with them. She was terrified - what if they broke down the door? What would they do to her? She didn't know if she should call the police, and if she did, would that make her life there in the apartment hell from then on as they sought retribution?

She moved back into her little apartment and turned off the TV, as well as the overhead lights, leaving just the one lamp on. She gathered up the cards and rewrapped them in the silk cloth before putting them back in the box, deciding that she'd curl up in bed and hope they'd stop the noise soon.

By the sound of things, they had moved on to the next door, their yelling and banging echoing throughout her apartment and making her want to cry. She loved living in this apartment, but there were a couple of tenants that spoiled her city lifestyle, and she had the extreme misfortune to live right across from two of them.

She listened to them for at least an hour, yelling, banging on doors, until finally someone must have called the police. She peeked out of her spyhole again to see the noisy neighbours going back into their apartment, but not before they pointed at her door and made a threatening cut-throat gesture, and spat towards her door.

Her heart raced with fear, she didn't want them thinking she'd called the cops on them, but she also didn't want to open the door to them, either. She climbed back in bed, frightened, cold, and worried she'd get no sleep at all now. She wished they'd just shift out or be evicted. She decided to call her real estate agent in the morning and have a word with them, rental agent to rental agent, and see if she could sort something out.

She yawned, thinking that maybe she could fall asleep after all. As she drifted off to sleep, she heard them arguing again, but this time not as loudly. She turned over, her last rational thought as she drifted off to sleep was a hope that they'd just overdose and be done with it.

Chapter Five

The banging at her door woke her, and for a moment she was unsure where she was, or if she'd heard anything at all. Then the banging came again, and Sarah got up, pulling her robe around herself. She tiptoed to her door, hoping that the druggie neighbours hadn't decided to come and take their revenge in the middle of the night. She peered through her spy hole to see a policeman standing there, another stood a bit further back and she could only see the side of his leg.

She opened the door but left the chain in place. "Hello?"

"Hello, we're sorry to bother you, Miss, but we've had a few complaints about the noise in the building last night. We've been trying to contact your neighbour across the hall, here, but there's no answer. We wondered if you saw them leave at all?"

"No, sorry, I've been asleep in bed. I haven't heard anything for a while now."

The young policeman smiled at her. "Sorry to disturb your sleep in, thanks for your time."

Sarah shut her door and frowned. Sleep in? Wasn't it still night? She walked back to her bedroom and groaned when she saw the time on her phone. She had exactly seventeen minutes to get dressed and head to work.

She threw on anything she could dress in quickly

and put on her quickest face ever. On mornings like this she was almost happy to have straight, thin, hair. She tied it up in a bun and pulled her shoes on. Grabbing her briefcase and keys she ran to the elevator, breathing a silent thanks that it was on her floor. She would make it to work if she hurried, and if the traffic let her across the road without any issues.

She didn't make it out of the foyer, there were police everywhere, and tape blocking the front entrance. Her mobile rang and she fumbled it out of her jacket pocket.

"Hello?"

"Hey, Sarah, it's Paul. I'm across from your building and I see what's going on. I've called work and told Matthew we'll probably be late. I'll come around the back and pick you up, meet me in the side alley."

He hung up before she could answer, so she hurried out through the back entrance just as Paul pulled up in the alley. She glanced up before opening the car door and frowned as she saw someone standing further down the alley, someone tall, dark, but obscured by the shadows so she couldn't see him properly.

"What's going on?" Sarah asked as she climbed into the car. "There's police tape blocking the front."

"Two druggies got into a fight out the front, ended up stepping in front of a tram. Both didn't make it. I saw the road was blocked and turned on my radio. Hell of a thing, hey?"

"Cops knocked on my door this morning, asked me about the druggies that live in the apartment opposite me. Shit, do you think it's them?"

Sarah woke with a fright, the alarm close to her ear. She must've fallen asleep with her phone in her hands last night when the idiots were arguing. She was glad she didn't have to race like she did in her dream and stepped into the shower. She put the radio on with her shower speaker and listened to the morning news but changed to iPod when it was just a sports report.

Sarah thought she'd leave early and get something to eat at the cafe on the way, grabbing her briefcase and keys as she headed out. The actions gave her a weird little feeling of deja vu, a remnant from her dream, she supposed. She had to wait ages for the lift, someone was holding it at the third floor and the other one hadn't moved at all from the ground. She waited several minutes before it finally came up and was surprised to see a security guard in the lift. He nodded to her as she got in, but he put his hand over the floors as she tried to press the ground floor button.

"Sorry, Miss, there's been an incident. You'll have to get off at the first-floor car park and take the stairs down to the street," he said, and pressed the first-floor button.

"Shit, what happened?" Sarah asked but the door opened on the next floor to let a few more people in, and the guard told them the same thing without answering her question. He had to do that on every floor and Sarah guessed the other lift wasn't working for this one to be so busy. As everyone exited at the first floor, the guard touched her arm.

"Sorry, I didn't mean to be rude, just so many people getting in and out. Seems there's a couple who OD'd in the other lift last night, and the building management called my company in to help manage things and work with the cops. Should be okay to come in normally by this afternoon."

"Thanks, have a good day," Sarah told him as she walked out of the lift. The car park stairs exited away from the front foyer, so she couldn't see anything from there, and when she tried to walk around the front there was police tape and two police cars, along with two ambulances blocking the road. The traffic was being detoured around the block, but Sarah was able to cross the road and walk to work, casting glances over her shoulder as she did, but she still couldn't see anything. She called into the coffee shop and grabbed her cappuccino and a bagel before work, happy that Joan was there to let her in the front door again.

She was eating her bagel in the kitchen and looking at the paper when Paul came in and put on the kettle. "Hey, I see your building was on the news this morning."

"My building? Oh, yeah, there was a druggie overdose last night."

"No, not that, or maybe that happened as well," Paul rinsed his cup in the sink. "There was a knife fight in the foyer and two people died. Both lived in your building. Yeah, look, it's in the paper there, look at the front."

Sarah had found the paper open on the table; she didn't see the front when she'd sat down. She closed the paper and felt cold stealing its way through her stomach. It was her loud neighbour, looking rather stoned in a mug shot, but it was definitely her.

"This woman lives right opposite my apartment. She was screaming and fighting with her boyfriend all night."

"Well, she won't be doing that again. They stabbed each other to death." Paul sat his coffee down. "How did they afford an apartment in your building?"

"It's some housing initiative thing, every building these guys manage allows ten percent of their apartments to low income or people receiving government benefits."

"Of course you'd know that, it's your job."

"Yeah, but it's a pain as well, means every floor has two or three apartments with junkies and shit."

"Two less now, by the sounds of it." Paul picked up his coffee and headed out of the kitchen, turning back at the last minute. "I got two new sales guys starting today, nice boys. One of them has a brother looking to get into rental, if you need anyone else in your department."

"Not at the moment, but I'm meeting a few people later in the week who have large apartment blocks, if I win them over we could be looking."

"Hey, lots of luck with that, big bonuses could be coming your way!"

Sarah stood up and gathered up her bagel

wrapper. “That’s the plan,” she said, her mouth feeling dry as ashes with the thought of people dying in her apartment building.

Walking out into the main office, Elyse’s bright smile made her feel a little better. This morning was her staff meeting for all of the rental agents, and when she could tell they’d heard about the stabbings she filled them in on what happened at her building. Everyone listened respectfully, and Sarah realised this was the second fatal occurrence this week, three people dead, all in some way connected to her. It made her feel a little sick, but she had a big day and tried to ignore the thoughts that popped into her head.

The meeting went well, all her agents were nice young people, vibrant and enthusiastic, and their good humour was infectious. She left the meeting with a smile on her face, bumping straight into Paul and his new salesmen.

Sarah could feel Elyse poking her in the back as she was introduced to the young men, and when they walked away Elyse guffawed and spun around. “Wow, they are super hot, did you see them?”

“Of course I did Elyse, I’m not blind. They’re the new salesmen Paul just hired.”

“I’m thinking they’re my future husbands, husband one and husband two, right there.”

“They are pretty cute, but I wouldn’t date anyone I work with,” Sarah sat at her desk and shook her mouse to wake up her computer. “I’ve worked in places where relationships ended badly, and it was so uncomfortable for everyone! I’m not getting into that, not here."

"Yeah but you're the boss. I can play, it's different."

"And what if it doesn't work out, Elyse? It'd be so awkward."

"Yeah, maybe. But also, how hot are they?"

Sarah laughed and waved her off. "Go, girl, you have four inspections before lunch, remember?"

Elyse saluted. "Yes, sir! I'll meet you back here for lunch?"

"Okay, my friend Kelli is meeting me, you'll like her. We'll be at Tarantino's at one thirty."

"Catch!" Elyse swayed her hips as she walked past the sales desks on her way out and Sarah shook her head, seeing the new guys both turn to watch the pretty girl go.

There were about a thousand emails to answer and Sarah needed to make a few phone calls. She was still on one when Kelli was ushered through by Helen, the other receptionist. Sarah mouthed *five minutes* and pointed to the seat opposite her desk. Kelli sat, looking around the office, and when she saw the two new salesmen sitting at Paul's desk, she smoothed her skirt and ran a hand through her hair. Sarah noticed and made a face at her friend.

Finishing her call, Sarah grabbed her handbag and stood up at the same time as Paul did.

"You off to lunch?" he asked her.

"Yeah, this is my friend, Kelli, we're meeting Elyse at Tarantino's." She saw Kelli's fervent glance in her direction. "Would you three like to join us?"

"Sure, that'd be nice."

"You guys'll like it, it's literally five minutes down the road," Kelli added as she flashed her brilliant smile at them.

The two young men nodded and smiled back as they followed Paul out of the door, Sarah and Kelli taking up the rear.

"Jesus Sez, you work with like the most hot guys on earth. Even the old guy, what's his name?"

"Paul, and he's married."

"Yeah, him, he looks like fucking Brad Pitt!"

"He's forty though, too old for you."

"Yeah, no, I like that dark haired newbie guy. What's his name?"

"Braden. The blonde's Reid. I'll introduce you properly in the restaurant."

"Be still my heart!" Kelli giggled as she followed the men up the block.

Elyse was already there; she was just walking in the door as the wait staff scurried to get them a table in the busy lunch rush. Paul introduced the young men to Elyse and Kelli, and Sarah cringed when the girls openly flirted with them. Paul just sat back, bemused at the girls' actions. Lunch was enjoyable, the new men were witty and well spoken, as most successful salesmen were. The hour passed quickly, and Sarah laughed and chatted along with everyone, until the conversation turned to the deaths at Sarah's apartment building. Kelli looked shocked, worried for her friend, and frightened at the thought of people dying where she had walked just days before.

Sarah leaned over to her as the others started to throw their money in for the cheque and whispered to Kelli. "I wanted to talk to you about the druggies, but also some weird things that've been happening since the weekend. You home tonight so I can call?"

"Actually no, I'm going to my mum's for dinner, but I'm home tomorrow. And when you say strange, like, how strange?"

Sarah pulled out her purse. "I'll explain later, it's nothing sinister or anything."

"You sure?"

"Beyond sure." Standing, the girls air-kissed and hugged. "Thanks for coming, honey, talk to you soon."

Kelli smiled as she said goodbye to the others, and Sarah was pretty sure she slipped her card to Braden.

Chapter Six

"Are you going to be okay going home?" Helen asked as she and Joan carried their cups to the kitchen.

"Yeah, it's fine. You know, it's probably safer now that they're gone, they used to scare the shit out of me if I got into the lift with them." Sarah turned off her computer and stood up to leave. "I used to pretend I got a call so I wouldn't have to be in there with them."

"I don't blame you, honey, what a bunch of freaks. You know what?" Joan turned and leaned against Sarah's desk. "You should start a petition or something for the residents to stop putting those druggies into the building!"

"I actually emailed the building management today to ask what they're doing to keep us safe."

"Good idea. Oh, I forgot to tell you," Joan said as she moved towards the kitchen. "I like your hair, that wave really suits you."

Sarah frowned, knowing she hadn't put a wave into her hair this morning, but shrugged the comment off. She said goodbye and headed out, wanting to get to the supermarket on the corner and grab a few things. She had to dodge the stoned guy standing out the front, he just stood there, staring at the lights on the hoarding, and Sarah noticed a few people laughing and filming him. The police were coming towards him, and as Sarah picked up a basket, she saw them gently take him by the arm and lead him away.

She wanted to make a healthy meal, something light after the big lunch today, and browsed through the aisles. She was just picking out some fruit when she felt like someone was watching her. She glanced out from under her lashes but couldn’t see anyone.

She turned the other way, pretending to look at something else, when she saw him. Just like in her dreams, there was a very tall, very dark man standing there. He was just at the end of the aisle but was half behind a stack of soft drinks, so she couldn't see him properly. She walked a few steps down the aisle as someone bumped into her and she glanced at them, they apologised and moved away but now the man was gone.

Sarah walked up the end of the aisle and down the next, unable to locate him, not even really sure he had been watching her. She gave up her search, took her shopping to the checkout and saw the dark man again. He was leaving the supermarket, his back turned to her, so she couldn't see who he was or what he looked like.

Sarah paid for her groceries and walked back to her apartment, pleased that the police tape was gone, and there seemed to be nothing to remind her of what happened there that morning. The foyer had been completely cleaned, and the carpet in front of the lifts had been changed. The pale greyish-green carpet had all been pulled up, replaced with a bright blue carpet, and the walls had been cleaned and painted.

Both lifts were waiting at the ground floor, but Sarah didn't want to get into the one where the bodies were found so she stepped into the second lift and rode it alone to her floor. She wondered if there would be anything different at the apartment across from her, but it was closed and quiet, no one around, and Sarah let herself into her place and started to prepare her dinner.

She heard her phone ring and answered to her mother. She didn't think that her mother would see the news and realise people had died in her daughter's building, but of course her mother had. As soon as the news screened, she rang and was quite panicked and frightened.

Sarah didn't have the heart to tell her mother that the deceased used to live right across from her, so she played the incident down, assuring her mother she was safe and didn't have to come home all the way to the country and be coddled until she went insane.

She hung up and her dad rang next. Her parents had been divorced since she was a baby, and her relationship with her dad could often be turbulent, but tonight he was just expressing concern and worry for her safety. She'd no sooner hung up from her father when her brother Sam rang and she rolled her eyes as she answered.

He was cool, though, just making sure she felt okay, but he knew his little sister wasn't stupid and would never put herself in danger. She wanted to tell her brother about the cards, but held off, worried that he'd think she was just overreacting due to the recent events. She told him about Elyse, though, thinking she might try to set them up together, and also about Noel, the recently deceased maintenance man. Sam sounded interested in Elyse but was worried she may be too young for him as there was an eight-year age gap. Sarah reminded him that their parents had been ten years apart in age, and so had their mother's parents. Sam finished the call, promising he'd think about it, and Sarah found Elyse's photo on the website, screenshot it and sent it to Sam. He answered back immediately that he was interested, making her laugh aloud before finally going back to her half-prepared meal.

Sarah poured a glass of wine, aware she'd been drinking a lot more than normal this week, but with the week she was having no one could blame her. She took her meal and wine and plonked down on the couch, the TV on, and thought she might watch the news to see if they mentioned her building.

While she ate she watched, then browsed social media on her phone as she sipped her wine, occasionally looking up at the television. It wasn't until after she'd washed her dishes that she touched the cards, flicking through them briefly, deciding that she would download and print the instructions tomorrow at work so she could really get an idea of using them.

She yawned, thinking it was time to shower, and stood in front of the bathroom mirror, before gasping with shock. Her hair was indeed wavy and looked somehow thicker and even longer than it had been that morning. Sarah ran her hands through her hair, and it really felt thicker. She couldn't understand it, she hadn't done anything different, she hadn't even washed her hair this morning.

She washed it now and marvelled at how thick her hair felt. Her whole life she had bemoaned her thin, fine hair, and had tried vitamins and supplements to thicken it, though nothing ever worked. She rinsed her hair off and wrapped it in a towel, and sat back on the couch, her fluffy robe wrapped tight around her to keep her warm.

She flicked through the cards until she found the one with the long haired girl she'd admired the night before. She touched the hair, remembering how she'd felt when she saw it. The cards were strange, but surely they couldn't make her hair grow thicker? That couldn't be possible.

Could it?

She sat that card down on the table and looked at the next one. It was full of lush, green plants, beautiful blossoms and blooms, and a tiny cat sitting right at the bottom, hardly visible. Sarah's own house plants were a bit sticky and faded, she didn't look after them properly, she knew that, though she always wanted them to be lush and beautiful, just like the card.

She touched the little brown cat at the bottom of the card before placing it back in the deck, then flicked through until she found the card with the dark man. It had changed, and she was completely sure this time, there was no doubt in her mind. The foliage was lower, she could now see the firm swell of his buttocks, the curve from the small of his back smoothing over those strong, taught, glistening muscles. She touched the card, her finger tracing all the way from his spine down to his buttocks, and felt herself grow warm, eager, and turned on with the sight of his body.

Sarah was attracted to blue or green eyed blonde men, the opposite to her dark olive skin and dark hair. She'd never dated a dark man, never shown any interest in dating anyone that didn't have white skin, but this picture made her feel very aware of her libido. She touched the curve of his neck, the strong jawline, noticing that he had turned just a fraction more, but she still couldn't see his face. The background did appear a little lighter, and she could see his shoulders more clearly. He looked tall, very tall, and very strong.

She wondered what it would feel like to have those arms wrapped around her…

Catching herself, Sarah wrapped the cards back in the silk cloth and put them in the little wooden box, sitting them on the coffee table. She looked at the box and frowned. She'd paid attention to two cards tonight, well, not counting the card with the dark man. She would see how her hair looked in the morning, and if her plants looked any different. She'd know then if things were just in her imagination, or if something strange was really happening. She yawned again, deciding to go to bed. She touched the cards one more time before she turned out the lights.

The alarm went off before Sarah even realised she had been asleep, and she stretched and yawned. No dreams had graced her sleep, and she woke feeling refreshed and in a good mood. She looked around her apartment at her plants as she walked to the bathroom, but they looked exactly the same. No sudden growth had occurred there, and when she looked in the mirror her hair looked exactly the same as the day before - no extra growth, no extra thickness.

She smiled at her reflection. Too much wine during the week had made her imagination run a little crazy, she decided, as she reached for her toothbrush. It didn't explain the changing view of the man in the card, or how her hair was thicker than before, but Sarah made a conscious decision to ignore that, and just get on with her day.

Chapter Seven

"I think we can work together, Sarah. I like what you bring to the table," the handsome man shook her hand, and tapped the folio on the table. "You're offering a far better rental package, and I'm happy to let you have all of our buildings, from here in Brunswick, right through to St. Kilda."

Sarah smiled warmly. "You won't be disappointed, Mr Kolac, we'll treat your folio as a top priority."

"Call me Alan, please. I have full confidence in you and your team. As you know I've been very disillusioned with the old guys, and that's why I severed my contracts with them."

Alan stood, and Sarah and Elyse stood as well, Elyse handing him a large document folder. "These are the contracts, Sarah's already signed them."

"Thank you, ladies, I'll walk you to the elevator."

"That's okay, we can find our way out, I know you're busy. Thank you again, and I'll expect the contracts to be mailed later today?"

"I'll have them couriered over to you." Alan shook their hands as he held the door to his office open to the girls.

The two walked to the elevators quietly and didn't speak until the elevator doors slid closed.

"Oh my fucking god! You landed every single property they own!" Elyse jumped up and down and squealed. "You've just made millions for our company! I mean, literally millions, annually!"

Sarah smiled and wrapped her arms around herself. "I can't believe it. I mean, sure, I thought I had him for the one apartment block, just not *every fucking property*!"

"Ring Matthew, he'll have an absolute heart attack, I swear."

"No, let's just walk in all calm and hand him the contracts when they come by courier, yeah? Give him a surprise when I take them in for him to sign?"

"That's perfect!" Elyse hugged her as the lift doors opened. Just as Sarah walked out of the lift a man was dashing into the next one, a dark man, tall, and Sarah whirled to catch a better look at him, but the doors closed before she saw anything. She frowned but put it down to coincidence and walked with Elyse out to the car.

"Hey, I meant to tell you, I love what you've done to your hair," Elyse opened the door and got in as Sarah started the car. "Is it a different shampoo? It looks thicker and even a bit longer."

Sarah flipped down the sun visor, the mirror on the other side showed her hair to be quite a bit thicker, and there was a definite wave to it. She ran her hand through her hair and tossed it to one side, marvelling at the thickness and volume. Something was happening to her, something strange, but good.

She parked right in front of the office, it was a two-hour parking space, but there was only an hour and a half left to the day so she should avoid a ticket and locked her car. Elyse was grinning ear to ear, and Sarah put her fingers to her lips in a *shhh* gesture. Elyse nodded, but still smiled as they walked into the office.

"How'd it go?" Joan asked as Helen spoke on the telephone.

Sarah winked at Joan and also gave her the *shhh* gesture, and Joan smiled and nodded. The girls walked back into the office, not saying much to anyone as they went back to their desks. Not a half hour passed before the courier turned up with the contracts, and Joan ushered the courier straight into Matthew's office.

Elyse winked at her as they watched Matthew start to sign so he could give them back to the courier before he pressed his intercom on his desk.

"*Sarah, can I see you in my office, please?*"

Sarah brushed her skirt down and walked quickly into Matthew's glassed office, a demure smile on her face. "Can I help you?" she asked.

"Am I reading this right? We have control of all of the Kolac Enterprise buildings?"

Sarah smiled wider. "Even the commercial properties, including warehouses."

"Wait there for a minute," he said as he quietly signed the contracts. He put them back into the courier's envelope and handed them to the fellow before Joan led him out. Matthew stood up and regarded Sarah.

"You didn't think to check with me first?"

"No, Matt, I didn't. I didn't want to give him any reason to think we couldn't handle his business, and if I had to check with you before I signed, he might have started to wonder if I was capable. I didn't want that to happen."

Matthew frowned. "That's damn presumptuous of you, girl." His frown changed into a smile and he grabbed her in a tight bear hug. "You've just landed the biggest rental deal we've ever had! Jesus, Sarah, this is beyond amazing! Fuck me, I am floored. Absolutely floored."

"Can't breathe," Sarah gasped and Matthew let her go.

"Sorry, geez, that was a little inappropriate. But wow, just wow. And your bonus, well, Christ, you could put a deposit on a house!"

"Really? You think I'll get a decent amount?"

"I'm sure of it! I'm going to call the owners now, they'll probably want to speak to you, too. Go back to your desk, I'll let you know how it goes."

Sarah opened the office door and saw every face turn to look at her, Elyse must've let the cat out of the bag. They all started to applaud as she walked out, and she could feel her cheeks burning red. Elyse was standing as she applauded and ran over to hug her. Paul was next, and then the new guy, Reid, Sarah feeling self-conscious as he hugged her.

"Sorry," he whispered into her ear. "I just couldn't resist."

She looked at him and he winked at her, moving back to allow the other sales and rental staff access to her. Sarah was enjoying the accolades but started to become a little overwhelmed, and thankfully Matthew noticed and called for everyone to get back to work. He indicated there was a phone call for her, and Sarah knew it would be the owners of their franchise. She went back to her desk and took the call, accepting the paise and gasping when they estimated her bonuses.

She wanted to scream out her joy but thought maybe she'd just message her parents and her brother, then sent another text to Kelli.

They all texted back immediately, excited for her, proud, though her dad gave her a mini lecture about not wasting the money. Typical dad. She went through her last emails and signed off on a few reports as the day drew to a close, and Elyse spun her chair around to lean on Sarah's desk. "Wanna grab a quick meal to celebrate? Your shout, of course."

"Yeah, sure, that sounds good. Where'd you want to go?"

"How about the veggie place, the new one? Has amazing reviews."

Sarah thought about it for a second. "Okay, sure, though I'm not a vegetarian."

"Me neither, but it's nice to eat healthy sometimes. Or if you want, we can go to the barbeque place?"

"Nah, that's too far down, and you have to wait for ages to get in there. Though I have got my car, we can drive over to the burger place, Harry's Burgers?"

"Yes! I've always wanted to go there. I'll grab my coat and leave my car here; you can drop me back on the way home."

"Sounds like a plan." She turned to see Braden

and Reid about to leave. “Hey, you two, wanna come to dinner and celebrate Sarah’s big break?”

The men exchanged glances and nodded. “Sure, yeah, that’d be great!” Sarah glared at Elyse, but the girl was incorrigible. “Should we all go in one car?”

“No, that’s okay, you and me will go in my car, and we can meet the guys there,” Sarah interjected before the guys could accept Elyse’s offer.

She unlocked her car as Elyse explained to the guys where the burger place was located, and then leaned over to open the door for her new friend.

“Why didn’t you want the guys to come with us?” Elyse asked.

“Look at my back seat, Elyse. There’s no room.”

Elyse looked back and burst out laughing. “Oh my god, you’re a pig! Your car is disgusting!”

Sarah pulled out into traffic and grunted at her co-worker. “I’m still your boss.”

“Yeah, and you’re a pig. Oh my god, you have to clean this up! What if you had to give the other managers a lift or something?”

“Good point. I’ll clean it up on the weekend, I guess. It’s just such a pain to carry everything up to my apartment.”

“So don’t. Most of that stuff can be thrown out, and just take a bit up every night. There’ll be less on the weekend that way.”

“Look out for a park, there’s Harry’s on the corner.”

Elyse tapped the window. “There’s a spot there, can you reverse park?”

“Like a boss,” laughed Sarah as she zipped into

the parking spot. “Great, it’s starting to rain.”

“With hair like yours that’d be a pain. Does it go all curly frizzy when it gets wet?”

Sarah got out of the car. “I have no idea.”

Elyse looked puzzled but didn’t say anything. The guys were just going into the burger place as the girls ran across the road, and Sarah stopped as she got to the door, that feeling of being watched catching her. She looked around but couldn’t see anyone.

“You okay?” Elyse asked.

“Yeah, I just thought someone was watching me,” Sarah answered.

“Was it that dark guy there?” Elyse pointed and Sarah saw a figure, obscured by a shadowy doorway, and was sure he was tall, dark, and definitely watching her. He seemed to know she was looking, and he moved back.

“Did you see what he looked like?” Sarah asked.

“Nah, he was real dark, though. Maybe African, or Aboriginal, I couldn’t tell from here. Do you know him?”

Sarah shook her head and followed Elyse into the restaurant. The men were waiting at the bar and joined them as the waiter led them to a table. The place looked warm and inviting, and Sarah was pleased when Reid pulled out her chair for her, Braden noticing and following suit for Elyse.

They ordered their burgers, all passing on any alcohol, and Sarah had to admit she enjoyed the chatter, the men keeping things light and easy, though the attraction between Elyse and Braden was obvious. Elyse kept touching the dark haired man's arm, or face, and he reached out more than once to tuck her blonde tresses behind her ear. Reid met Sarah's eye when the two bent close and started whispering, and he rolled his eyes.

"Think you have an interoffice romance happening," he whispered to her.

"Just what I need. Not," Sarah laughed with the attractive man. He was exactly what she was attracted to in the opposite sex - tall, attractive, and fair haired and skinned. Well dressed and well spoken, his clipped British accent intrigued her.

"So how long have you been in Australia?" she asked him.

"Five years, I'm a permanent resident now. Came here with my family, though I was going to stay behind when they came."

"Why would you stay behind?"

"Well, I'm the oldest, I was twenty-one, and had all my friends, girlfriend, a life there."

Sarah sipped her orange juice. "What changed your mind?"

He smiled at her, and Sarah felt her stomach flip at his straight white teeth. "Girlfriend found someone else better than me. My best friend. So, I came. Haven't regretted a single minute."

"Would anyone like dessert?" The waiter had four dessert menus in his hand.

"Sure, why not?" Sarah held out her hand. "Diet's out the window anyway."

"Why do you need to diet?" Reid asked, genuinely puzzled.

"You're sweet," Sarah flipped open her menu. "Elyse, you want to share a slice of cheesecake?"

Elyse looked up. "What?"

"You want to share a piece of cheesecake?"

Elyse shrugged. "Sure, I'll share a piece with Braden."

"I'd prefer the lava cake," Braden said and handed his menu to the waiter.

"I'll share a slice of cheesecake with you," Reid offered.

"And coffees," Elyse handed her menu to the waiter. "Cappuccinos all round, please."

They ate their dessert and chatted, Sarah enjoying Reid's wit. Every joke he told seemed funnier because of his accent, and Sarah's face started to hurt from laughing. She didn't realise how late it was until the waiter placed the check on the table and she looked around, the restaurant empty of all patrons, except for them.

"Come on, guys, it's a work night," Sarah grabbed her purse and put her share of money down, the others following suit.

"This has been an awesome night," Elyse smiled warmly at Braden, and Sarah noticed they were holding hands.

"Yes, thanks everyone, it was very enjoyable. Let's go, Elyse, I'll drive you to your car."

Sarah thought the girl would protest and say she was going with Braden, but instead she just kissed him lightly on the cheek and followed Sarah out into the night. Sarah didn't think to look for the dark man, she just ran across the road and got in her car.

"Looks like you and Braden hit it off."

"We sure did. Oh, Sez, he's awesome! I can't believe how perfect he is!" Elyse put her seatbelt on as Sarah pulled out. "He's such a nice guy. He raised his little brothers and sister when his parents died, the youngest one just went to Uni this year. What a honey!"

"Wow, that's a huge commitment, poor guy. Here's your car, I'll wait while you get in. See you at work tomorrow?"

Elyse leaned over and kissed her on the forehead. "That you will, boss. Congratulations again. You did good."

Sarah waited as promised until Elyse pulled out, and then drove around the corner and through the alley that led to the car park. As promised, she filled her arms with as much as she could carry and took it upstairs. She dropped half at her door as she fumbled for her key and kicked it inside when she finally got the door open.

Shoes, handbags, and two or three jackets all got put away, and Sarah took a rubbish bag and put it on her briefcase so she could fill it with rubbish from her car in the morning. After such a big day she was tired and decided on one glass of wine before bed. She turned on the television so the apartment wasn't silent, and sat on the couch. She didn't notice at first but sitting there she couldn't believe her eyes.

All of her plants were different, all had grown exponentially, they were lush, green, and beautiful.

She put her wine down and turned on all the lights, amazed at her little indoor jungle. Even the plants in her bedroom and bathroom were huge, and she unlocked the door to look on the balcony. The plants were the same out there, it looked like a little slice of a botanical park. She stood looking at the transformation when she heard a tiny meow.

Being on the seventh floor, Sarah knew that there was no possible way a stray animal could find its way onto her balcony, but she heard it again. The call seemed to be coming from above her, and she looked out from her balcony, looking up at the roof. She had to lean out a little, and that always freaked her out, but she could hear the pleading call, and knew there had to be a kitten stuck on her roof.

The kitten must've been able to see her, the call intensified, but Sarah couldn't see anything in the dark. She pulled a chair over and stood on it, lifting her hands up and screaming as the kitten jumped into her hands. She nearly overbalanced, so jumped off the chair and hurried inside, the small animal in her hands.

The kitten was brown, a rich, mink like colour. Sarah didn't know cats could be a chocolate brown like this. It was looking at her with its bright blue eyes and started to purr. She had no idea where it could have come from, but it was a bag of bones, the poor thing was starving.

She had some tuna in her pantry so opened a tin and emptied it onto a plate, the kitten jumping onto her kitchen bench to attack the food.

Sarah patted the poor little thing, and it purred as

it ate. She sat a bowl of water next to the food, then looked for something to use as a kitty litter. She had a cardboard box and tore up some strips of paper and put it inside. Hopefully the kitty would get the idea, she didn't want it dirtying in her apartment. She knew she could quickly run to the supermarket, but it was late, and dark, and she didn't want to be out on the street at night.

The kitten finished the entire plate of food and meowed at Sarah, so she put it into the makeshift litter box. The kitten squatted, doing exactly as it should, and Sarah picked up the little thing when it was finished.

"You poor little baby!" she crooned. "How long were you stuck up there, poor baby. Come on, sit on the couch with me, we can put up a *found* poster in the foyer for you tomorrow. Poor kitty kitty."

The little thing purred louder than its little body should be capable of and nestled against her as she walked back to the couch. When she sat down the kitten crawled up her shoulder and nestled under her hair, purring into her ear. Sarah sipped her wine, smiling to herself. She hoped no one claimed the little thing; she had always wanted a pet and knew the building allowed them, she had seen other cats in the hall, and people taking their dogs down the lift to walk them.

She changed channels on the television and didn't even realise she had picked up the cards until they were in her hand. The card with the plants and the picture of the cat was on the front and she drew it close to her face to examine it. The cat was brown, just like the kitten, and it had bright blue eyes.

She frowned. Something was going on. Obviously the cards were magic, or enchanted, or something, she wasn't sure of the terms. Clearly the plants had grown while she was at work, and her hair had grown and thickened, she couldn't see it in the mirror, but she could feel it and see it as it hung over her shoulders.

She looked at the next card. This one was a slim woman, large breasted, small waist, and a firm, round arse. She sighed. Up until this week she had been to the gym every second morning. She struggled to keep her weight to this level, getting a waist as slim as the picture, or as slim as Elyse's seemed impossible.

She looked at the next card. This one showed a beautiful necklace on a very ornate table, beside the necklace was some jewellery and a glass of wine. She moved to the next card, and this one held the dark man. She smiled when she noticed the bushes had dropped even lower, she could see most of his firm buttocks, and they were pretty damn good. She wasn't a sexist person, and didn't believe in objectifying either sex, but she also was human, and female, and had been alone for quite some time.

There was no doubt this man, this picture, was hot. Like, smoking hot. She turned the card over, looking at the intricate patterns on the other side. The pattern alone was beautiful, a swirling, brightly coloured collage of gum leaves, wattle, swirling vines, and what looked like a lyre bird in the middle. She'd like that as a print on her wall, it'd look brilliant with her new green foliage. She turned it back and looked at the dark man, his profile taking forever to reveal itself.

Sarah was fairly certain she would see the whole man soon, each day he turned just a fraction more, and she got to see more of his delicious physique. Wrapping the cards up and putting them away, her thoughts turned to Reid and his clipped British accent. He was pretty much every box ticked on her list, if she had a list, of what she'd like to have in a man. Feeling a bit warm and fuzzy she lifted the little kitten off her shoulder and sat it on the couch as she went to take her shower. The kitten sat on her clothes and waited for her to finish, then climbed up her robe and sat on her shoulder while she brushed her teeth. She looked at her hair, amazed at how thick and luxurious it looked now, and it had indeed grown a good two or three inches.

She wasn't sure what to think, whether to keep looking at the cards, or to tell someone, or maybe to throw them away. She decided to tell Kelli when they got together before Hannah's party on Saturday night. Maybe she'd ask her to get changed here, and then show her the cards. See what she thought. She yawned and looked at the kitten, the tiny thing was snuggled up into the collar of her robe and was purring like a tiny freight train. She wasn't sure where to put the little thing to sleep, but as she went to bed the kitten climbed up and found a spot on the end of the bed, turning around about a dozen times until it found its comfort, then immediately fell asleep.

Sarah wasn't far behind the little kitten, and drifted off into a deep, restful sleep almost immediately.

She woke, not sure what had woken her, but then she saw him. His strong, tall body stood out in a black silhouette against the shuttered window, and as he turned Sarah realised he was naked. His manhood was large, and firm, not quite erect but not far off, and she couldn't drag her eyes from it. He pulled back the quilt that was covering her and reached towards her.

He touched her neck, his hands warm against her skin, and Sarah felt her pulse in her temples. Her breath quickened as the man touched her neck again, this time his fingers trailed down her collarbone to the cleft between her breasts, and he smiled. It was dark and there was a shadow covering most of his face, but she could see his perfectly white, straight teeth against his full lips. He pulled the quilt back further and climbed into bed, holding himself above her and to one side, his manhood now touching her thigh and making her breathe even harder. She felt her need grow, her desire for him strong, overwhelming, and she reached up and touched his chest. His skin was smooth and warm, his muscles taut, and he leaned forward pressing his mouth against hers, his tongue pushing its way between her lips and into her mouth.

He kissed her, long and hard, and her back arched with passion, her thighs parting, her lips pressing against his as she kissed him back. Gently, she pulled at him, guiding his body over hers, and he lowered himself onto her, though held his weight in those arms, those strong, muscular arms.

Sarah gasped as he moved to enter her, a cry on her lips as she felt his hardness enter, and though she was willing, though she was ready for him, the size of him was what made her cry out. She gasped and buried her head into his chest as he thrust harder, her hips lifting and joining his rhythm, her heart beating in time with his.

The alarm woke her, and Sarah wiped the sweat from her brow. She'd never had a dream like that before, and she was left feeling weak, shaken and exhausted, as if she'd really had sex with the strange dark man. She climbed out of bed and stumbled towards the shower.

Chapter Eight

Sarah enjoyed the rest of her working week, she enjoyed the fact that nothing else happened that was as traumatic or bizarre, and especially, no more deaths, and that was just fine by Sarah. Her hair had slowed in its transformation, she hoped it would keep growing the same way, but of course had no way to figure out if that was going to happen.

Her plants continued to flourish but were now growing at a normal rate. She made sure she attended to them, watering them and turning them around to greet the light, and trimming any wayward stems, or dried leaves.

No one claimed the kitten, and though Sarah left the notice in the foyer at her building, and a poster on the door facing the street, she secretly hoped no one stepped forward to claim the little brown cat. She did have the nagging feeling that the cat was a manifestation from the cards but strived to let that thought disappear into the back of her mind. She was growing very fond of the little scrap of fur and had bought a litter tray and at least a week's worth of food, along with a score of kitten toys to keep the little thing happy.

She also had not touched the cards for a few days, having put them in her bedside table drawer and made a concerted effort not to touch them again. Not that she would admit to being scared of them, though if she was truthful with herself, she *was* quite scared, but she also wanted to see if the things that were happening stopped happening, or if they continued. She also was experiencing a massive week, with the new contracts and properties she had to hire three new property managers, and Matthew trusted her to interview and make the decision with little to no input from him. As much as she loved having that responsibility, it was also quite daunting.

Sarah felt that she would be judged on the performance of her new staff, if they failed, it would be a failure on her part for hiring the wrong people, so she made sure she was tough on her interviewees. She knew Reid had a brother he wanted her to hire, but she thought it best to keep family out of the equation for now. She would need more staff as things were sorted out, and she could always give his brother a chance later on down the track.

And while she didn't dream any weird dreams, and didn't see anything strange, anything *card-like*, she did occasionally feel like she was being watched, and rarely, just every now and then, caught a glimpse of a tall, dark man, just on the edges of her periphery, always in the shadows, always where the shadows moved.

Friday night came around quickly and though Sarah was working in the morning, she still intended to head out for Friday night drinks with the team. She felt she had to, not only to celebrate her big win for the week, but to welcome her new guys to the team. Elyse invited Reid and Braden to join them, who then asked some of their fellow sales guys to come, and somehow the rental team ended up with seven property sales guys at their Friday night drinks.

Sarah had warned everyone that they all needed to be up early, Saturday was a big day for real estate, and she needed her guys sharp, the same with the sales team. It wasn't just that, Sarah didn't want to be exhausted for Saturday night. She was very much looking forward to Hannah's party, and to seeing Kelli. She needed a big, fun, hair down and too many drinks type of party, and Hannah always delivered on the fun side. She also needed to share her weird week with her best friend.

She was still going to tell Kelli about the cards. It would be hard to avoid, Kelli was sure to notice the veritable jungle in Sarah's apartment, and her little brown jungle cat. And her hair, of course. Kelli was well aware of Sarah's dissatisfaction with her thin, stringy hair, and her great wish to have long, thick, wavy locks. One look at Sarah's gypsy waves and Kelli would know straight away something was up.

She didn't know if Kelli would believe her, but out of everyone she knew, Sarah thought Kelli would be the most likely to take what she said seriously and help her look into the weird cards. Sarah also wanted to see if Kelli found anything in her box that might be a little bit weird, maybe another set of cards, or anything, really, that seemed like it was more than what it looked.

"Hey, Sarah, we'll meet you there," her new guys called to her as they walked out with the rest of the staff. Sarah finished up her email and sent it, then grabbed her handbag. She was going to walk down with Mason, another of the rental staff.

They met at the pub on the next block over, it was a great place that Sarah really liked. A rooftop garden area was the perfect place for Friday night drinks, the guys had already ordered a round and there was a plate of tapas on the table.

"Matthew put money on the tab for us!" Braden told them as they walked in. "We hope it's okay that we ordered something to eat?"

Sarah smiled at the attractive man. "Sure, it's better that people have something to eat. Is everyone here?" She looked around the table, and everyone gave her a nod and assurance that everyone was there.

"I just want to say, before we start drinking, that this isn't an official work function, but guys, act like it is, please. I don't want to see anyone get wasted, especially you new people, all five of you! Yes, even you sales guys. You know you all have to work in the morning, and I won't be accepting any calls to say you're not well, cool?"

Everyone nodded.

"Next, let's welcome our new property managers, Andrew, Piers, and Seth. You guys are my first new hires, like, ever, so you better not let me down, you hear?"

The three boys smiled and clapped their hands.

"Why'd you only hire guys?" Elyse asked. "We've only got a couple of girls on the rental team!"

"All the girls that attended for the interview were bitches, Elyse, you would've hated them." She paused for laughter. "I'm not a sales manager, but let's also welcome Reid and Braden to the Westwood Real Estate family. I hope you guys are super successful!"

They raised their glasses to Sarah and received the applause with grace.

"And before anyone forgets," Mason stood up, glass in hand. "Let's have a round of applause for our almost new department manager Sarah, for winning the biggest contract ever in the history of Westwood. You new guys are here because of her big win, so you kinda need to kiss her feet, too."

Sarah laughed and lifted a foot into the air. "Such dainty feet they are, too!"

The laughter that flowed was genuine, and Sarah grabbed a handful of the tapas and sat them on a napkin next to her glass of wine. Elyse leaned in and whispered in her ear.

"I think I want to fuck Braden."

Sarah squealed and slapped her shoulder. "You dirty slut. You just met him! You haven't even been on a date yet!"

"Yeah, right. Do you think I should wait a couple of days?"

"I think you should wait a couple of weeks, girl! Get to know him at least. I mean, more than a couple of days, really see if he's what you want to risk your job over." Sarah would have to remember to tell her brother that Elyse was off the cards.

Elyse sat back, a frown on her face. "You saying

you'd fire me?"

"Shit no, idiot, I'm saying if things don't work out you may feel like leaving, you know, if it gets awkward and shit. You know what I mean? If it all goes pear shaped it could be real weird, and one of you'd probably leave. That's what I meant."

"Oh, I get it. Yeah, you're right. He's super-hot, but he is a salesman. He might just be telling me what I want to hear, yeah?"

"Yes! That's exactly right! You need to take things easy for a bit. And get fucked for thinking I was threatening you!"

Elyse laughed and ate some of Sarah's food. "He is super-hot, though."

"Yeah, he is. I'm not blind."

"Yes you are. You don't even see Reid is like crushing on you so bad."

Sarah wrinkled her nose. "Hundred percent I'm not blind, but I have to take the same advice I just gave you, girl. And even more than you, because I'm a department manager. But I have to say it's so fucking hard! He's really pretty, and those eyes are amazing. Seriously."

"I know, right? Argh!" Elyse shook her head, making her blonde hair fly around in a halo around her head. "Maybe I'll wait, okay, yeah, I'll wait, but if he asks me on a date I'm for sure going."

"Just don't fuck him."

"Okay."

"I mean it."

"Fuddy duddy." Elyse laughed. "Hey you're working tomorrow, right?"

"Sure am."

"Do you mind if I take off like a half hour early? I have a party to go to, and it's like in Frankston, so I'd like to get going early, if that's all right?"

"Elyse, I've got a party too. If you gave me some notice I could have covered you, but I've got opens all day, and you're rostered to help Seth on that one. It's his first day out in the field, you can't leave him alone."

Elyse looked unhappy, but took a drink and didn't answer, moving off to talk to Braden and leaving Sarah alone. She frowned as Reid came over with another glass of wine for her. "I don't think I can have any more than this, so last one, thanks."

"You looked pissed off. Something happen with Elyse?"

Sarah shrugged. "I kind of feel she is pushing our new friendship to get favours. I could be wrong, though. I hope I am. Anyway, how's it all working out for you?"

Reid smiled at her and Sarah felt her heart quite literally flutter. "I wouldn't worry about her, she's young, and probably doesn't even think before she speaks. And me? Good, I made my first sale today, so I think Paul likes me. Not as successful as you, not yet, anyway."

"Always aim high, good way to be. I guess you have some open houses tomorrow, you might get lucky again."

Reid leaned in close, his breath warm on her neck. "It's all about getting lucky, Sarah."

She hesitated, lost for a moment in his breath, in his scent, in his words, before she realised she was about to do what she had just cautioned Elyse against.

"Not just luck, hard work is needed to be successful," Sarah recovered, and took a sip of her wine.

"I'm willing to work as hard as I need to, for as long as it takes," Reid replied, his bright green eyes flashing under his thick eyelashes.

"Good to hear," Sarah stood and excused herself, joining Mason and some of the other property managers. She chatted about nothing significant for a while, refusing to turn or look for Reid. She thought perhaps she'd better go home, it was getting late and she didn't want to leave the poor kitten alone for too long as it was going to be alone the next night as well. She looked around to see who could walk her down to her car when she felt someone watching her.

Thinking it was Reid, she didn't look behind her, she didn't want him to walk her down to the car. The temptation for a goodnight kiss would be too great, so she leaned over and grabbed Mason's elbow.

"Hey dude, can you walk me to my car? I'm taking off."

"Yeah, me too," Elyse came over. "I should head off as well, before I get myself in trouble."

"How much have you had to drink, Elyse?"

"Sezzy, don't worry, I'm fine!"

"She's not fine," Sarah looked at Mason. "You

live near her, right?"

"Yes, absolutely. You're coming with me, Elyse, I'll give you a lift home, and I can bring you back in the morning."

Elyse shook her head, giggling.

"Boss's orders!" Sarah looped her arm through Elyse's, and Mason did the same on the other side. "Night everyone, see you all in the morning!"

The feeling of being watched persisted, and Sarah was surprised to see Reid standing at the other end of the bar, his back turned to her, talking to Braden and a few others. So who was watching her, making her feel like this? She turned her head just as a dark shape moved from her view, a glimpse of a very tall man disappearing down the stairs at the rear of the open rooftop.

Elyse stumbled and Mason righted her, causing Sarah to forget the dark man as she helped get the drunken girl down the front staircase and bundled her into Mason's car.

"What if she upchucks in my car?"

"I won't throw up!" Elyse burped and swallowed, then laughed. "I don't think I will, anyway."

Sarah shrugged. "If she throws up, the company will have your car cleaned, okay?"

"I'd just rather she didn't chuck, if that's okay."

Sarah tapped on the roof and hurried to her own car, almost embarrassed to drive such a short distance. Mason watched her until she started her car, then did a U-turn, Elyse's head hanging out the open window on the passenger side. Sarah laughed as she drove home, parking out the back of the building and hurrying inside, as always, a little freaked out about coming home late, and by herself.

She didn't feel safe until she opened her own front door and was greeted by her little brown kitten, the tiny thing climbing her clothes to nestle on her shoulder, under her hair. Sarah reached up to pat the soft kitten. “We really should think of a name for you, little one.”

Chapter Nine

"Hurry up, Andrew, I have to go, I've got a friend coming to mine and I don't want her waiting outside for me," Sarah called to her new rental guy as he fussed about with his papers.

"Sorry, I'm not in a routine yet. I've put all the keys back and filed all the applications, this is just my notes, I'm taking them home to sort them out, if that's okay with you?"

"Sure is. Have a good weekend, I'll see you on Monday. Good job today."

Andrew was stuffing the paperwork into his briefcase as Sarah left, waving to Joan on the desk. Kelli was meeting Sarah at her place, but they were going to walk down the street and have a late lunch somewhere before getting ready for the party. She wanted to go up and change out of her high shoes, but Kelli was waiting at the front door for her.

"Hiya! Have you been waiting long?"

"Nope," Kelli leaned over to kiss her cheek. "You wanna put that upstairs first?"

"Mind reader." Sarah used her pass to open the foyer door. "I've got something to show you, too."

They didn't speak on the ride up to her floor as they weren't alone in the lift, and the other occupants were weirdos that Sarah wasn't comfortable with. They got off the floor before hers and Kelli burst out laughing.

"Seriously, did they just bathe in gutter water?"

"They always stink, and it's weird, because I think he's a lawyer. Can you imagine being in an office with him?"

"What about the missus? She smelled just as bad!"

Sarah rolled her eyes as the lift opened, and they nearly bumped into a group of cleaners with their trolleys, mops and buckets. Kelli laughed again as they dodged them, then headed down Sarah's hallway. They stopped at Sarah's door, but faced the apartment opposite, as the door was open and someone was inside.

"Are they cleaning, renovating, or moving in?" Kelli wondered as she twisted her head for a peek

Sarah turned back to her door, turning the key and opening it ready to escape if confronted by anyone. She slid her briefcase in and turned to see if she could see anything other than the half-closed door and a vague shape behind it.

"New carpet," Kelli pointed. "And I can smell paint, too."

"They needed to fix it up, that druggie person probably ran a meth lab in there. It would've been filthy; she was always filthy, and the boyfriend wasn't much better. They were gross."

"Well I hope you don't get someone worse."

"Nah, I won't. I emailed the letting agent and they said they'd keep this floor for private tenants, no welfare cases here."

"Thank god for that."

"Amen," Sarah smiled. "Anyway, I'll just change my shoes so I can walk comfortably down the street. Come in for a sec."

Sarah stepped back to let her friend in, watching for her reaction. She had to notice the difference from just a week ago. Kelli was still trying to get a look at the person opposite, she only turned when the kitten mewed.

"You got a kitty cat?" she gasped. "Oh my god, really?"

Kelli finally stepped in and closed the door behind her, her eyes on the tiny brown scrap of fluff that circled Sarah's feet before climbing up her clothes to nestle under her hair.

"It's so cute! Give it to me!"

Sarah handed the kitten to Kelli and walked further into the apartment, trying to lead Kelli in and see what her reaction would be.

"What have you called her?"

"I don't even know if it's a her," Sarah said. "I thought I'd wait a week, see if anyone claimed the little thing. It was on the roof of my balcony, I had to get a chair to get it down."

"Definitely a girl, she has tiny little lady bits. And how on earth did she ... holy shit, Sarah, did you raid a garden centre?"

Sarah laughed. "These are the same plants from last week, Kells."

"Bullshit. Your plants were all sad twisted things that were always wanting a drink and a feed, these things are, well, they are a tropical garden!"

"Something's been happening since last week, Kelli, something weird. And not just my plants, it's the cat, and even my hair!"

"What do you mean, your *hair*? That's just extensions."

"No it isn't, this is my hair. It's my real hair. Well, it's my own hair that's just gone mad since last week."

Kelli grabbed a handful of Sarah's hair and lifted it up, looking for the extension tapes. She handed Sarah the kitten and ran her fingers through Sarah's scalp, looking for any clue as to how the new hair was attached to her friend's scalp.

"I'm telling you, it's my real hair!"

"I don't get it. Like, how did your hair and your plants grow like this in just a week? Less than a week, shit, I saw this place on Sunday and your plants weren't like this."

"In the box you got from the market, you know from the last stall, did you get anything weird?"

Kelli frowned. She looked around the room before answering. "Weird, like how?"

"Well, I got this," Sarah walked over to the couch and picked up the wooden box. "It's a set of fortune telling cards, and from what I could look up they're based on some really ancient ones, but with a twist."

"What do you mean, a twist?"

Sarah sat on the couch. She placed the kitten beside her and opened the box, unwrapping the cards and handing them to Kelli. She gazed at them and handed them back.

"They're ugly. And they smell kinda funky. What've they got to do with any of this?" Kelli sat down on the couch.

Sarah flicked through the cards and found the one with the girl whose hair she had admired and showed it to Kelli.

"So?"

"So, I liked her hair. I wished I had hair like that, now I do. And this one," Sarah found the card with the plants and the cat. "This is the one I looked at before my plants grew. And there's more, I've been having really weird dreams lately, and then they come true."

Kelli snorted.

"I'm serious! I dreamed about Noel, the dickhead service guy that I fired, I dreamed he got hit by a fire engine."

"Yeah, it was a strange way to die, no wonder you dreamed about it."

"I dreamed it before he died! And the druggos, Kelli, I dreamed about that too, the night before they died, as well!"

Kelli tipped her head to one side, and Sarah could tell she wasn't sure if she should believe Sarah, or if she was being fed a big pile of horseshit.

"And there's another thing."

Kelli's eyebrows raised, but she didn't say anything.

"This one, it's the strangest one. Hang on, I'll just find it." Sarah shuffled through the cards to find the dark man and couldn't find him at first. She flipped through the cards a second time and realised the reason she couldn't find the card the first time. The dark man's card looked exactly as it had the first time she saw it. His back was squared, and the foliage was over waist high. Sarah frowned. Why had the card changed back to the original position? She held it close to her face, really examining it, when Kelli snatched it out of her hands.

"Hey, he's hot! I wish the bushes were a little lower. I could really trim that hedge, you know what I'm saying?"

"That's just it, Kelli, they were lower, or cut, or something."

"What are you saying, Sarah?"

"I'm saying that every day I see a bit more of this guy, like, he turns just a tiny bit, just a fraction, and the bushes are lower. But now he's right back to the start, like he hasn't moved at all." Sarah flicked through the cards again, just in case there was more than one dark man card. Frustrated, she sat the cards down and took the dark man card from Kelli. "I don't know why he's turned back, but that's just one thing. You see, every day he doesn't just turn around, but I think I see him, on the street, or in the supermarket."

"Like he's following you?"

"Yeah, um, no, maybe. I don't know. But Kelli, I can feel him when he's there, I feel him watching me. It's the weirdest feeling."

Kelli chewed her bottom lip, her gaze on the pile of cards. She then looked around the room at the plants and noticed the plants on the balcony were just as lush. She finally turned and looked at Sarah.

"Okay, I'm not sure what I think, or if I really believe everything, but the plants are definitely different, and your hair is completely changed. And I can see that you believe it, so that's good enough for me. Shit, Sarah, I'm a bit freaked out about this. This is super weird, and you don't look like you're freaked out at all."

"No, no, I am, trust me. Super freaked. But also, and this is weird, too, it almost feels right, in a way. Like, the druggies and Noel dying is sad, I guess, but Noel was an arsehole, and the druggies were, well, druggies."

"And the plants? And your hair? Why wouldn't you wish for money or something?" Kelli stood up. "Shit, you did, didn't you? That's how you got the contracts for all those properties? Shit, Sarah!"

"No, I didn't wish for money, and I had those contracts almost won before the cards. I've been talking to that guy since the second day of my job. And I have another guy that I'm pretty much sure I'll get to sign as well, and he's got even more buildings. The only other thing I looked at in the cards was a necklace and jewellery, but I didn't get any jewellery."

Kelli nodded. "Did you wish for it?"

"I like it, but I didn't really want it. It was too fancy, like you'd wear to a ball. And I didn't wish for the other things, not really, but I did like them a lot, and when I think about it, I suppose I did *sort* of wish for them."

"What about Mr. Hot Black-man?"

"You know I like the blonde guys, Kells. But he does have super wide shoulders, he looks like he would be a stunning human. But not really my type, well, not normally, anyway."

"Yeah, he's more my kinda guy. Though I am super crushing on Braden right now."

"I don't want to talk about that, you know how I feel already."

"Yeah, I do. Are there any other hot guys in the cards?"

Sarah started to lay the cards out on the table, and Kelli leaned over to look at them, though Sarah noticed she no longer seemed to want to touch them.

"She's pretty," Keli pointed to one card. "And I like that, what is it, a lake? It's so peaceful and like a paradise."

Sarah kept arranging the cards out in long rows.

"What are these people? Are they aboriginal? I mean, I see there's kangaroos, and that's a lyrebird, but then here there's a peacock, they're from Africa, aren't they?"

"India, I think," Sarah put down another card. "See this? There's a tiger, that's definitely Indian, but then there's wild horses, and an elephant, but here's an emu, and that looks like Uluru. There's some that're obviously Australian, but I don't think lions are Australian, though this looks like a dingo."

"What's that?"

"That's a Tasmanian tiger."

"Bullshit. There are no tigers in Tasmania!"

"Not anymore, but there used to be. They're not real tigers, they're like a dingo or something, but they're extinct. Like a hundred years ago I think."

"Wow, he's more your type!" Kelli pointed to

the card Sarah had just placed on the table. "Looks like a Mr. Blonde Surfer-dude!"

"Yep, that's my taste, right there. I wonder why all the girls are facing forward, but all the guys have their backs turned to us? It's strange, right?"

"Sezzy, everything about these cards is strange. Did you try looking them up on the internet?"

"Yep. I found some sets that looked like they're similar, I told you that before, but these are, I guess, customised? Anyway, I couldn't find the exact ones, but I found some that are close."

Kelli pulled out her phone and took a few pictures of the cards. "I'll search for you as well. Now, put on your shoes, I'm starving. Let's go and eat, we can talk more over lunch. Leave the cards here, though. I don't want a fire engine to run over me."

"Not funny."

"I wasn't joking."

Chapter Ten

"Thanks for driving, Kelli, but I don't mind if you have a drink, I can drive home. I've changed my mind about drinking after all that's happened with the cards. I think I'd rather just keep in control."

Kelli turned off the motor and handed Sarah her keys. "Are you sure? Okay, I'll have one drink, but if I have more than one, please feel free to drive us home."

"I'll grab the present from the back, can you get my handbag?" Sarah reached over the back seat. "I am really looking forward to this, I hope it's not a total lame party."

"Hannah has never thrown a lame party in her life. I think she was born hosting amazing functions, and I seriously cannot wait."

Sarah straightened her dress as she stepped out of the car, the present clutched to her chest. She followed Kelli around the side of the building to the entrance, the decorative lights reflecting off the helium balloons that surrounded the door. The music was loud, but not deafeningly so, and Kelli was walking in time to the beat. Sarah frowned and grabbed Kelli's arm.

"You invited Reid and Braden?"

"Who?"

Sarah pointed to the two men standing by the entrance talking to the hired security guard. "The two guys you met the other day at lunch."

"Shit, seriously? I have no idea why they're here, but I didn't invite them. I barely know them." Sarah walked up to Braden and slapped his shoulder. "What're you doing here, dude?"

Braden turned to Sarah, his face reflecting pure surprise. "What? Hey Sarah, how come you're here?"

"Hannah's been our friend since school," Kelli stepped forward. "How do you guys know her?"

"We only met her a few times, Reid here is Declan's cousin."

Reid smiled at Sarah. "Hi, fancy seeing you here."

Sarah sighed. He was so dreamy, she didn't want to look into those green eyes, or see those full, pink lips.

"You're Declan's cousin? We've never seen you at any of their parties or anything."

"I was in Sydney before my family came here. We've only been in Melbourne for two months, so I'm not surprised we didn't meet before now."

"Let's get inside, guys, I think they're going to serve the food soon," Braden said as he turned to walk inside, Reid starting to follow. Reid turned back, just for a moment, and smiled at Sarah before following Braden inside.

"He's got the hots for you," Kelli teased.

"I know! And he is absolutely gorgeous, but we work together, nothing can happen."

"What, is that like a rule or law or something?"

Sarah hooked her arm through Kelli's. "I'm a

manager, it's not professional, and if things didn't work out, can you imagine how shitty it'd be?"

"Yeah, I can, remember, I'm the girl who dated the principal at my first school placement, right?"

"And dated the club manager at the bar you work at."

"That worked out okay, though."

Sarah laughed. "Only because he transferred states, you idiot. C'mon, let's go inside."

The hall Hannah hired for the night was old but beautifully renovated, a bluestone former church with massive, exposed beams, hardwood floors and stained-glass windows. The decorations were tasteful as well as extravagant, Hannah had combined exotic flowers, fairy lights and delicate lace bunting to make the old church look like an enchanted wonderland.

The tables were decorated with an equal amount of restraint and fantasy, and Kelli went to find their allocated seats while Sarah took the present to the table set aside for this, finding it was already overflowing. Hannah was standing by the table and grabbed Sarah in a hug as she sat the present on top of another.

"My god, Sarah, thank you for coming! Have you seen how amazing everything looks?"

"We never expected it to look anything but amazing, girl. You're about the best interior designer I know."

Hannah laughed. "I'm the only interior designer you know, but thanks, I'll take the compliment. Where's Kelli?"

"Right here!" Kelli bounced up behind Sarah. "You look stunning, that dress is brilliant. It's gonna look amazing in the photographs."

"Speaking of which, turn around, here's my photographer! She'll be snapping all night." Hannah grabbed Sarah and Kelli in each arm and turned her brilliant smile to the camera. Sarah tried to angle her body, so she didn't look too large next to the two slim girls, and wished she'd picked an outfit that minimized her curves. The photographer snapped a few shots and then the girls moved aside so others could get a picture with their hostess as Kelli showed Sarah to their table.

Reid was already seated there, and Braden was off talking to a group of people at the next table. Kelli leaned in so she could be heard over the music.

"So, Reid, tell me all about your handsome friend there," she smiled.

Reid laughed. "I don't know a lot, we've only been working together this week, both hired on the same day."

"But you invited him along to an engagement party?"

Reid nodded. "Yeah, I originally had a date, but she cancelled. I knew the place was already paid for, and I didn't want to let Declan down and have an empty seat. Braden wasn't doing anything, and he actually knows some of the people from his footy club or something. I did ring ahead and check if it was okay to bring him."

"Hey, I'm not the party police or anything. I just

wanted to know a little more about him. Like, does he have a girlfriend?"

"No he doesn't," Braden leaned in between Kelli and Sarah, surprising the girls. Kelli giggled and Sarah nearly rolled her eyes at her friend's obvious flirting. Though she knew Elyse had her eyes set on the handsome man, Sarah was happy he was showing interest in Kelli, it would make the workplace a lot easier to negotiate. She knew Elyse would be disappointed if these two hooked up, but it would absolutely save Sarah from any more awkward conversations about fraternising in the workplace.

Braden pulled a chair out beside Kelli, and Sarah thought Reid was going to follow suit and sit beside herself when the other people sitting at their table joined them, all checking their name tags and taking their allocated places.

The entree arrived straight away and Sarah turned to talk to her friend, but Kelli was engrossed in conversation with Braden, so she turned to her other side. The young lady there smiled at her, but then touched Reid on the sleeve. "Hey, I hope you won't mind, but can I change chairs with you? I'd like to sit next to my sister, if that's okay?"

Sarah groaned inwardly; she didn't think she could resist the charms of the young salesman if she had to sit next to him the whole night. Reid smiled at the young lady and lifted his plate, allowing her to slide over. Sarah filled her mouth with food so that she wouldn't have to speak, but Reid just nodded at her and seated himself before tucking into his meal. He didn't speak at first, perhaps he knew she was trying to resist him, and Sarah was grateful for that.

She could just imagine what Elyse would think if Sarah hooked up with Reid, but Braden was out of her reach with Kelli. She sighed and Reid touched her hand.

"You look like you have the weight of the world on your shoulders, Sarah."

She shrugged. "Not really, I was just thinking how gorgeous it all looks, you know, the decorations and the old church."

"It's the old church I love, I'd really like to buy a place like this one day and convert it into a home," Reid sipped his wine. "They normally have beautiful floors, hardwood, and really high ceilings. You could put in a mezzanine level and still have plenty of head height."

"You've thought about this a lot."

"Yeah, I guess so. You know what it's like, you're in so many people's houses that you can't help but start to plan what your own will be like. I've seen some brilliant church conversions before, and some warehouses, which is my next choice after a church."

Sarah pushed her plate away and picked up her water, thinking she'd better keep her wits about her, she didn't need alcohol to dull her common-sense tonight. A tap on her shoulder made her turn around, and she felt her insides flip flop when she saw who had hailed her attention.

"Ben. I didn't think you were still friends with

Declan."

"Yes you did, you know we've been friends since kindergarten."

"Maybe I was just hoping, then," Sarah sipped her water and turned back, but Ben didn't take the hint.

"Hey, pal, would you mind if I sat here for a minute?"

Reid shrugged and stood up. "Sure, go for it, I'm going to chat to Declan."

Ben slid into the vacated seat and put his hand on Sarah's shoulder. "You look absolutely fantastic."

"I know."

Ben laughed. "I always loved your sense of humour. It's one thing that kept us together even when we were fighting all the time."

Sarah turned to face her ex-boyfriend. She remembered when she'd loved that face, when she'd kissed every inch of it, and stroked that powerful jawline. "No, we just stayed together because we were young and had nowhere else to go."

"I guess we did flog a dead horse a bit, especially at the end there. But we've grown up a lot now, and I'm really happy to see you, Sarah. You look amazing. I like a little bit of weight on you, you wear it well."

"You just called me fat, right?" Sarah laughed at the horrified expression on Ben's face.

"I, no, um, I didn't mean it like that, seriously, you look fantastic."

Sarah laughed again. "Thank you, I think."

Ben ran his hand down Sarah's arm and smiled at her. "You really do look tasty, you know that? God, Sarah, I miss all the times I tasted you. I've never met anyone like you, not ever, and I don't think I ever will. You weren't just my first, you were my best."

Sarah felt all the old feelings come rushing back. The love, the confusion, the friendship. But she also felt the anger, the betrayed trust, the heartbreak. Ben was her first love and he would always hold a special place in her heart, but he'd also been her first heartbreak. He'd cheated on her and left her for one of her friends. That's something you just don't forget.

"If I was your best then I worry about what kind of girls you've been seeing."

Ben kept stroking her arm. "Maybe we can go outside, for old time's sake. I've got my car here. You know you always liked car sex, and I'm parked right away from everyone else, too."

Sarah pushed her chair back and faced him. "You think I'll just rush outside with you and fuck you in your car? Is it still the same car I helped pay for?"

"I keep it because it reminds me of you, Sezzy.

"Don't call me that. Only my friends call my Sezzy."

"Come on, girl. We'll always be friends." Ben took her hand. "Come on, we can be back before dessert, if you like."

"Hey, Ben." Kelli leaned over Sarah and cupped her chin in her hand. "You still living with Ali?

Isn't that her over there?"

Ben shrugged. "What's it to you? You were always sticking your nose in where it doesn't belong."

"It belongs with my friend, Ben, and that means it's right where it should be. Why are you stroking her arm? Won't Ali be upset if she sees that?"

"Mind your business."

"Maybe I should call her over. Hey, Ali!" Kelli called out.

"Stop, Kelli," Sarah said. "I don't want to make a scene."

"You're not, Mr. Cheater here is the one making a scene. I want to see if Ali knows he's asking you out to the car for a quickie."

"No I didn't!" Ben protested.

"You talk too loud, fuckface. We heard every word. Didn't we, Braden?"

"Sure did. You're sprung, dude. Maybe you should just move away now, before things get ugly."

"Are you threatening me?" Ben stood up, his hands clenched in fists.

"He'd better not be threatening you, that's my job," Hannah spoke from behind Sarah's shoulder, startling her a little. She hadn't realised her friend was so close. Hannah smiled, all her teeth showing, but the expression didn't touch her eyes. "I'm pretty sure Sarah wants nothing to do with you, Ben. I wouldn't have invited you or Ali at all but you're one of Declan's oldest friends. Ali, though, none of us want her around much, so maybe you'd better just go and keep your girlfriend on a tight leash, okay?" Hannah patted his shoulder. "Now, Ben. Off with you, boy."

Ben scowled, but when Braden stood up, he nodded at Hannah. "Sure, Ali's probably missing me."

"Hmmm, not so much. She's busy flirting with Dec's cousin. The tall, extremely handsome British cousin. You know girls just love that accent, right?" Hannah laughed as Ben grunted and stomped off to find his girlfriend, while Braden and Kelli joined in with her laughter.

"Sorry, Sarah, I didn't think he'd bother you," Hanna took the recently vacated seat and hugged her friend. "I hear Ali and him aren't getting along at all, and I guess he thought he could plough his old fields."

Sarah smiled. "What are you, a farmer? Seriously, thanks, he's such a sleaze bag."

"Douche asked her to go out to the car for a quickie!" Kelli shook her head. "Like she'd scrape the bottom of that barrel again."

"Even if you wanted him back, we'd never let you, you know," Hannah picked up Sarah's untouched wine and took a mouthful.

"She's right, you know," Kelli kissed Sarah's shoulder. "You don't need that shithead in your life."

"Hey, I've never met him before, and even I don't like him," Braden added.

"Oh, goody, main course! I'm starved, I didn't eat properly for two days with all the planning and shit. I'll catch you guys later, okay?" Hannah didn't wait for a reply, she flounced off to find Declan and take her seat. Sarah pulled her chair back into the table as Kelli took her hand.

"Are you okay, babe?"

"Not really. You know how I feel about him." Sarah squeezed Kelli's hand. "How can you love someone and hate them all at the same time?"

"No, you don't still love him, do you?"

Sarah sighed. "No, not anymore, but I did for a long time. For way too long. I can't believe he came over to me, though. Remember at Dec's birthday? He totally ghosted me, he had nothing at all to do with me. Now he wants to bump uglies in a car?"

"Guy's an arse, Sezzy. I heard Ali is cheating on him, and good on her. He deserves to feel what it's like."

"Maybe," Sarah moved so the waitress could put her plate on the table. She felt the hairs on the back of her neck stand up and her hand froze halfway to her mouth. She knew that feeling. She hadn't felt it for a couple of days, but she knew it. The dark man had to be here. She put her fork down and looked around. She couldn't see him, but she could feel him. He was here. She was sure of it.

"You okay?" Reid asked as he took his seat beside her. "You look like you saw a ghost."

"Nah, just an arsehole," Kelli answered for her, and Sarah looked over at the stained-glass window. She wasn't sure if she saw the silhouette of a very tall, dark man, or if it was a party guest having a smoke. The feeling of being watched passed and she smiled at something Kelli said, even though she'd missed the comment.

Sarah picked up her fork and forced the food into her mouth. Reid put his hand on her shoulder. "You sure you're okay? Look, if I'd known that he was your ex, or a douche, I wouldn't have given him my seat."

Sarah turned to him and gave him an apologetic smile. "There's no way you could've known, Reid. It's okay, don't let him spoil the night."

Chapter Eleven

"You were gone for ages, Kelli," Sarah glanced over her shoulder and changed lanes. "You sucked face, am I right?"

Kelli giggled. "Yes, we made out. I went outside for a smoke with him and we hit it a little bit."

"You hit it? You fucked him?" Sarah turned the car around the next corner and drove onto the freeway. "And a smoke? Kelli, you don't smoke!"

"Well, sometimes I do. And it wasn't that kind of smoke. Some guy had a joint and we tried it out," Kelli laughed. "It makes an alcohol buzz so much better."

"You're incorrigible," Sarah admonished. "So, does this mean he asked you out, or you just had fun?"

"He asked me out to dinner on Wednesday night. And to lunch at work on Monday, so yeah, maybe we'll start dating. He's really nice, Sarah. Super hot. Does your work hire only attractive people?"

"You saw them when you came into lunch, and there are some really wonderful specimens of humankind there. I didn't think about good looks when I hired my new rental guys, though."

"So, you hired fuglies, based purely on their experience?"

"Of course not. I hired hot guys based purely on their experience."

Kelli giggled. "So are you going to date Reid?"

Sarah turned into the alley beside her building and parked. “No, I can’t, I told you, we work together. But he’s soooo cute!”

“I think you should go for it. Just keep it quiet, though.” Kelli undid her seatbelt and grabbed her shoes from the floor. “And no, I didn't fuck Braden. I just kissed him. He’s a good kisser.”

“T.M.I. Kells. Come on, let’s get upstairs. I am stuffed, I just want to go to sleep.”

“I’ll sleep on the couch, if that's okay?”

“Yup. It’s actually more comfortable than my bed, I’m sure. I’ve fallen asleep there more times than I can count.”

Kelli yawned and followed Sarah into the building. They didn’t speak in the elevator, walked silently to Sarah’s door, and were surprised to see the door opposite was open a crack.

“You think someone's moved in?”

“Don’t know. Don’t care tonight. It’s late, Kelli, and I’m still a little rattled from Ben’s big sleaze.”

“Such a douchebag, that Ben. Come on, let's just have a peek, the door’s open, we can just, you know, bump it a little?”

“No! Kelli if the door swings open, you’ll see straight into the lounge room, and if someone is sitting there then they’ll see you looking right at them.”

“So?”

“So, I have to live here, and make eye contact every time we open our doors at the same time. Don't touch the door, please.”

Kelli took a step forward and the door slammed

closed.

“Great, they heard everything we were saying. So that won't be super awkward the first time we meet.”

“They’ll get over it. Besides, they don’t know me, or you.”

“Let’s just get inside,” Sarah yawned. “I’m falling asleep on my feet.”

“Okie dokie,” Kelli replied as she followed Sarah inside the apartment.

Sarah smiled as the kitten came running to her, running up her clothing to purr under her ear as it rubbed affectionately on her neck. She reached up to scratch the kitten with one hand as she pulled open the linen cupboard with the other, retrieving a pillow and blanket for her overnight guest. Kelli was already brushing her teeth with the spare toothbrush Sarah kept for her.

“You want PJs?” Sarah asked.

“Sure, or a nightie, even a t-shirt. I’m not fussy. Hey, you wanna try telling my fortune before we go to sleep?”

Sarah groaned. “I literally am falling asleep on my feet, so no, I don’t.”

“You should put them under your pillow, you know,” Kelli pulled off her dress and pulled the nightie Sarah gave her over her head. “I read that you sleep with them under your pillow to connect with them. Or sync with them, or something. Here, take them to bed with you.”

“Sleep with my hot black card man? Sure. Good night girl.” Sarah kissed Kelli on the cheek. “Let's have a mega sleep in, then go and get brunch."

"That's a bonza plan, honey. Nighty night."

Sarah yawned again as she sat the kitten on her pillow and pushed the card box underneath, before changing into her pyjamas. She couldn't stop yawning, and when the kitten turned around a dozen times before settling into her hair to sleep, Sarah just left it there, listening to the purr that was louder than the little cat itself.

The phone kept ringing, annoyingly waking her up before eight am. She hated getting up early any day but waking up early on a Sunday was enough to put her instantly in a foul mood. The phone stopped so she turned over, but the respite was very brief, the ringtone starting all over again. She fumbled for the phone, her eyes not quite opening enough to see who was ringing.

She had a sudden thought that maybe something was wrong, maybe her mum was sick or her dad had a heart attack, and her heart started to pound in her chest.

"Hello?" Sarah's voice was croaky, and she cleared her throat. "Hello?"

"Hey, Sarah, sorry I woke you."

"Who is this?" Her brain was spinning, trying to figure out who was calling her this goddamn early on a Sunday morning.

"It's me, Sarah, it's Ben. God you sound so good in the morning, your voice is all sexy and sleepy."

"Why the fuck are you ringing me? Didn't you get the hint yesterday?"

Sarah could hear him exhale, then he drew a

deep breath. She was confused as to why he was ringing her, and why this early.

"I'm downstairs, Sarah. Come down and talk to me. I need to see you; you have no idea how much I missed you. Please come down."

"Fuck off, Ben. Go home to your skank girlfriend and leave me alone." Sarah hung up and lay her head back on the pillow.

The phone rang again, and she could see it was Ben calling back. She didn't answer, but he just kept ringing. Sarah sighed and answered the phone, thinking she had to get him to understand that there was no way she would ever go out with him again.

"Go away," she answered.

"Sarah, I'm begging you, please, please come downstairs." *He sounded like he was crying.*

"I told you to fuck off. I don't want anything to do with you Ben. go away, just fuck off and go away, can't you understand me? Fuck off!"

"Sarah, I'm standing next to your car. If you don't come down, I'll do something to your car. I'll fuck it up, I swear."

"I'm calling the police, fuckwit."

"Please, Sarah, please! If you don't come down, I'll kill myself. Right here on your car. I swear I'll kill myself. How's that gonna look for your job, or your apartment building? But if you come down and talk to me, I'll go away. I promise. If you look me in the eye and tell me you never want to see me again, I'll leave and you'll never have to talk to me ever again. I swear on my mother's life, Sarah."

"Bullshit. I'll come down there and you'll just

carry on, we'll have a screaming match and someone will call the cops. So no, Ben, I'm not coming down, and you'll just go home."

"I will kill myself, Sarah. I'm broken, I am. Ali cheated on me and she's pregnant to the other guy. I just don't know what to do with myself. Please come down, just talk to me. That's all I want, I promise. Please, Sarah, please."

"Argh! You're so annoying! If I come down, it'll be just for a second. I'm still in my pyjamas, and I'm not getting dressed. That's all you get, a few seconds, understand?"

"Oh, yes, thank you, thank you, you won't regret it, I promise. Thank you so much."

Sarah hung up and stretched, then grabbed her black wool coat. She wasn't going to get dressed, but she also wasn't going down in just her pyjamas. She slipped it on and snuck quietly out of the apartment, careful not to wake Kelli.

The lift took no time at all to arrive, this early on a Sunday the place was a veritable graveyard, and she rode down fairly confident that she wouldn't bump into anyone. When she turned to walk out the back of the foyer, she could see Ben leaning on her car, waiting for her. She scowled as she opened the door, not giving him any encouragement at all.

"Okay, I'm here. What the fuck do you want?"

"Don't be like that, Sezzy, please. I just wanna talk. I just wanna see you, okay?"

Sarah folded her arms and cocked her hip. "What do you want?"

"I love you; you know that. I've always loved

you. I think I forgot it for a little while there, but I was young, you know, and we fought all the time. I just needed to get out, stretch my legs a little, you know?"

Sarah rolled her eyes, but Ben wasn't discouraged.

"I know I was wrong; I know that now. I'm so sorry for hurting you, I'm so very sorry. I know how you felt, believe me, I know now. I can't believe I let you go. I was crazy to do that, crazy. But I know what I lost, and I'll do anything to get you back, Sarah. Anything. Just ask, and I'll do it. Anything at all. Just name it."

"There's nothing you can do, Ben. You stuffed up. You didn't just fuck around on me, you fucked my best friend. So, you lost me, and then we both lost her. That's it. Now you've got to lie in that bed you made, and that's it. I'm never taking you back. Not ever, you hear me? Not ever."

Ben walked up to her, his arms out, hands held up in supplication.

"I love you so much, Sarah. With my whole heart and soul, I love you. I adore every bit of you."

"No you don't. You just don't want to be alone."

Ben moved closer, and Sarah backed up. "I do love you; you have no idea how much. I would die for you. I would."

"Shame you couldn't be faithful for me. Now I've done what you wanted, and you promised you'd go away and never come back, so go, and go now."

Ben moved closer, but he put his hands in his jacket pocket.

"You can't tell me you didn't love me back then."

"Whatever, that was then. I don't love you now."

"Don't say that."

"I don't love you, Ben, I don't even like you. Just looking at you makes my stomach turn. Please go away. I don't ever want to see you again."

"Don't say that. It's not true. Why are you saying this to me? There's someone else, isn't there? Is it that blonde pretty boy that was sitting next to you at the table?"

"Go home Ben. Just go home."

"It's him, isn't it? He's been fucking you, and you let him. Well, he can't have you, Sarah. You're mine. You'll always be mine; you know that, you've always known that."

"Ben, you're starting to scare me. Please go home, get some sleep. I don't think you've been to bed at all, have you?"

"You know me so well, like no one else ever could. Just tell me you love me, Sarah. Just tell me the truth, that you love me too."

"Ben, I told you, I don't love you. I don't. Nothing you can say or do can change that. It was over back then, and it's still over. Can you understand that? We'll never get back together. Never."

Ben took his hands out of his jacket, and Sarah felt her knees go weak when she saw he was holding a knife. It looked like a carving knife, and the overhead light glinted off the blade, reflecting in his eyes. Sarah looked at his eyes and realised that they had a wild, crazy look about them.

"Go home, Ben. Get some sleep. We can talk later. You need to go home."

"If I can't have you, no one will. You hear me? If I can't have you, then you'll never have anyone touch you ever again."

"Don't say that, Ben. If you love me, you'd never hurt me. You wouldn't do anything to hurt me, would you?" She tried to keep her voice light, confident, as she backed up, sliding along the glass doors, her hands behind her, feeling for the handle.

"We can be together forever this way, Sarah. It's the only way. I can never leave you, and you can never leave me, not ever again."

Sarah felt the door handle and moved her key pass up to open the door.

Ben realised what she was doing and lunged at her, the knife held out to stab her in the chest. Sarah didn't think, she reached out and hit his arm from underneath, flicking the knife up, but he recovered and lunged again. Sarah grabbed his wrist and pushed with everything she had. She put one foot up behind her on the door frame and pushed with all her strength, moving the knife up and away from her, and Ben stumbled. His grip slipped, just a little, and Sarah pushed harder. Ben's hand bent backwards and the knife plunged straight into his chest.

He looked at her, his face suddenly white, then looked down at the knife sticking out of his body. His white shirt showed a large red mark, blood soaked through his shirt and flowed down his waist.

He opened his mouth to speak, but no sound came out, just blood. It splashed onto Sarah's face as Ben coughed, then he fell forward, on top of Sarah, knocking her to the ground and landing astride her small frame.

Sarah could feel the blood covering her and she pushed Ben off, watching as he rolled over, his eyes staring lifelessly at the ceiling. She sat up, looking at her hands which were covered with blood. So much blood, it was all over her, dripping from her hands, pooling in her lap, and spreading from Ben's lifeless body.

Sarah screamed.

She screamed and screamed, her throat raw and bleeding, but she still screamed...

Sarah woke and sat up with a jolt, a scream trapped in her throat. Her bed was soaked with sweat, her sheets tangled, her heart hammering in her chest and her bed clothing clinging to her. The kitten yawned and stretched, then looked at her through half lidded eyes.

She looked over at her bedside clock. It was ten thirty and she could hear the television on in the lounge room. Kelli must've woken up and was watching TV; Sarah could hear the sounds of some reality show playing. She took a deep breath, blew it out and took another, trying to calm her panicky heart. When she felt half human, she swung her legs out of bed and walked into the main room.

"Good morning," Kelli turned to look at her friend. "Fuck, what's wrong with you? You're as white as a ghost Sarah, and your clothes are dripping wet!"

Sarah sat on the arm of the couch, her bare feet on the seat. "I just had the worst nightmare, Kelli. It was a dream like the other ones I told you about."

Kelli picked up the remote to turn down the sound on the television.

Sarah looked over at the kitten as it ran out of her room and into the bathroom, a race to use the litter box. She looked back at Kelli, then down at her hands as she described the dream, Ben, the blood, and the knife. Kelli just looked at her, not reacting, not talking, just listening to everything she said.

"It didn't come true, though. At least, not yet. I didn't go downstairs, and Ben didn't ring me."

Kelli picked up her mobile and flicked through a few things before handing it to Sarah. There was a news alert describing a fight between a young couple in Melton, resulting in a fatal stabbing. Names had not yet been released, but there was a picture.

The picture showed police tape, a body covered with a tarp lying next to a car with personalised number plates.

"That's Ben's car," Sarah gasped.

"I thought it looked like his car, but I just thought something must've happened in his street or something. Sarah, do you think it's him? Do you think you dreamed about his murder?"

"I don't know. I don't know. I'm going to have a shower; I am soaked with sweat. Why don't you turn on the news, and maybe message someone, see what you can find out?"

"I don't think anyone'll be awake yet, but I can try. Go, have your shower. I'll let you know what happens."

"Okay, yeah, thanks. I'll be quick."

"Take your time, Sarah. Wash your hair, de-stress. There's nothing you can do right now."

Chapter Twelve

"I can't believe it," Declan ran a hand through his hair then scrubbed it over his red eyes. "I mean, we all just saw him last night!"

Hannah hugged her fiancé and put her head on his shoulder. "Ali, too. I mean, I didn't like her, I'm not gonna lie, but she didn't deserve to die like that."

"Does anyone know what happened?" Kelli asked as she looked around at the shocked faces at the table. Aaron, Declan's best friend, turned as the waiter came over with a handful of menus, which he sat down before respectfully moving away, aware of the sombre mood of these patrons in the cafe.

"Looks like he and Ali had a fight, and he stabbed her, or she stabbed him, but they both got stabbed," Alek, another close friend of Ben's told them. "All I know is that they both died within minutes of each other. Ben was out on the road, Ali on the front step."

Silence fell over the eight people, and they sat like that for a few moments, mute with their grief and shock.

"Hey," Aaron broke the reverie. "Did you guys know Ali was pregnant? I heard them talking about it last night, and when I tried to congratulate Ben he told me to shut up. Was real pissed off about something."

"It wasn't his baby," Sarah spoke quietly. "Ali

cheated on him, and Ben said it wasn't his baby."

"He told you that?" Hannah was shocked. "Really? I had no idea, though I can't say I'm surprised at the fact Ali cheated."

"Yeah, she was with someone else when she met Ben, she cheated on her boyfriend at the time with him. I guess once a cheater always a cheater."

"Really, Ben was no better," Alek said. "Guy really couldn't keep it in his pants. All due respect, Sarah, but he did cheat on you over and over."

"So I found out. Look, I know I'm not exactly a fan of Ben's and I also know all you guys really liked him. If you want me to go…"

"No, Sarah, stay. We know he wasn't perfect, we know that," Declan placed a hand on Sarah's arm. "But he could be a good guy as well, you know? I mean, of course you do, you were with him for four years, right?"

"Yeah, I was, and I think he always wanted to have kids, too, so I don't know why he was so certain that the baby wasn't his."

"Well, it depends how far along she was, I guess." Hannah looked around the table. "Ben had that six-week business trip to Cairns, remember? So, if she got pregnant when he was gone then he'd know for sure the baby wasn't his. How awful, that's both of them and the baby died? It's just too horrible!" Hannah sniffed and wiped a tear from her cheek as Declan hugged her.

"Waiter's hovering. Anyone want to eat anything?" Alek asked.

"We can get coffees, yeah?" Hannah asked.

"Oh, we can't, sorry, we actually have to meet my mum. Shit, we're late, Sarah," Kelli looked at Sarah, giving her a *don't say anything* look. "Thanks guys and let us know when the funeral is and all that. See you all later, okay?"

"Don't let this take the shine off your engagement, Hannah," Sarah stood up and grabbed her purse. "It's terrible, I know, but don't let this be what you remember about this weekend."

"Hannah and I will make sure we keep the happy memories, and thank you," Declan stood to give the girls a hug, Hannah stood as well and kissed their cheeks.

"Thank you both for coming, I know it's hard on you Sarah, and Kelli, you were never a fan of Ben, but the respect is appreciated."

Sarah held the door for Kelli and waited until they were a few steps away before speaking.

"Your mum?"

"Hey, it's all I could think of on the spot, okay? It's nice that you went along and all, but you really couldn't stand Ben anymore, and shit, Sarah, the dream and seeing all that must've completely spun you out. Sitting there and talking like you didn't see what happened is just, well, crazy."

"Thanks for getting us out of there. Really."

"I'm starved, I really want to eat, can you eat?"

Sarah nodded. "Yeah. I'm not starved, but I'm hungry. I just want to get away from the coffee shop. We could go back to Brunswick street?"

"Sure, lots of nice places there."

Kelli pulled her keys out of her pocket as Sarah

stopped, looking around, a puzzled expression on her face. "You okay?"

"I think he's here, somewhere."

"He? He who?"

"The dark man, the guy on the cards, the one I told you about."

Kelli took Sarah's hand and looked around. There were a few people around, but none of them were a tall, dark skinned man. "I can't see anyone that looks like the guy you described. Also, you didn't say that he was the guy on the cards, either. You just said he was a dark, mysterious guy. Come on, let's get in the car."

Kelli hopped in, put on her seatbelt and turned the key in the ignition, starting the motor before she spoke.

"You sure the card guy's near?"

"I do, though I don't know if it's the guy that's on the cards, but I'm sure that he's got something to do with them. The feeling I get when I know he's around just freaks me out, Kells."

Kelli checked the road was clear and then did a U-turn, slowing to let a man run across the road. She felt her stomach lurch as she saw the man was tall, very tall, and dark skinned. She could see his bare arms; his shirt sleeves were rolled up. His back was to the girls so they couldn't see his face, but Sarah gasped, and Kelli knew she'd seen him and felt the strange feeling she spoke about yesterday. He continued across the road then disappeared into the shadows on the other side of the street.

"You don't know if that's him," Kelli offered.

"Yes I do, and you do, too. I can see it on your face."

"Where did he go?" Kelli slowed and looked but had to drive off as cars were coming.

"I can't see where he went," Sarah was turned all the way around in her seat. "It always happens like that; I get a glimpse and then he's gone. I'm just glad you saw him, too. I was starting to think I was hallucinating him."

"Well, I definitely saw him, though I can't tell you what he looked like. For someone running across the road, don't you think it was strange that he didn't turn around or check where the car was?"

Sarah didn't answer, she just chewed her lower lip, her expression dark. Kelli decided to let it go for now and concentrate on driving, she was planning on going through the whole cards story again once they were sitting down to eat.

"Anywhere in particular you feel like going?"

"Let's go to Alfred's. They do a great brunch," Sarah suggested. "There's always parking around the corner if there's nothing on the street, too."

"Coolio," Kelli laughed as she found a parking spot right out the front and reverse parked with ease.

"Impressive parking," Sarah said as she undid her seatbelt. "I'm normally good at parking, but that was neat."

"Why thank you, and I know I'm not normally good at it, so I'm as surprised as you."

Kelli smiled at the very handsome young man that held the door open for them, stepping to one side to let them through before he walked out, a takeaway coffee in one hand.

"He was tasty," she said as she held up two fingers to the waitress walking their way, and the black-aproned girl pointed to a table at the front window.

"You okay at the window?" she asked them.

"Sure, I guess. Nothing out the back, in the garden?" Sarah asked and the girl nodded, grabbing two menus from the counter as she walked them through the cafe and out to the open eating area at the back. Kelli had been here before and liked it as much as Sarah, the overgrown plants, flowering and lush always lent a cheery feel to the atmosphere of the place.

Kelli sat down but Sarah put her bag on the table. "I just need to use the ladies."

"Don't get lost," Kelli quipped and picked up a menu. Truth be told she wasn't nearly as hungry as she had told Sarah. Her main motive for getting into a cafe quickly was to sit down and pick Sarah's brain about the cards and what they could mean. She also wanted to know what else Sarah had found in her box, if there was anything else weird that she should know about.

"Decided on what you want?" Sarah pulled out her chair and sat down. "I feel like eggs and avo, maybe, no, not maybe, definitely bacon."

"Maybe pancakes, I think. Or waffles, I'm not sure. I feel like I need a sugar hit."

"Go the waffles then, they're awesome here. Cinnamon, chocolate ice cream and rum soaked raisins. Uber yummy."

"Sounds disgustingly fattening. I'm in. So, tell me about the box of shit you got with the cards."

Sarah waited to answer as the waitress came up and took their drinks order. She didn't say anything until their coffees arrived, then put too much sugar in her cappuccino and stirred it until Kelli wanted to smack her.

"You can't remember what you got, or you're keeping it a secret?" Kelli prompted.

"Sorry, I was kind of lost in thought. You know, Ben, and all that craziness." Sarah sipped her coffee. "What did you ask me again?"

"I wanted to know what other weird shit you got in the box of things the cards came in."

"Oh, there was nothing else special at all. Just a lot of rubbish, actually, stuff that I'm not surprised didn't sell. Handkerchiefs and things, I stuck most of it on the giveaway shelves in the foyer of my building.'

"You don't think any of that stuff was, I don't know, haunted? Or possessed?"

Sarah shook her head. "No, not at all."

"How do you know that?"

"Because they didn't feel different. The cards felt different right from the first time I touched the box. It was a weird feeling, like they belonged to me, I think. They sort of felt warm when I touched them - it was so strange, Kelli. None of the other stuff felt like that at all, it was just rubbish."

Kelli moved her coffee aside as the waitress took their food order, then leaned forward, elbows on the table. "You felt they were *different* the first time you touched them?"

"Absolutely. They felt right. That's hard to explain, I know, but that's how they felt to me. And I don't do anything to make the dreams happen, but they seem to come when I've been hurt or upset during the day. Like Noel, the maintenance guy, he really upset me. I couldn't stop thinking about it, and then whammo, he was gone."

"Same with the druggies?"

"Yeah! They banged on my door and argued in the hallway, up and down, all fucking night. I wanted to bash their heads together! And then Ben, well, you saw how he carried on. Though I didn't wish any of them dead, not for a second."

"Are you sure?" Kelli paused as their meals arrived, waiting for the waitress to leave before she continued. "Maybe you wished it just a little bit?"

"The druggies, yeah, I think I hoped they'd overdose or something, but not Noel. And definitely not Ben. I never hated him, not really. He was my first love, and in a way, I think I still loved him."

"No, really?"

"I didn't want him back, not ever, but he always gave me goosebumps when he touched me, like electricity. Even when we were fighting, he could still do that to me. I'd never have slept with him again or anything, seriously, but I still had a little thing for him."

Sarah started to eat, and Kelli mused over what she'd been told. "So, if we had a fight, do you think my life would be in danger?"

Sarah's hand stopped midway to her mouth, the forkful of food frozen there. She put her fork down, her face suddenly pale.

"Fuck Kelli, I never thought of that. Shit, what happens when I have one of my blow ups with my dad? Or get pissed off with my mum, or my brother? Oh god, Kelli, what do I do?"

Kelli frowned. She had no answers for her friend, and now had serious worries about her own safety. "I can see the thought upsets you, and that might be enough for you to have a dream about me. We need to be really careful until we know what's going on."

Sarah started to cry, and Kelli felt a panic grow. If Sarah was upset enough to cry then chances are she would dream about this, and dream about fighting with Kelli, or a member of her family. "Sarah, I know you're scared, but you can't get this upset. You could be damning me if you get this upset. Seriously, we need to pull it together and get you thinking happy thoughts already."

Sarah used her napkin to wipe her tears and then blew her nose. "You're right, exactly, I need to focus on something else. I need to destroy the cards, throw them in the rubbish."

"They'd still be around if you did that. I think you need something more final, more radical."

"Burn them? That's the only way to be sure, to get rid of them. When we're finished here let's go get them and burn them in the park. If we try and do it in the apartment, I'll set the alarms off." Sarah pushed her plate aside. "I've lost my appetite."

"You need to find that appetite, and you need to get happy real quick. For my sake, Sezzy."

Sarah nodded and pulled her plate back. Kelli desperately tried to think of something to say, to change the subject and bring Sarah's mood up.

"Have you been up to your mum's lately?"

Sarah frowned, then realised what Kelli was trying to do. "I should go soon; she's got a new horse and I'd like to ride with her. I know she gets lonely, and I feel bad about that, so I really should go."

"Not just you, but that brother of yours, too. You need to go and take her out to lunch or something. My mum loves it when I shout her lunch. Gets half cut and says stupid things, I can't stop laughing."

"Oh my god yes, I remember that time I went with you two, what was that place? That old pub that had that buffet?"

Kelli smiled. "She loved that place so much. And the free wine you get with the meals even more. Remember she stole ours? She couldn't walk straight after that!"

Sarah started to laugh, and Kelli felt her trepidation lift, just a little. "Your mum never embarrasses you like that when you take her to lunch?"

"No, not anymore, but it used to be her favourite thing, remember?"

Kelli knew this could lead to some bad memories, so she turned the conversation again. "Has she still got that old whippet? The skinny old bag of bones?"

Sarah smiled and nodded, putting food into her mouth and chewing. She swallowed, her smile still in place. "Yeah, old man Zac. He's such a good dog, and my mum loves him so much. I think he likes me better than her, though. Every time I go there, he goes bananas, he never does that to her when she's been away."

"My mum is still the crazy cat lady. She's got eleven of them now."

"Her house must stink!"

"Nah, which I was surprised at, I have to say. She's got that weird outdoor cage thing, and the cats can go out through the laundry window. She keeps their poop box out there, so the smell stays outside."

"Litter box, not poop box."

"Whatever," Kelli laughed. "I could smell your kitty's box when I went in your place. I mean, it wasn't bad, but eleven cats could be a nightmare."

"Yeah, I've had houses on my portfolio that stunk of cat piss. Disgusting."

Kelli ate for a little, not sure if she should keep the conversation going or let the quiet carry on for a little longer. Sarah finished her meal and pushed her plate over, and the waitress swooped in to clear their table.

"Can we have two more coffees, please?" Kelli asked as the waitress carried their plates away.

"So, you never told me what was in your box."

Kelli grimaced. "I haven't looked in it, and if I'm honest, I don't think I will now. I don't want to find cards, or something worse."

"What could be worse?" Sarah asked.

"I don't want to know!"

This made Sarah laugh, and Kelli wanted to push the humour a bit more.

"What if there's voodoo dolls or something?"

"Maybe a spell book? Or a cursed object like on that TV show you like? What did they have that I couldn't stop laughing about?"

"Ballet slippers and a porn magazine that were cursed."

Sarah laughed harder, remembering her amusement at the thought of a cursed pornographic magazine. "What if there's cursed undies? You could have a cursed vagina, oh my god," Sarah was crying now with laughter and Kelli couldn't help but join in.

"I wouldn't put on any undies I found in a box, Sarah. Hey, can you imagine if there was a cursed vibrator? No, a cursed butt plug?"

That was more than Sarah could take, she was having trouble catching her breath, she was laughing so hard, and the other patrons were looking over, wondering what the joke was. The waitress brought over their coffees, her amusement clear at Sarah's hilarity.

It took a few minutes for the laughter to die down, Sarah's face flushed and her eyes red, but she looked happy. Kelli felt enormous relief at that, hoping it was enough to steer the dreams away from herself and, hopefully, keep her from dreaming at all.

Sarah stirred her coffee, wiped her eyes on her napkin and took a deep breath. "I haven't laughed like that in ages!"

"It's good to see you laugh. You've had a very strange week this week."

"Yes, I have, but I've had some great things happen, too. I won that contract, and I'll be getting a heap of commission from that. Like, seriously, it will be a massive bonus!"

"Shit, I forgot about that! Have you thought about what you'll spend it on? A holiday, maybe?"

Sarah shook her head. "I was thinking of going overseas, but I think I might bite the bullet and put a deposit on a property. Maybe an investment apartment or something. I'll have to talk to my mum's boyfriend; he'll work out the best way to go about it. He's an accountant, so he can figure out the tax and that shit."

"Wow, a property owner! That'd be awesome. You could buy a house and rent out the rooms to pay off the mortgage, and still live there. Be nice to get out of the apartment."

"Yes, it would, but I don't think I could afford anything close to the city, and I don't want to live in Melton or Broadmeadows. I love being able to sleep in till eight thirty and then just walk across the road to work. If I lived in an outer suburb, I'd be driving most of the day. Been there, done that, don't want to do it again."

"I'm hearing you! Maybe another apartment then, somewhere in the city? Or close by? Or maybe you should just get an investment property. Listen to me, I'm no help at all."

Sarah didn't laugh, instead she frowned and sat

her coffee cup down.

"He's here, isn't he?" Kelli asked when she saw Sarah's expression.

"I definitely feel something, the hairs on my arms are standing up." Sarah looked around the outdoor dining area. "No one else has come in, and you can't see the main cafe from here, so I can't tell where he might be."

Kelli looked around as well, agreeing with Sarah. "Maybe he's in the little boys' room?"

"He would have passed us to get there. But I can feel something, and it's really weird. Like, my stomach is turning over."

"Are you going to hurl?"

"No, but it's really uncomfortable."

"Do you want to go?"

Sarah shook her head. "No, no I don't think so. If I walk through the cafe and he's there I'll freak. If we stay here, he'll either leave or come through here. No chance of me missing him if he comes through here."

"Can I get you anything else?" the waitress asked.

"Yeah, two more coffees please, and can I ask you something?" Kelli smiled at the young girl. "Is there a really tall black guy in the cafe? Maybe he just came in?"

The waitress shook her head. "Not unless he literally just walked in. Is there something wrong?"

Kelli's smile widened. "Oh, no, not at all. We've been waiting for a friend of ours, but he thinks we're in the main part of the cafe."

"Oh, okay! If I see him while I'm in getting the coffees, I'll tell him to come out here."

"No, don't," Kelli tipped her head to one side. "I'd like to surprise him, maybe just let us know if he's there?"

"Oh, sure thing, mum's the word!" She picked up the used cups and walked back into the cafe.

"Shit, what if he's there? What will we do?" Sarah asked.

Kelli shrugged. "I'm thinking I'll go around the front and stand at the door, then you come through. If he tried to leave without you seeing him, I'll stand in his way. I'll even film him."

"What if he's dangerous, Kelli? What if that makes him angry? We don't want to trigger anything."

"Jeez, I didn't think about that." Kelli chewed on her bottom lip, trying to think of a new plan. "Let's just see what the waitress says when she comes back. If he's here we can walk out and look at him. It's something that could happen anyway, and he can't think that we're picking on him."

"Okay, but I'm scared Kelli. Really scared."

"Me too. I don't want to die. I really don't." Kelli looked up as the waitress brought their coffees.

"Sorry ladies, no tall black guy out there. No black guys at all. Can I get you anything else?"

"No thanks. And thank you for that." Kelli waited for the girl to leave then ran a hand through her hair, not sure if she was relieved or upset that the guy wasn't there. Mostly she felt relieved.

Sarah was looking at her, a question in her eyes

and a plea in her expression.

"Let's just drink our coffee. Maybe the feeling will go, and we can leave. Have you had the feeling before and he wasn't there?"

Sarah frowned. "Um, I think so, maybe once. I can't remember really, but I think so."

"Is he still around?"

Sarah nodded, her face white.

Kelli sipped her coffee, burning her tongue. She waited for Sarah to put sugar in hers and then leaned forward, wanting to whisper to Sarah. "There are gaps in the fence, what if he's on the street watching us, listening to us?"

"Well now I'm even more freaked out, Kells. Fuck."

"Drink your coffee, act normal. We don't want him getting angry or anything." Kelli picked up her coffee, blowing on it before she sipped it this time. "Let's just take it slow and steady, don't be upset at anyone but him."

"He doesn't upset me. Not really, he more frightens me. No, it's not even that," Sarah sipped her coffee and smiled, but Kelli could see it was fake, put on for her possible audience. "I think I'm freaked out that I can feel him, but if I really think about it, he doesn't make me feel scared, I think. It's the whole situation that scares me."

"What do you think he wants?"

"I have no idea. He seems to come mainly before someone dies. Or before I have the dreams, that is."

Kelli's lip trembled; she couldn't stop it. She was very scared. "Do you think you'll dream about me?"

"No, Kells. No, I don't. I love you, you hear? You haven't done anything to upset me or hurt me, so I really believe that I will not dream about you. I believe that."

Kelli felt an errant tear escape and trickle down her cheek. "I love you too, Sezzy. With all my heart."

Sarah's lip quirked to one side. "Well don't go all gaga on me now."

"If I was gay, you'd be the one I'd go for."

"I wouldn't go you. Not my type."

The girls actually laughed at that, but it was a dry, hollow sound that didn't last long.

Sarah drank her coffee, then she smiled. A real smile this time.

"He's gone. The feeling is gone, Kelli."

"Phew. Thank the gods for that. I'm dying to go to the ladies, hang tight, I'll hurry." Kelli nearly ran to the toilet, not wanting to leave her friend alone for too long. She was washing her hands when she felt a tingle down her spine, almost a premonition, and she hurried out to find Sarah standing, her bag in her hands. She passed Kelli her purse and looked towards the front. "He's back, and I don't want to wait here anymore. I want to get out of here and go home."

"Okay, yeah, sure. I'll pay the cheque and we'll go."

"I already gave the girl my card, it's paid for. Let's go." Sarah led the way, Kelli right at her shoulder, as they entered the cafe. Just as they did, they noticed a tall man, a very dark man, turn and walk out the door. Sarah gasped and Kelli felt positively sick.

"I'm going after him!" Sarah exclaimed.

"No, please don't," Kelli begged. "I think I'd rather you not see him than enrage him."

Sarah whirled to face her and Kelli could see that she was angry and frightened, but the look on Kelli's face was enough to stop her rushing out of the door.

The waitress handed Sarah her card and waved towards the door. "Oh, hey, there was a tall guy in here just a second ago. But he turned right around and left before I could come and get you."

"Thanks, that's okay. Did you see what he looked like?"

The waitress smiled. "Internet date, huh?"

"Um, yeah, that's right. I brought my friend for back up, just in case he was a weirdo."

"Oh, bummer. Do you think he saw you and left?"

Kelli frowned, then shook her head. "Yeah, maybe. Hey, did you get a look at him? Can you tell me what he looked like?"

The waitress shook her head. "No, sorry. I was making a coffee, when I looked up he was already heading back out. I just saw his back. He's a bodybuilder, isn't he?"

"Yeah, sure, that's right. Thanks." Kelli led Sarah outside.

"That's about the closest I've been to him," Sarah sighed. "I nearly saw him, did you see, he turned just as we went right through the door? It's almost like we surprised him. Maybe he doesn't know what I'm thinking."

"Or maybe he does and he's playing with you."

Chapter Thirteen

"You sure you want to go up alone?" Kelli asked.

"Yes, I am. I'm fine, Kelli. Really tired, though. I think I'd like to veg out and not interact with anyone. That's safe, yeah?"

Sarah studied Kelli's face as her friend did the same to her, both looking for signs of fear, stress, and panic. Kelli did look scared, but she also looked as tired as Sarah felt.

"Go home Kelli, you need some sleep, too. I promise I'll call you if anything else happens."

"Promise?"

"I promise." Sarah slipped out of the car and slapped the roof. Kelli didn't drive off straight away, she waited for Sarah to enter the building foyer before she left. Sarah felt grateful to have a friend like Kelli, someone who'd watch out for her, would have her back no matter what. She had assured Kelli that she wouldn't dream about her, but truth be told she wasn't that sure herself. She had no control over what she dreamed, and she was terrified that she would dream of one of her friends, or her family.

She didn't have a real good relationship with her father, and an even worse one with her father's girlfriend. If she were to argue with them, were to get upset with them, what would happen? She had no time for the girlfriend, but her father loved that woman, and she wouldn't hurt him. She rarely fought with her mother or brother now that she was an adult, but they were all human beings, and there were times that they didn't get along. She didn’t want to risk anyone just because they didn’t see eye to eye.

Kelli had forgotten about getting rid of the cards, but Sarah hadn’t. She didn’t think giving the cards away would work, or even donating them to a charity shop. She didn’t want to pass the curse they seemed to hold onto anyone else, and she didn't even know if it would pass on. She could get rid of the cards and still be stuck with the curse.

The elevator took forever to come, someone must have the door propped open on one of the levels. It usually happened when people were shifting or bringing things upstairs, and Sarah was getting annoyed.

She took a breath, trying to keep her volatile temper under control. She didn't need any random person to die just because she got pissed off at them. She pressed the button for the second lift, the one where the druggies had died, and the door opened immediately. Sarah looked at it for a moment before getting in.

“Not sure about ghosts?” a voice from behind startled her, and she turned to see a man standing there.

“Oh sorry, didn’t mean to give you a fright,” he smiled, his perfectly white, straight teeth showing through his full lips. “I get a bit freaked out about that lift as well, I don't think I’ve taken it since it all happened."

Sarah stepped into the lift and he followed her. "I think someone must be shifting, the other lift has been on level five for ages."

"That would be my fault. I'm shifting from the fifth floor to the seventh. I hired a bunch of guys from Airtasker to get my stuff from one apartment to the other."

"You left strangers alone with your stuff?"

"Yeah, but just for a minute. I had to move my car, I parked it in the loading bay. I foolishly decided to get a new bed suite all on the same day."

Sarah looked at the doors of the lift, they hadn't closed.

"Um I think you need to press a button before the doors will close, ma'am."

Sarah smiled a little at being called ma'am. She was only twenty-five, she didn't think she was old enough to be called that.

"What floor?" she asked.

"Fifth. I should see what's holding them up." Sarah stabbed the buttons and stepped back.

"I'm Michael, by the way."

"Sarah," she looked down at her feet. He was really handsome, and very tall. She liked the way his hair, while combed back and neat, had an errant blonde curl that twisted above one eye. Sarah looked back up and felt her cheeks grow hot under his steady gaze. His eyes were sapphire blue, and his lips were tilted at one side, giving him a roguish grin.

"It's very nice to meet you, Sarah. I hope I bump

into you again."

The elevator door opened, and Sarah smiled back at him. "Same," was all she could think of saying. He stepped out and she could see three guys trying to wrestle a long television unit into the elevator. Michael glanced back at Sarah and rolled his eyes as the doors closed, making her laugh. Kelli was not going to believe that when she told her. She felt stupid at the one response she gave him, of all the witty, clever and enticing comebacks all she could manage was *same*.

The lift opened at her floor and she walked to her apartment, finding the door to the apartment opposite her was open and there were two guys inside manoeuvring a refrigerator into position. What were the chances that two people were shifting to the seventh floor on the same day? She opened her apartment and stepped inside, the kitten rushing to her in excitement. She let the little thing climb up her shoulders as she looked through the peephole, waiting to see who was shifting in. It wasn't a long wait; she saw the guys with the television unit, then Michael carrying a large cardboard box.

This could be awkward, she thought. She wouldn't be able to leave the apartment unless she'd done her hair and make-up ever again. She patted the kitten on her shoulder and turned to the bathroom, needing to clean out the kitty litter and make sure the feed and water bowls were full. After she'd done that, she glanced in the bathroom mirror and was shocked to see how thick and luxurious her hair looked, and it seemed so much longer today. Everyone was going to notice, and she had no idea how she'd explain it to anyone.

She walked to her bedroom, changed into her comfy around-the-house clothes and turned on the television, the card box sitting on the coffee table almost accusingly.

Pouring herself a wine, Sarah sat down, wondering what she could do about the cards. Her phone message tone sounded and she picked it up, seeing Kelli had messaged her to check if she was okay. Rather than messaging back Sarah rang her and told her about Michael and the apartment across the way.

"*Oh shit, you think he saw us last night?*"

"Bugger, I forgot about that. Yeah, probably. Anyway, I'll deal with that if he brings it up."

"*We forgot to burn the cards, Sarah.*"

"Look, we don't know if that will work. We don't want to set the guy free if he's bound to the cards or anything. What I'm saying is I need to find out more about them, about what we can do to stop them."

"*How are you planning to do that? Ask a psychic?*"

"Actually, that might be a good idea. Find someone that knows about these sorts of things and ask them what we should do."

"*So how do you find someone like that? Google?*"

"No, I think I'll ask my mum. She's got a good knowledge of tarot cards, but I don't know about other types of cards, and she knows an indigenous lady that's right into dreamtime and shit. I think I'll ring her."

"*Okay, but Sarah, be careful you don't get angry or frustrated with her. You don't know what triggers the dreams, and you'd never forgive yourself if someone you love got hurt.*"

"I know, the thought of it terrifies me. I'll let you know how I go."

"*Yes please, and let me know about Mr. Dreamy-Eyes, too. Talk later.*"

"Bye Kells."

Sarah took a sip of her wine before she called her mother. She didn't beat around the bush, she told her mother everything, and once she started talking, she couldn't stop, spilling it all out, and only finishing when she couldn't stop crying. Her mother was silent for a while, then she spoke quietly.

"*Don't touch the cards tonight. Don't even think about them, if you can. Take the box and wrap it up in something, cling wrap or something like that. Wrap it up real tight and stick it in the freezer, right at the back. Put things in front of it so you can't see the box if you need to open the freezer, understand?*"

"Y...yes," Sarah sobbed.

"*Do it now while I'm on the phone. I'll wait. You hear me Sarah?*"

"Yes Mum. Hang on."

Sitting the phone down she walked to the pantry and found the box of cling wrap. She wrapped the card box over and over, using up the whole roll of wrap. Then, just as she was told, she took it over to the freezer and put it right at the back, piling packets of frozen vegetables and ice cream in front of it. Once she was done, she went back to the phone.

"You still there Mum?"

"*Yes, I'm here. Now Sarah, you have to promise me you won't touch them, no matter what. Don't look at them, don't touch them, don't even think about them if you can help it.*"

"Okay."

"*If you still have dreams tonight, get a large jar of honey and put the whole wrapped bundle in it then stick them back in the freezer. I'll see what I can find out about the cards and what to do about them. Do you want me to come there?*"

"No, that's okay, I know you have to work. Should I do the honey now just to be safe?"

"*No, I don't think you'll have to. I think the freezer will keep them quiet for now. Just as long as you don't touch them.*"

"Then what should I do?"

"*Just leave them, sweetie, leave them alone until we can figure out what to do. There're people not far from here that know about this sort of thing. I'll find some answers for you, I promise.*"

"Thank you for believing me. I love that you never doubt anything I have to say. I love you Mum."

"*That's because you don't lie to me. I love you more, Sezzy.*"

Chapter Fourteen

The sun was warm, almost too warm, and Sarah sipped her cocktail as she adjusted her hat, so its shade covered her face. The island was stunning, she didn't know why she hadn't taken an overseas holiday before now. Oh, she'd done the Thailand thing with Ben when they were just eighteen, but spent the time drunk and partying, not really taking things easy, or relaxing at all. This beach was just what the doctor ordered, as the saying goes, with its azure sky, still waters, long, white beaches and palm trees.

She lay back on her sunlounge, her brown legs tanning darker, a stark contrast against her white bikini. She sat her cocktail down on the little table beside her sunlounge and watched the sailing ships on the horizon, far away, adding to the postcard perfect view.

"Can I plait your hair?" a little dark-skinned woman asked, and Sarah smiled and nodded.

"How much?"

"For you, very good price. Very good. I look after you."

"Okay, sure, do you want me to sit up?"

"Yes, little bit, please, you sit this way," the woman demonstrated a position and Sarah twisted around, removing her hat to let the woman have access to her hair.

"You have very long hair, very thick. More hair

than me, very pretty."

"Thank you, it's fun to have it long but it's so hot against my neck. Could you maybe braid it so it sits up from my neck and shoulders?"

"Yes, I do like that, I make you happy. You very pretty, I make your hair very pretty too. All very pretty."

Sarah smiled and sipped her cocktail as she felt the girl start to work on her hair. Having very thick, wavy, waist length hair was pleasant in the winter, but in this tropical heat it was a burden. Having it braided up off her face and neck would help keep her cool and make swimming so much easier. She watched some seagulls fighting over some titbit on the sand, obsessed with the fight and ignoring little children that ran up to try and catch them, almost successfully.

"You got boyfriend? Pretty girl must have many boyfriend, yes?"

"Nah, I don't have a boyfriend," Sarah replied. "I'd like one, though."

"Maybe you find boyfriend here on holiday. You maybe have lucky holiday, find plenty rich man."

Sarah laughed. "That'd be nice, but all the men I've seen here seem to be with someone or are really old. Maybe I should find a rich old man, a sugar daddy, yeah?"

The woman laughed. "No need old man. Plenty young man. You come restaurant dinner you see many young man, many single man. All on business trip."

Sarah nodded and the woman jerked her hair a

bit.

"I've seen those men, I think they're all married, just here on a business junket. They want a good time, not a good wife."

"No, some man not marry. I ask them. That man there not marry. Tall man. Very handsome, very rich. He be good boyfriend for you."

Sarah looked to where the woman was pointing and she gasped. The tall dark man was walking along the beach. He had a camera in his hands and would pause to take pictures of the sailboats, his head turned away from her. Sarah was sure it was the man from her cards, the man that was always on the edge of her peripheral vision, and again, his face was not revealed to her.

"There, I finish your hair. Very pretty. You like it. You pay me now."

Sarah didn't have a mirror, so she reached up and gently felt the thick braids, admiring the tasteful way the woman had lifted her hair up from her face, forming a French braid then twisting it back into a double chignon. She knew this would look classy, and hopefully would last for the rest of her stay. Satisfied with her service, Sarah handed the woman some notes from her purse, knowing the tip she gave her, while not much in Australian dollars, was probably a week's wage in her country.

"Oh, you very nice girl. Very generous. Here, I call handsome man for you, look," the woman stood and called out to the dark man.

"Skuse me, skuse me, mister, you come here,

okay, mister?"

The dark man stopped walking and lowered his camera. Sarah's heart was in her throat as he turned, the sun behind him momentarily hiding his face, but then...

...she woke with a gasp, sweat beading on her forehead and making her underarms itch. She felt the irritation of not seeing the dark man's face in her dream, while also understanding that whatever face she saw in a dream had no guarantee of being the *actual* face of the dark man. She rolled over and checked the time. It was two thirty, not time to get up. She didn't know if she could go back to sleep after that dream, and her kitten seemed to understand, mewing and slipping into the space between her chin and her shoulder, right up into the nape of her neck.

"We need to think of a name for you, little kitten," Sarah said as she scratched the kitten's scruff. "I guess I'll think of something sooner or later." She yawned and smiled as the kitten mewed sleepily, the loud purr buzzing in her ear. She needed to get some more sleep, she had work in the morning and didn't need to be dog-tired on a Monday. This week was going to be another big week work wise, she hoped, with appointments to see the CEO of a large investment building company. If she was successful in winning their contracts, she could be financially set up for quite some time. The kitten stopped purring, sleeping soundly, and though Sarah wanted to turn over she didn't want to disturb her little ball of fluff.

The alarm went off and Sarah was surprised to see it was eight o'clock. She hadn't realised she'd fallen asleep but was glad that she did. The kitten watched her while she showered, sitting on the bathroom vanity while she blow-dried her hair and did her make-up. She fed the kitten before getting dressed, and as Sarah checked her outfit in the mirror she thought back to the dream.

She'd have to text Kelli and let her know she had a safe dream, though Kelli would probably already realise that Sarah hadn't dreamed about her. She checked the time before putting on her shoes, smiling and patting her kitty before grabbing her bag to leave.

As she opened her door, she saw Michael closing his, and he smiled at her, a warm, friendly smile, and Sarah felt her cheeks turn red.

"Good morning, neighbour! What a pleasant surprise, I wondered what floor you lived on."

"Well this isn't super awkward," Sarah laughed.

"Not at all, it's nice to know I have a gorgeous neighbour. I'm going to have to think about all the excuses I can use to knock on your door, like borrowing a cup of sugar, etcetera."

"Seriously, I'd freak out if you did that. I'd never be able to slop around in my grungy house clothes."

Michael laughed. "I actually won't be home much; I've still got a lot of work to do and I fly up to Sydney a lot. I've got a day off to settle in, then back to work tomorrow."

"That's where I'm off to right now, I'll grab a coffee on the way."

"Mind if I walk with you? I was actually just going to go out and grab a coffee and something for breakfast. My Airtasker guys forgot to plug in the fridge, so all that food is wasted. Might've lasted in winter, but not summer."

Sarah locked her door. "Sure, you can walk with me. I can't stay long, though, I have to be at work."

"Not a problem, Sarah. I'm just glad for the company."

Sarah turned and walked down the hallway, Michael by her side. She hadn't remembered how tall he was, he had to be at least six feet and maybe three or four inches. He was too good looking, far too good looking, and he made Reid look positively plain. Though it would be strange if she started dating him, she thought, being that he lived right across from her. Could be awkward if they broke up, though if Sarah bought an apartment with her bonus that wouldn't be an issue.

She almost laughed at her musings, the guy had only asked to accompany her to the coffee shop, not asked her out on a date. And with her fortune card problem, maybe dating wasn't such a good idea.

"Penny for your thoughts?" Michael asked as he stabbed the lift button. "You look like you were a world away just then."

Sarah looked up at his face. "Just thinking about work. Got a lot of meetings this week, some rather important ones."

The lift door opened, and Michael gestured in first. "I didn't ask what you do for a living."

"You first, Michael. What keeps you so busy and

flying interstate?"

"I'm sure it's all terribly boring, but I'm in IT, in securities."

"Insecurities?"

Michael laughed. "I didn't word that very well. IT securities is what I'm in. Just got a promotion not long ago and transferred down from Sydney to run the Melbourne branches. Your turn now."

Sarah stepped out of the lift and was impressed at the way Michael held the front door open for her. *Nice,* she thought. *An actual gentleman.*

"I'm a property manager, actually I'm the head of the rental department at Westwood Real Estate, just down the street here. I've only been there a month today."

"You're lucky, living walking distance from work. I hate the morning peak hour commute. Drives me insane."

"I hear you! I worked in Berwick before this, though at least it was mostly driving against the traffic. I can't tell you how many times I was late due to some accident."

"You'll never have to worry about that again, now."

Sarah ran across the road, Michael by her side. He held the door to the cafe open for her, and when she tried to pay for her coffee, he waved her away, ordering exactly the same as she did, right down to the bagel. He then walked her to work, and Sarah wondered if he was going to follow her inside. She needn't have worried, though.

"Well, you have a great day at work, Sarah.

Thanks for the walk, and I look forward to doing this again sometime."

"Thanks for paying for my breakfast, you didn't have to do that."

"That's right, I didn't. But I wanted to. And when I take you to dinner, I'll be paying as well." He smiled at her and turned before she had a chance to protest, running across the road, dodging cars to make it to the other side.

Sarah felt her cheeks grow warm again, and turned to see Helen and Joan watching her, their smiles wide on their faces. She rolled her eyes and pushed the door open.

"Good morning girls," Sarah said as she walked in.

"Good morning, Sarah. So, tell us, who was that absolutely gorgeous man? Seems like you had a fantastic weekend!" Joan stepped out from the reception counter. "Did he stay over? You can tell me!"

"No, oh my god, Joan, you're incorrigible! No, he lives in the apartment across from me, he just shifted there, into the druggies' apartment, the ones that died last week. He used to live on the fifth floor, but I've never seen him before the weekend."

"So how come he walked you to work?" Helen asked.

"We walked over to the coffee shop at the same time and just got to talking, that's all."

"If I were twenty years younger, I'd be doing more than just watching through the window. He is absolutely gorgeous!"

"Yes, he is a stunning human, I'll admit. I only just met him. Let me get to know him, make sure he's not an axe murderer or anything."

"He's too pretty to be an axe murderer," Joan said as she walked back behind the desk.

"You don't have to be ugly to be a murderer, look at Ted Bundy," Helen countered. "He was as handsome as all get out; it's how he lured the girls."

Sarah shook her head as she opened the door to the main office, listening to the women talk about how sexy serial killers actually were. She took her coffee and bagel into the staff kitchen where three or four of the sales staff sat and pulled up a chair next to Paul. He moved the newspaper over for her to share with him as she ate.

"Good weekend?" he asked.

"Not too bad, had a party Saturday night. Friends got engaged, but then a mutual friend, actually my ex-boyfriend, was murdered on Sunday morning."

"No shit! Sarah, no offence, but you are a dangerous person to know!"

Sarah thinned her lips. "Yep, that's me lately. I feel like avoiding all of my friends and family."

"Still, you didn't really know the druggies, or even that douche Noel, so maybe I'll take that back."

"Good morning everyone, boss, other department's boss," Baden came in, a smile on his face. Reid followed him, winking at Sarah. She still found him super attractive but was very glad that she had Michael to obsess over now and could fend off the advances of the young salesman with thoughts of the cute neighbour of hers.

She finished her breakfast and stood up, wiping down the table before she threw her rubbish in the bin. She had a lot of emails and reports and couldn't spend any more time in the kitchen. Besides, she could see Reid was positioning to sit next to her, and she wanted to avoid any awkwardness, especially after the party.

The week passed much like that, busy days, avoiding Reid, and keeping a lookout for Michael, though she didn't see him again. His apartment seemed empty, and Sarah thought he must've stayed in Sydney. She kept in touch with Kelli and her mum, and her brother rang when he found out about Ben, promising to go to the funeral with her for support. She knew her brother used to like Ben, not that they were great friends or anything, and only stopped talking to him when Ben's cheating came to light.

She had a quiet week card wise, no sightings of the dark man, no more dreams, and there was no change to her hair or plants. They stayed the same, and although the abnormal growth stopped, it also didn't recede, either. She wondered if the last dream she had was not fatal to anyone and short lived due to the cards starting to freeze, but didn't want to think about things too much in case she triggered something.

Matthew gave her the afternoon off on Friday to attend the funeral, and first thing Friday morning she had the final meeting with the CEO of the property development company to get his decision on giving her the contracts to represent his rental properties. She wanted to dress demurely for the funeral, but business like for the meeting, knowing she probably wouldn't have any time to get changed in between the two events. Her brother would be picking up Kelli and meeting her outside of work, so she had to hurry her meeting and get back in time.

She caught a taxi to the CEO's office and arranged for the same taxi to come by and pick her up after the meeting, taking the stress out of finding parking spots and meters and possibly getting booked. She didn't want any stress; she needed the meeting to go as planned. Her plan was, of course, to win this contract, and she had worked very hard this week to impress that company, as well as taking the effort to transition all of the other properties from her previous contract win over.

Joan had been her right-hand man, so to speak, helping her coordinate, write the tenants letters and working to manage and assign all of the properties. She had spoken to Matthew about giving Joan some kind of reward as the woman had stayed back late and bent over backwards to make sure Sarah had every support she needed. Matthew agreed, though he also mentioned that if Sarah won any contracts today, she may have to hire her own personal assistant.

Chapter Fifteen

"I told Kelli she should sit in the back, but she said your head was too big for the front seat." Sam leaned over and looked at his sister as she did up her seatbelt. "Congratulations, by the way. That win today must make you the most successful property manager they've ever had."

"I know, right! I can't get the smile off my face, which is going to be super inappropriate at a funeral."

Sam turned to face the road and pulled out into traffic. "Yeah, you better think about something other than the stacks of money you're about to get. Otherwise they'll be expecting you to dance on his grave or something. You've really got the cat that caught the mouse face on right now."

"Jesus, Sam, you sound ninety. But yeah, I need to get my mind off it for now."

"Not yet, Sezzy, I want to know what your boss said when you told him."

"I didn't have time, and he was at a lunch meeting with the investors. I put the contracts on his desk, so he'll see them when he gets back. I expect a couple of texts later. I did tell Joan to remind him I'm at a funeral."

"So, Kelli tells me you have a little supernatural problem," Sam looked at Sarah's reflection in his rear-view mirror. "You didn't think to come to me with any of this?"

"Quite frankly, no, I didn't. You are about the biggest sceptic I know and would find reasonable explanations for everything that happened."

"I'm not sure I understand what's happening, or even if it's all supernatural, but Kelli's freaked out and she says people have died, and that Ben's death may be related. I was surprised when I heard how he'd died, he wasn't the sort that would knife anyone, and I don't think his girlfriend was, either. And someone to get hit by a fire engine with sirens and lights blazing? What are the odds, seriously?"

"I thought you'd tell me I was crazy and imagining things and find a rational explanation for everything that's happened."

Sam turned into the church parking lot and found a park straight away. He turned off the engine before making eye contact in the mirror again. "I can't think of a single explanation that would make your hair grow about seven inches and thicken up like a Spanish princess in a week. I gotta ask you though, couldn't you think about me when you touched the hair card?"

Sarah smiled at her brother. His thinning hair at such a young age was something he was very self-conscious about, and she felt a pang of guilt for not thinking of him when she touched the card.

"Your hair looks like mine used to, of course mine never got that long." Sam sighed and scrubbed a hand over his head before taking off his seatbelt. "I guess we better do this, then."

There were a few people milling about the front of the church, and Sarah was pleased to see she knew all of them. They stopped and spoke very briefly before they were ushered inside, and Kelli groaned when she saw the coffin was open and people were milling past to view the body.

"Do we have to look at him?" she hissed to Sarah.

"Fuck no," Sam whispered back. "I'm not up for nightmares tonight, no corpse viewing for me."

"Same same," Sarah added. "I have enough problems with dreams now."

They took their seats towards the back of the church as they were the only ones that would let them sit together, the church was nearly full and more people were arriving, slipping into seats or standing at the back. The service was as Sarah expected it to be, praises flowing around what a wonderful man Ben was and how much he loved his family, how the man could do no wrong and was looking forward to married life with his fiancé.

"I didn't know they were engaged," Sam whispered.

"Neither did I, and I don't think anyone else knew, either. No one mentioned it before now."

At the end of the service everyone was invited to walk past the coffin and pay their respects, but less than half the attendees stood and shuffled past. When they were done, they were asked to move outside, and the pallbearers carried the coffin to the limousine. The cemetery was next, and then they went back to Ben's parents' house for the wake.

Caters had been engaged, they walked around the large entertainment room that opened on to manicured gardens and handed out napkins, offering finger food and trays of refreshments. Sarah hovered close to the French doors that led to the garden, a prime position to collect food from the trays as they passed by her. Sam was right there and grinned at her over a mouthful. "I guess I'm not the only one that didn't have lunch," he smiled as he swallowed.

"I don't know how you two can eat when Ben's just been put in the ground." Kelli looked distraught. "And we pretty much know what happened to him."

Sarah took Kelli's arm. "I know you're frightened, I do, but I promise you, I will never dream about you. You couldn't upset me like that."

"You can't promise," Kelli sighed. "Sarah, you don't have any control over what you dream."

"No, that's right, but since I've put the cards in the freezer, I only had that one dream, and it wasn't bad. No one got hurt, and there's been nothing ever since. I think my mum will find an answer, and this will all be over."

"Have you tried contacting the woman that gave you the box?" Sam asked.

"No, we didn't. She was just some random at the market, I don't have any way to find her."

"Why don't you call the market organisers? Tell them the stall that she was on and ask for her details, say she gave you some stuff and you found something the woman may not have realised was valuable, ask them to pass on your details to her. If she thinks money's involved, she'll contact you quick smart."

Sarah hugged her brother. "You were always the smart one!"

"Don't you forget it, either."

"This is all your fault, you know," a woman's voice made the three turn around. "You caused all of this!"

"W… what?" Sarah stammered. "What are you saying?"

"You fucking whore, this is all your fault and you know it!" Ben's mother screamed as she pointed at Sarah's face.

"Mrs. Dellon, I know you're upset at losing your son, but Sarah -" Sam started.

"Shut up, shut the fuck up! It's all your sister's fault, my boy would still be here now if it weren't for her." She slapped Sarah hard across the face and Sam jumped forward, grabbing the woman as others rushed in to help restrain her. She started to scream, angrily trying to claw at Sam, desperate to reach Sarah. When she couldn't escape, she collapsed to the floor sobbing. Sam only let her go once her husband and others had hold of her, lifting her up and leading her away. She whirled against their arms and pointed at Sarah. "If you'd only let him sow his wild oats, he would never have ended up with that scum Ali and he'd be alive right now! Why couldn't you just accept he liked to fuck around? I did, my husband has never been faithful, but I shut up like a good woman, and let him do what he needs to do. If you did the same, he'd still be alive, you stupid whore."

Sam grabbed hold of Sarah as her close friends surrounded her, Hannah and Kelli comforting her while Ben's dad dragged his sobbing wife away.

"We should go," Sam said. "I'm not having my sister be treated like this, not by some lunatic."

"We're going too," Hannah said as Declan joined her.

"I think most of us are going to leave. We really didn't need to know about the Dellon's dirty secrets, and your brother's right, Sarah, no one should treat you like that."

Kelli was white, her eyes large with shock, and Sarah was holding her cheek where she'd been slapped. She looked up at her brother and handed him a napkin. "She scratched your face, Sam."

"I think she was trying to gouge my eyes out, stupid old crow." Sam wiped his face and looked at the napkin. "Let's go, girls."

Sarah turned to look back as they walked to the car and was surprised to see that Declan was right, almost everyone was leaving all at once. Ben's mum had always been volatile and a little unhinged, but it seemed the death of her only child made things so much worse, accelerating her erratic behaviour to a point that no one wanted to witness.

"What're you guys going to do now?" Kelli asked Hannah.

"I think we'll head home. Trauma overload for this week." She turned to Sarah. "Are you okay, Sezzy?"

"I'm a bit rattled, but I'll be okay."

"Well, look after yourself, and I'll message you

during the week. Love you heaps," Hannah leaned in and kissed Sarah on her unslapped cheek before giving Kelli and Sam a cheek kiss as well. Sam shook Declan's hand and waved to them as she unlocked the car, letting Sarah take the front seat this time.

"I'm taking you both to get something to eat, then I'll drive you back to your cars, okay?"

"Sure, thanks," Kelli answered quietly, but Sarah didn't respond.

Sam didn't ask for anyone's preference, he just drove to Collingwood's Best Burgers and parked out the front. It was still relatively early for dinner, so there was plenty of room and they had no problem getting a seat.

No one said anything about the funeral as they placed their orders, keeping conversation very sparse and light until the waitress delivered their drinks.

"I know what you're both thinking," Sarah said. "The cards are in the freezer, everything should be fine, Ben's mum should be safe."

Kelli looked at Sarah, her face still pale and drawn with worry. "You don't know that for sure, though. There's no way you could know that. Those cards are powerful, and I can't see how a freezer can do anything to them."

"It's not the freezer, it's the symbolism. She's freezing the power and the control they have. That's what the freezer does."

Sarah turned to her brother with a frown. "You talked to mum about this?"

"She rang me, yeah. Of course, I didn't really believe her, you know how she is with her crystals and shit, but just looking at Kelli, who doesn't believe in fortune cards, and I believe. I believe this much, anyway."

"So if I don't believe it, it won't work?" Sarah looked very alarmed. "If I think the freezer won't work then it won't, is that what you're saying?"

Sam shook his head. "You didn't believe in the cards before they started working, but that didn't make a difference, did it? The power was already there, and it didn't need you to believe. The freezer thing is the same, believe it or not it'll still work. If you leave the cards there, if you keep them frozen, then that's how they'll be, frozen."

"Mum said that maybe if the freezer doesn't work, I should put them in honey. I'm going to message her and ask if I should do that. I don't want any room for error here."

Sam nodded as Sarah messaged, and Kelli gulped down her wine and signalled for the waitress to bring her another.

"I'm happy to drive you home, Kelli, you can pick up your car tomorrow," Sam told her.

"Yeah, I think that's a good idea," Kelli gave him a weak smile.

"You're not working tomorrow?" Sarah asked her as she placed her mobile down on the table.

"Nah, day off. Thank god, I can get half blotto and then sleep in."

Sarah's phone buzzed and she picked it up, frowning as she read the message. "Mum says she's asked around and not to put the cards in honey. The honey could feed the cards, it could make them more powerful. She said don't touch the cards, and if I can help it, don't even open the freezer if she thinks there could be something that happened that might trigger them."

"I'd say something definitely happened that might trigger them," Kelli took a gulp of her wine as the waitress arrived with their burgers.

The phone buzzed again and Sarah sat her burger down to read it. "She says she's working on what to do to either take their power away or destroy them. She says hi, too."

"Hi mum," Kelli said and bit into her burger.

"Well, that's it then. Cards stay in the freezer, and you don't open the freezer tonight. Do you want to sleep at mine, get right away from them?" Sam asked.

"Nah, I actually don't think distance makes a difference. I think once they attached to me then it wouldn't matter where I was."

"Yeah, I'm inclined to agree," Kelli nodded.

"I have no idea how this works, but okay. So let's eat and talk about anything else except cards and people who piss us off," Sam suggested.

"Well, that ruins the whole conversation," Kelli grinned, amused at her own attempt at humour.

Chapter Sixteen

"Well, I'm glad you didn't dream last night," Kelly took a sip from her orange juice, the straw a bright pink paper one with random patterns of stars and half-moons. "I'm not ashamed to admit I was positively shitting myself."

"I tried so hard not to think about it. Like, I get what Sam was saying about trying to lucid dream and make sure I have control over what happens, but I was too scared to try. I mean, I didn't want to risk anyone's life or anything, I wanted to maybe practice on a day when I was having a normal dream, not one the cards control or anything."

"Yeah, I get that," Kelli looked up as the waiter came over to clear their table. "Why are we in this cafe anyway? Didn't Ben bring you here all the time?"

Sarah shrugged. "I used to bring him here, you remember how tight he was, he never paid for anything, even when I was just a student!"

"Yeah, I remember. You paid for the whole trip to Thailand, am I right?"

"Yeah, you're right. Anyway, I didn't want to pick this place particularly, but the property I'm managing is just around the corner and it's the closest place."

"I didn't think you came out in the field anymore, super contract seller Sarah."

"Yeah, I do. Saves money for the company, and

we don't actually have enough staff at the moment. I need to hire more people. If you ever think about ditching teaching and your hospitality job, I'd hire you in a second."

"There are days where I'd seriously consider it, trust me. Not today though. I'm sure you'd get a dozen people easy if you put an ad up."

"Yeah, but then I have to interview them. That shit takes forever!"

The little brass bell above the door rang as it opened, but neither girl turned to look at who walked in. The cafe was busy, the door tinkled constantly. The waitress placed the cheque on the table and Sarah asked for a takeaway cappuccino to take with her.

"Do you want a takeaway coffee too, Kelli?"

"Nah, I'm good. Thanks though."

The waitress accepted Sarah's card, smiling as she took it away to process the sale.

"I've got to get back to work. You're lucky to have school holidays off, so much less stress."

"And so much less money," Kelli stood up and grabbed her jacket from the back of the chair and slung it over her shoulder. "Hence the second job in hospitality."

The waitress brought Sarah's card and her coffee, thanking them for their patronage, and turned to walk back to the counter.

"Thank you!" Sarah called to the barista as she opened the door, ignoring the shout from a woman at the counter.

Kelli grabbed Sarah's arm. "Fuck! Did you see

that?"

"See what?"

"That was Ben's mum at the counter screaming at you?"

"Fuck, let's get out of here. Is that your car across the road?"

Kelli nodded. "Good, drive me to my car, it's in the carpark at the end of the block."

"Let's hustle, quick, before the lights change."

The doorbell tinkled behind them and Sarah ran out onto the road, not turning to see if it was Mrs. Dellon or an innocent cafe patron.

"Come back here you fucking cunt!"

"Shit shit shit," Kelli ran after Sarah, searching for her keys in her jacket pocket. They had to stop in the middle of the road to let a car past, and Ben's mum took this chance to start crossing.

"You fucking whore! You killed my son, and you think you can just walk around like nothing? I'm going to kill you, you fucking bitch. I'm going to send you straight to hell."

Kelli had the keys and Sarah ran to the passenger side of the car, waiting for the beep beep *that signalled the door opening.*

"Hurry up Kells! Crazy is nearly here!"

"Don't you get in that car, don't you dare!" Mrs. Dellon stopped to let some cars pass, but she was only two lanes from catching up to the girls. Kelli fumbled and dropped the keys, and Sarah squealed as Mrs. Dellon launched herself at them, just as Kelli picked up the keys and pressed the open button.

Sarah ripped her door open, Kelli a half heartbeat behind her as Ben's mum launched herself at the car. Her hand just hit Kelli's door as a police car raced around the corner, lights flashing, and hit Mrs. Dellon.

The angry woman launched into the air, her blood splattering over Kelli's window before her body crashed down on the roof. The police car skidded, trying to stop before it clipped a car coming in the other direction and rolled, ending up on its side, the lights in the front still flashing.

The girls sat still, not breathing, shock and fear paralysing them momentarily. A slithering noise sounded in the car and Kelli took a breath and screamed. Sarah just sat there, her urine staining the seat as her bladder let go.

Mrs. Dellon's face appeared at the top of the windscreen and slowly slipped down, her blood and something thicker, something that Sarah thought looked like brains, smeared the window as she slid down and rolled onto the bonnet of the car. Her intestines were still looped over the windscreen, and Kelli stopped screaming long enough to vomit on her lap.

Sarah woke up with her heart pounding, her first instinct to check she hadn't peed the bed. Relieved that she hadn't, she sat up and tried to breathe slower, she needed to calm her racing heart and terrified mind. Her mobile rang, this time she nearly did pee herself, and grabbed it off the nightstand.

"*You dreamed again. I fucking knew you would,*" Kelli didn't wait for a reply. "*Ben's mum was killed early this morning, it was on the television, on the morning show.*"

"Bullshit."

"You telling me you didn't dream?"

Sarah sighed. "Yeah, I dreamed. I dreamed she was hit by a police car and ended up on the roof of another car, major injuries. Dead on impact."

"Well, close, she was hit by a speeding car and ended up on a police car. They have dashcam on the whole thing, though they didn't show it of course. What the fuck, Sarah, did you touch the cards?"

"No, I didn't, I swear. I didn't even open the fridge or freezer. I came home and showered and went straight to bed. What's the time?"

"It's early, seven am. I know I woke you up, but I'm not sorry. Sezzy you have to do something, I mean it. I am completely freaked out. How long until your dark man decides we're getting in the way and takes us out? Or kills off your bosses because you work too hard?"

Sarah felt a tear escape from one eye and squeezed them shut, hard.

"I don't know what to do, Kelli. I really don't. I'm so frightened, and I don't know what to do."

"Call your mum, see what she thinks. But I'm also thinking that maybe I should keep away from you for now, I am seriously terrified. I can't tell you how scared I am."

"Me too, and you're right, don't even message me, don't do anything to make me think of you. Can you message Sam and tell him the same thing? I'll hang up now and call my mum. I need to figure out what to do."

"How will I know you're okay?"

"I don't know, Kelli, but don't call, don't do anything to make me think of you. Promise me that, please."

"I promise. Okay I'll hang up now and I'm going to ring Sam. Sezzy, I love you, don't forget that, girl."

"I won't Kells," Sarah answered, but her friend had already hung up.

Sarah dialled her mother, knowing she was a very early riser and would answer the phone immediately. She let the phone ring out twice, her anxiety growing as her mother didn't answer. The kitten stretched, yawned, then went back to sleep, her place on the pillow beside Sarah now her permanent sleeping spot.

Sarah jumped when her phone buzzed and she was relieved to see it was her mother.

"*Sorry baby, I was just out feeding the horses.*"

"Mum," Sarah's lip quivered, and her mother knew straight away something was wrong by the tone of her voice.

"*Tell me what happened, baby,*" she soothed.

Sarah told her everything about the funeral and the dream, then what happened to Ben's mother, promising that she hadn't touched the cards, hadn't even opened the freezer.

"*We need to step things up a bit, Sezzy. Get some tongs or something and take the cards out of the freezer, make sure you don't even touch the wrapping. Put them in something, a container, like a Tupperware or an ice cream container. Fill it full of water and heaps of salt, then seal it and stick it back in the freezer. Do it straight away.*"

"Will that stop them, Mum? Will it stop people dying? I'm so scared to talk to anyone. I told Kelli and Sam not to call or message me anymore. I'm so scared that I'll dream about them." Sarah was crying as she talked to her mother.

"*I'm working on things as fast as I can. That link you sent me with the similar cards helped, and I'm actually meeting some people today and we'll be working on fixing this. I'll call you as soon as I know something. Don't cry, baby, please. I promise I'll get this fixed.*"

Sarah thanked her mother and hung up, trying to calm herself. She didn't need to go to work with red, puffy eyes. She got out of bed and rummaged through her kitchen drawer until she found the serving tongs, and then an empty takeaway food container. She followed her mother's instructions before placing the whole wet mess back inside the freezer, then went to have a shower, hoping that a long, very hot shower would relax her and soothe her fears away.

Checking the time she saw she still had at least an hour before work, so she decided to go and treat herself to a sit down breakfast in the cafe, where there would be no television news, no distractions, no refrigerator, no thoughts of what's in the freezer or the things it could do. She opened a can of food for the kitten and grabbed her briefcase. She looked around at her place, at the abundant and luxurious plant life, at her long hair as she caught her reflection in the mirror, and at the little kitten, purring as she ate.

She locked the door as Michael was doing the same to his, and she worried that he would walk with her. How could she tell him to keep away, to not talk to her, just so he could be safe?

"Oh, good morning, Sarah. You're out early."

"Appointments, no rest for the wicked," she managed a limp smile.

"I hear you! I'm just going to my car, off to Sydney again. Probably gone for another week this time."

"No luggage?"

"Already in the car. I forgot my mobile, just came back to grab it. Glad I did, I got to say hi, at least."

Sarah felt warm inside. "Well, have a great trip, stay safe!"

"I hope so. Lots riding on this trip. At least I can take the lift down with you," Michael smiled and for a moment Sarah forgot her woes. He was so warm and friendly, and when the elevator doors closed Sarah caught a drift of his aftershave, causing her knees to feel weak. It was a quality, very expensive scent, and it made her even more attracted to him. He stopped at the first-floor car park and turned to her before he left the elevator.

"Maybe we can have dinner sometime when I get back?"

Sarah took a deep breath. "Sure, I'd like that."

"Can I have your number?"

Sarah reached into her pocket and pulled out one of her cards. “Sorry for the hubris of the gesture.”

Michael looked at the card then smiled as he pulled a card out of his own pocket and handed it over. “Well, I’ll see you later, then.”

“Yes, absolutely,” Sarah replied as the elevator doors closed.

She was still smiling as the doors opened to the first floor, and the smile didn’t fade as she walked across the road, dodging the slow-moving peak hour traffic with ease. The cafe door opened as she neared, and as she moved to walk in the hair on the back of her neck stood on end, goosebumps prickling up and down her arms. She looked around, there were plenty of people about, but none seemed to be her dark man. There were plenty of dark-skinned people, but none exceptionally tall, likewise the tall people she could see didn’t appear to be dark.

She put her head down and walked into the café, the feeling fading a little. All she could think was that she wasn’t followed in but, as she was unnerved now, she didn’t want to sit in the cafe to eat.

She ordered food to go along with her coffee and carried it to work, the feeling of being watched increasing when she left the café, and the sensation followed her all the way to work. Helen was just arriving and let her in, a relief as Sarah was having trouble balancing her coffee, meal and her briefcase. She didn’t want to know if she could manage it all while she got out her keys and opened the door and turned off the alarms.

"Wet the bed?" Helen laughed as she turned to Sarah, but the smile dropped from her face when she saw Sarah's expression. "Are you okay, hun?"

"I'm not sure, I think someone is following me."

Helen let her in then walked up the street a little, pretending to put something in the rubbish bin on the street before casually walking back inside.

"Was it a very tall, black man?" Helen asked her.

Sarah's face turned white. "Did you see him?"

Helen nodded. "I just caught a glimpse; he turned and went the other way when I looked at him."

"So you didn't see his face?"

Helen shook her head. "Has this been happening much?"

"Why, what do you know?"

"Joan and I saw a tall black man walking past the front a couple of times a day last week, every day. We can't see his face because of the sign on the window, we only noticed him because he's so tall, and it's unusual for him to be wearing a big black coat in the middle of summer."

Sarah sat her coffee and food back on the table, running a hand through her hair.

"Oh honey, you're shaking! Do you know this man? Has he been bothering you much?"

The stress and shock of the past week, added to the violent and graphic dream of last night, came crashing down on Sarah, and she broke down, crying and shaking. Helen grabbed her into her arms. "Oh sweetheart, what's he done? Did he hurt you?"

Matthew chose that moment to walk in the door, a look of shock on his face as he saw Sarah sobbing. "Trouble?"

Sarah nodded and Helen grabbed her arm, picking up Sarah's food in her other. "Grab your coffee, honey, let's go out to the tearoom and talk about it."

Matthew followed them and leaned against the bench as Sarah sat down. She told them about the eruption at the funeral and the subsequent death of Mrs. Dellon, and how she had felt the man following her all week. She told them how she had never seen his face, she didn't know him, but was careful to make no mention of the cards at all.

Matthew listened to everything, not making any comment, then turned and filled the kettle with water from the tap before flicking the on switch. He grabbed his cup from the cupboard before finally turning back to face Sarah. "You came here straight from your last job, didn't you? No time off in between?"

Sarah nodded, wiping her eyes with a tissue Helen handed her.

"When was the last time you had a holiday?"

Sarah let a little laugh escape her. "Holiday? I think I was eighteen, I went to Thailand for five days with my then boyfriend, Ben."

"The guy who just died?"

Sarah nodded.

"Hmmm," Matthew turned back to the kettle, pouring his tea and stirring the cup for a while, his face thoughtful. "This is what I'm thinking," he looked at Sarah and Helen smiled, already knowing what he was going to say.

"With the contracts you landed us we are sitting in a very good place, Sarah. You didn't just win the rentals, but all the sales opportunities as well. This last contract was mind blowing. You're not even a salesperson, but you got us so many properties, and an ongoing client that runs the biggest investment company in Victoria. Girl, we don't need to solicit any more work for years!"

Sarah nodded, wondering how bad her eyeliner had run.

"Well, we talked about you on Friday afternoon, after you left, and we need to reward you. Not just bonuses, they're yours, and you'll get them in the next two pay runs. No, we want to send you away on a holiday, the owners have shares in a resort in the Maldives, and they want to give you ten days in the resort. That won't be until after the financial year, though, so there's a bit of a wait until you can go."

Sarah's eyes widened and she shook her head, trying to take in what Matthew was telling her.

"Not just that, but due to everything that's happened to you last week, and now this week, I think you need to take a week off, maybe go home to your family and just debrief a little. I can't let you go today, I'll need your help bringing in new staff and bringing them up to speed, so if you can stay till Thursday then take off after that for a week, maybe ten days, how does that sound?"

Sarah started to cry again, and Matthew looked at Helen, gesturing for her to comfort the distressed woman. Helen sat beside Sarah and wrapped her arm around the younger woman's shoulder.

"I've called a temp agency and they'll send over a dozen people today for you to look at, I'm thinking you'll need five at least to take over existing contracts. Paul will step in and take over your role while you're gone, and your existing staff will take on the new buildings. I've had all weekend to figure this out, so all I need you to do is get everything ready for Paul and your guys and then I want you to go."

Sarah looked up at her manager, her large brown eyes shining with tears.

"Don't think we're trying to get rid of you or anything, you are far too valuable to us! We're rewarding your amazing achievement and trying to retain you as best we can, by giving you what you need. I'd already come to this conclusion last week after your boyfriend died, now these other things have just made me sure of my decision."

Helen squeezed Sarah tighter and Sarah nodded. "I don't know what to say."

"Say nothing, just eat your breakfast then fix your face up, you look like a mess," Matthew smiled at his attempt at humour and Sarah laughed, though it was a forced and hollow sound. Matthew took his coffee out of the kitchen, shutting the door behind him. Helen pulled the bag of food over and placed it in front of Sarah. "Do I need to nuke this?"

"No, it's just avo and tomato toast, fine cold.

Thank you, Helen, thanks a million. Can you believe what they're doing for me?"

Helen got up and re-boiled the kettle. "Honey, why are you surprised? You've just made the company millions, literally, over the next five years. They aren't going to let you go, so you better get used to us!"

Sarah hugged the receptionist, her heart warmed by the kindness and generosity she was being shown, something that she wasn't used to. Helen kissed her on the top of the head and left, also closing the door behind her, and Sarah thought they were giving her the room to herself, as the tearoom door was never closed. She needed the time to get her thoughts together. She wished she could message Kelli, or Sam, but knew that was a bad decision, so she messaged her mum instead.

Mum answered immediately, happy that Sarah would be coming, and happy that they could deal with the card situation in person rather than trying to figure things out at a distance. She kept the conversation very light and mum-like, saying how proud she was of her baby girl, how she was looking forward to seeing her and the things they could do on Sarah's visit.

Finishing her coffee, Sarah threw half of her toast away, looked in the little mirror on the wall and groaned. She pulled out her make-up bag from her briefcase and fixed her face, and then ran her hands through her hair, still not used to its thickness, the glossy dark waves falling to nearly her shoulder blades now. She tucked it around, lifted it up and tied it with an elastic she found in her make-up bag. Feeling a little better and looking a great deal better, Sarah made herself a strong black coffee before opening the tearoom door, a bright smile in place for all the faces that turned in her direction as she made her way to her desk. She drew close and frowned as Mohammed, her most senior rental agent, was sitting there.

He grinned at her and pointed to the glass walled offices set at the back of the main office, and Sarah gasped when she saw one of the offices had been filled with flowers and balloons, a big *Congratulations* banner hanging jauntily across the front. Her name was stencilled on the door, and a very shiny new key was hanging around the doorknob.

"Seriously?" she whirled to look at Matthew as everyone started to clap, standing up and congratulating her. She felt her face go brighter than red as an embarrassed sweat broke out under her arms. She accepted the handshakes of just about everyone there, then took a video of the office for her social media story. She mightn't be able to share her great news with her loved ones, but this way they could at least see what had transpired.

She opened her door and slung the key onto her keyring, laughing with joy when the balloons flowed out into the main office. The room smelled of blooms and heady scents of roses, and she filmed another video, then squealed with delight when she found a little bar fridge, and still in the box was a coffee machine, a packet of coffee capsules on the top.

A knock at the door made her look up, and a young man stood there, his briefcase clutched to his chest. “Can I help you?” Sarah asked him.

“Um, hi, I’m Robbie, your new personal assistant.”

Sarah put her hands on her hips. “No shit.”

“No shit, girl,” Matthew put his hand on Robbie’s shoulder and led him into Sarah’s office. “Robbie worked at our Altona branch, he was on reception. Did such a good job he got this promotion. Give him a try, and if he doesn't work out, we'll fire him.”

Robbie looked distraught until Matthew laughed. “Just kidding, he’s a good kid, and a very hard worker. Best part is you won't have to break him in, he knows the drill already. He’s also a bit of a computer wiz, so get him to set up yours and you’ll be ready to go in no time.”

Robbie smiled shyly and sat at Sarah’s desk, turning on her computer as Matthew started to unpack the coffee machine. “I’ve got the same type, it’s really good. I put full cream in your fridge, but I wasn't sure if that’s right or if you have soy or something like that.”

“Full cream is perfect. Matthew, I can’t thank you enough, this is all very overwhelming!”

“You have earned every bit of it, and another thing I forgot to tell you, don't feel pressured to continuously bring in huge amounts of new business. We know that’s simply not sustainable, and with the contracts you’ve already won, not even necessary." Matthew pressed a button and a plume of hot white steam shot out. "Well, coffee machine is ready to go, you just need to fill it with water. Have a good day and yell out if you need anything. I mean that, Sarah."

"Sure thing, and thanks again, Matthew."

Sarah lifted up the water chamber from the coffee machine and Robbie jumped up. "I'll fill that for you," he said as he reached for the chamber.

"I really need my computer set up first," Sarah said.

"All done and ready to go. Do you have your own coffee mug? Is this it?" he asked as he pointed at the cooling black coffee.

"Nah, that's just from the tearoom. I don't have a mug, I mean I did but I dropped it, ended up in a thousand pieces. Any mug will do. Thank you. Oh, do you know where the tearoom is?"

Robbie nodded and picked up the cold coffee. "I filled in for Joan when she went on long service leave last year. I like it here, much closer to home. This is a really good break for me."

"Me too," Sarah said to an empty office as Robbie hurried off to get the water. She sat down at her desk, her joy returning at the super comfortable chair she had been given. She moved her mouse to wake up the computer and logged into her mail, groaning when she saw how many there were. This was going to be a long morning.

Robbie returned with the water and set about making a coffee for Sarah, and when he placed it beside her she looked up and smiled at him.

“Please make yourself one as well. And when you get a chance can you gather up the balloons and sort of move them to the back, so my desk is clear?”

“Sure thing, boss.” Robbie hurried about then made himself a coffee, stopping at Sarah’s desk he handed her a new box of cards. “These are over on the bureau. Hey, you don't have to go through all those emails, that’s my job. I’ll go through them and filter out what you don't need or take care of the minor stuff. You haven't had a PA before, have you?”

Sarah shook her head. “Nope, but you are about to become my hero. Where’s your desk?”

“Just there, right in the front of the main office, see? Next to Elyse’s new desk.”

“Awesome. Right, I’m working on this email, the DeLancey file, so leave that one for me.”

Robbie nodded and grabbed his briefcase. “Nice to meet you, Sarah, and thanks for this opportunity.”

“To be honest, I didn't hire you.”

“No, I know, but if you hadn’t got the promotion, I wouldn't have gotten my promotion. A fortuitous chain of events for me.”

“Absolutely,” Sarah nodded as he left, and went back to her computer.

Chapter Seventeen

The week passed quickly, Sarah hired the new temps and one permanent property manager and organised everything for Paul's turn at her job while she was away. Paul had his own office but no PA, so he was happy to have Robbie help him for the time being.

Every morning, and several times a day, Michael would text her, telling her about his day, checking on hers, sending pictures of the city and sights, sometimes a selfie, and Sarah would do the same. She would smile every time the phone buzzed, and felt a strong attraction growing towards the handsome man. She told him she was going to visit her mother for a week and he was disappointed, she would leave the day before he returned from Sydney.

Sarah had warned her mother she would be bringing the kitten and her mum seemed unsure, which worried Sarah. Her mum was a crazy animal lover, cats being one of her favourite animals, and her reluctance to meet the new kitten was something Sarah found very strange.

She was taking the kitten anyway, and had her things all packed and ready, along with a large duffle bag of her own clothes. All her plants had been watered and placed in a shady area or inside, and she even put a couple in the sink with an inch or two of water to keep them sustained. She left the cards until the very last minute, packing her perishable food in a large supermarket bag and carrying it to the car. She double checked everything, then brought up the cooler that she'd purchased especially for the occasion from the car.

The kitten was sitting on the back of the couch, just watching her, occasionally grooming herself, then turning her bright blue eyes back on her master. Sarah scooped her up and tucked her onto her shoulder, then opened the freezer. The cards were right at the back in the takeaway container, and she used a hand towel to take the container out, wrapping the towel around it as she placed it into the cooler and slammed it shut with a relieved sigh.

She put them in the very back of the car, not wanting them anywhere near herself, and set off to her mother's house. The kitten made itself comfortable on her shoulder, purring as she drove out into the traffic, glad that she was going the opposite way to the main peak hour rush. Her mother only lived about two hours away so it wouldn't be a long drive, and Sarah had filled up her petrol tank the night before.

She was hungry though, so drove through a McDonalds to grab a takeaway breakfast. The kitten stayed hidden under her hair as she picked up her coffee and McMuffin. She felt the strange feeling of being watched when she stopped the car at the pick-up window, but tried to brush it off, turning up her radio and closing the window. The day was a pleasant one, the sun bright, white fluffy clouds in a sapphire sky as Sarah ate one handed, singing with a mouth full to her favourite song on the radio.

She'd promised her mother she would pick up some groceries in the nearby town before heading out to the rural property, and when the message tone went off on her phone Sarah knew it was her mother sending through a shopping list. She pulled into the IGA supermarket car park at Heathcote and was happy to score a park right beside the entrance. She grabbed a trolley and pulled out her mobile to check her mother's list.

Grateful that her mum didn't want much, Sarah pushed her trolley around the aisles, grabbing her items and ignoring the looks she was getting from people. It wasn't until she was queued up to pay that Sarah really noticed the eyes of everyone on her and felt decidedly uncomfortable. She didn't know why they were staring at her, so she smoothed down her shirt, checked her fly, and glanced at her reflection in the shiny mobile screen but could see nothing out of the ordinary.

People were pointing and talking behind their hands, to the point where Sarah wanted to leave the groceries and get out of there. This was almost as bad as the dark man feeling, and the sort of attention you got at school when you had a notice stuck on your back by the bullies in the year ahead of you.

Her turn at the check-out came all too slowly, and Sarah unpacked her groceries under the eyes of what felt like everyone in the supermarket. She pushed her trolley through and smiled self-consciously at the girl behind the register.

The girl's face lit up when she saw Sarah. "Oh my god! That's beyond adorable!" she gushed, and Sarah frowned in confusion.

Noticing Sarah's discomfort, the girl pointed at her shoulder. "Your little kitten. It's so tiny, but so damn cute!"

Sarah reached up and touched the kitten. Its head was poking through her hair and she smiled in relief. "Oh my god, I forgot she was there. I wondered why people were looking at me, I thought I'd sat in something."

The girl laughed as she rang through the shopping. "She's so tiny you wouldn't be able to feel her there! What's her name?"

"She hasn't got one yet. I only found her like two weeks ago. No one claimed her, so I guess she's mine."

"Oh, you'll have to think of a good name for her. I think she looks like a Lilly, I like that name for a cat. She looks too small to be away from her mother, though she might just be really small. I had a cat like that, the runt of the litter, but he ended up being an absolute monster! Is that cash or card?"

Sarah held up her card and thanked the girl. She wheeled the trolley to her car, suddenly worried the kitten would jump off and she would lose her, but when she tried to lift the kitten off her shoulder the animal dug in, her little, but very sharp, claws attaching like Velcro to her shirt. Taking the chance the kitten would stay, Sarah opened the car door to put her shopping away.

The feeling hit her as soon as the door was open,

and even the kitten growled, a comical sound coming from such a tiny larynx.

The dark man was near, and she could feel him, though she did wonder why the feeling hit her so hard once she opened the door. She worried about taking him to her mother's place, but didn't know what to do to prevent him. She loaded the shopping into the back seat and messaged her mother.

Just at supermarket. The dark man is following. Don't want him at yours, but don't know what to do.

She stood in the sun, waiting for a reply, aware that everyone that came out of the supermarket was amused at the kitten which peered out of the back of Sarah's hair, a little blue-eyed fluff that watched everyone that walked past.

Her phone beeped and Sarah opened the message.

Buy a bunch or two of sage and some garlic bulbs. Put them in the cooler before you leave. Hopefully that's enough.

Sarah did as her mother suggested, buying all of the sage on the shelf as well as several large bulbs of garlic, then shoving it into the cooler, packing it so tight that she could barely close the lid. She locked the car then ran into the bottle shop, grabbing a few bottles of wine for herself and her mother before returning to the car.

This time when she opened the door, she didn't feel the strange sensation, and decided she could continue her journey. She drove back down the street then around the block a few times before heading back on her way, the kitten settling down to sleep and the radio blaring.

The day was even more perfect as she drove through the closest town to her mother's land, but her buoyant mood had sunk with the dreaded feeling and turning up the radio hadn't helped at all. She passed a car pulling a laden down trailer as she crept up the hill, then turned off to a dirt road and drove another half hour before finding her mother's street.

Sarah had lived a good ten years at the property, but it no longer felt like home. While it was warm and welcoming, it was her mother's house through and through. Perhaps she felt that way because the gardens had changed and grown in the last seven years since she left home, the house was painted and modified, and the whole property was different than when she lived here.

Sarah knew it was her mother's partner that worked on the property and made all the structural changes, but the expansive native gardens were all her mother's doing. The house looked like a retreat in a native forest, and that would have been exactly what her mother planned it should represent.

An old whippet came wandering out to the car, and Sarah whistled with joy when she saw him.

"Zacky boy, you old bag of bones!" she laughed as she climbed out of her car and the dog wiggled his entire body with excitement at seeing her.

"I always knew he liked you better than me," her mother stepped off the long front veranda. "Look at him, behaving like a puppy again."

"He looks so old!" Sarah kneeled down and

cuddled the excited dog, who drew back a little before plunging his nose into her hair. Sarah heard the kitten hiss at the pointy snout exploring her hiding place, though Sarah didn't worry about the friendly whippet. He was a kindly soul, had never shown any prey drive in his entire life, even helping foster abandoned kittens on numerous occasions. “How old is he now?”

“He’ll be fifteen next month, and he’s really slowing down. I don't think he’ll be around much longer, sadly.”

“What will you do without him? He’s such a wonderful old dog.”

Zac withdrew his nose from Sarah’s hair and the kitten popped her head out, blinking her deep blue eyes in curiosity and surprise.

“So that’s the card kitten. It looks really cute. What’s her name?”

“She hasn’t got one, though the girl in the supermarket said she looks like a Lilly.”

“You took her into the supermarket? Well, it’s probably better than leaving her in a hot car. Speaking of which, bring that cooler into the garage, I’ve plugged in the old freezer.”

Sarah opened the hatchback and pulled out the cooler, following her mother into the opened roller door. She lifted the cooler into the open chest freezer and turned to her mother in surprise. “Why is there sand and seashells here?”

“It’s to throw the cards off, confuse them. Julia suggested it.”

“Who’s Julia?” Sarah stood back as her mother

tipped a large bucket of sand on the cooler and shut the freezer, putting a padlock through the catch and making sure it was securely fastened.

"She's the spiritual lady I told you about, her and her partner Ange are the ones that told me about the sage and garlic, and not to use the honey. They'll be working with us on finding a resolution to our little problem."

"Our little problem… I guess that's one way to put it. Are they here?"

"No, they'll come over tomorrow and have lunch with us, give us this day to ourselves. Come one, let's get the shopping inside and I'll show you around a bit, see what's changed since you last got here. Do you want a tea first?"

"Absolutely, I am dying for a hot drink. C'mon Zacky boy. Hey, where's your man?"

"He's in Perth for ten days, taking care of the family trust or something. I thought it was perfect timing, we can take care of things without him being all sceptical."

"Sounds like a good idea," Sarah lifted out the shopping as her mum grabbed her duffle bag and led Sarah inside. The house was everything you'd imagine an aged hippy would have; it was beyond a cliche. Beads, crystals and incense flooded her senses, and she noticed her mother had added to her collection since her last visit at Christmas.

"You have so much stuff," Sarah noted as her mother carried her bag into the end room, her old bedroom.

"Yeah, but it's *my* stuff, and I only have to

please me. I don't care what other people think. It's clean and tidy, even if it is a bit cluttered."

"You are the epitome of an aging hippy, you know that, right?"

Her mother smiled and wrapped her in a bear hug. "I know, and I don't care. I love you baby Sarah."

"I love you too, Mum."

"We'll fix this mess, don't worry about things for now, I promise we'll fix things."

Sarah felt her tears welling up and she nodded, afraid to speak lest she burst into tears.

"Okay, let's have a little morning tea before we go for a walk in the gardens."

A weird tapping sound made Sarah turn around and she squealed with delight. "You have a baby kangaroo?"

"That's Wally the wallaby, his mate Kevin the kangaroo will be along soon. I've just weaned them, but they're still very clingy."

"Can I pick him up?"

"Best not to, I have to get them used to being outside so they can be rehabilitated back into the wild. We don't get to keep them as pets, and there's always another baby needing a wildlife carer to help him get back to health."

As predicted, Kevin the tiny kangaroo hopped around the corner and Sarah couldn't help herself, she bent down and scooped up the bundle of soft brown fur and long gangly legs into her arms. The joey reached up and touched her face with his paw.

"He just loves that, he's the cuddliest joey I've

ever raised," her mother smiled.

"I wish you'd been a wildlife rescuer when I was still here."

"I worked too much then; I really didn't have the time. Now I do. If you came up more, you'd get to play with them when they're little. Bottle feed them and everything."

The kitten poked her head out of her hiding place in Sarah's hair, leaning down to sniff the native animal.

"Look, Lilly likes him," her mum said as she led Sarah back into the homely kitchen. Sarah smiled at the sight of fresh cooked scones sitting on the table, homemade jam and fresh cream adding to the spread. "I know you like scones, I'll just re-boil the kettle. You still want tea?"

"Oh, yes please! Is this raspberry or strawberry jam?" Sarah sat down and started to help herself, the kitten meowing at the sight of the cream. Sarah ignored the kitten, not wanting to teach her any bad habits.

"Did you bring food for the kitten? I only have adult food here," Sarah's mum poured the tea as she spoke. "My cats are all outside cats, so they shouldn't bother her."

"Hey Mum, why didn't you want me to bring Lilly?" Sarah asked, deciding to use the name bestowed on the kitten.

"To be truthful, I don't know if your dark man uses the kitten to spy on you and what you do."

Sarah's hand paused midway to her mouth. "What the fuck, Mum! I never even thought about that!"

"I'm surprised you didn't. It's weird that a living animal appeared right when you wanted one, it's super weird. Same as your hair, while it's beautiful, it's also super weird."

Sarah sat her scone back on the plate. "I feel sick."

"I'm sorry, I didn't want to upset you, you've had enough shitty things to upset you to last a lifetime. Let's change the subject, tell me about your promotion and that fantastic looking office!"

Sarah told her mother about her office, her PA, and how much she'd be expecting in her bonus. She also let her mother know about the trip to the Maldives.

"It's for two, you know."

Her mother wiped some cream from the corner of her mouth. "That's brilliant. Who'll be joining you in your tropical getaway?"

"I was thinking of taking you, actually," Sarah sipped her tea as she watched her mother's reaction.

"No, not really, you'd take one of your friends, or Sam. Why would you want to take me?"

"Because I love you, Mum. You've always been there for me and Sam, you'd do anything you could for us. We know how much you gave up to make sure we had everything we needed, and you missed out on heaps of things. Kelli, Sam and me can go another time, the company has shares in the resort so I get a super discount."

Sarah's mum started to cry. Sarah jumped up and hugged her, tears burning her eyes as well. "This was supposed to make you happy, not make you cry!"

"I'm crying happy tears, I am, I promise," her mum sniffed and wiped her eyes on a napkin. "I've never been overseas; this is just amazing! Oh, geez, I'd better get a passport!"

Sarah laughed and let her mother go. "Yeah, that might be handy."

"Let's go outside and have a look at the gardens and the horses. I need some fresh air, I think," Sarah popped her last piece of scone into her mouth. "I need to walk off all these carbs, too."

Chapter Eighteen

Sarah left the kitten asleep on her pillow, tying her robe about her waist and stuffing her feet into her slippers before walking out of her old room. The house was quiet, which was unusual; her mother always had music playing. She would put it on as soon as she woke up and leave it playing all day, even when she was outside.

She turned when she heard a meow, the kitten running towards her and climbing up her robe, taking her customary place on Sarah's shoulder. Scratching the kitten, she continued down the hall to the kitchen. Her mother was sitting at the table, the paper in front of her as she drank her tea.

"Good afternoon," her mum said as she lifted her gaze.

"It's not that late, is it?"

"No, it's only ten. I came in to have a cup of tea after working outside. I'm glad you slept in a little bit."

Sarah rubbed her eyes as she sat down. "This isn't sleeping in. I can often go till one or two on a Sunday."

"I'll make you some breakfast, what would you like?"

Sarah shook her head. "You don't have to do that, Mum, I can make something myself."

"I like to do it. I live all by myself, I rarely get anyone other than my man to cook for."

"Guilt trip much," Sarah yawned. "But thanks, it'd be nice to have breakfast. What's on the agenda for today?"

"Jules and Ange will come over for lunch, they've messaged me to confirm, and we'll talk about what we can do. Sam also messaged, the market got back to him and gave him the email address of the three people that booked stalls where you remember the getting the boxes. He's contacted all of them and will let us know his results."

"Good, good," Sarah looked over at the kettle as her mother put it on. "I don't suppose you have any coffee?"

"Don't drink it, you know that," her mother cracked eggs into the old frypan on the stove. "Did you bring any in your groceries?"

Sarah shrugged. "Nah, I'll just have tea. You want one?" Sara stood up and filled the kettle from the tap.

"Yes please love. No sugar, I've cut right back."

A knock at the kitchen door had both of them surprised, and Sarah's mum put the eggs on the table before she hurried over to open it.

"Rod! Good to see you, come in, come in."

"Thanks Alison. And who is this fashion model at your table?"

"Sarah, this is my neighbour Rod, he and his wife often come over to help out or visit or ride a horse."

"Nice to meet you," Sarah pulled her robe tighter. "Sorry about the pyjamas."

Rod laughed. "Girly, I spend whole days in my

bathrobe, so your fluffy pink gown is a step up from my old dog rug of a thing."

"Nice," Sarah cast a glance at her mum who shrugged and smiled.

"Anyway, I'm here as a favour for Jules, she asked me to come over and give youse this." Rod held out a large shoe box he'd carried in with him. "It's made special for youse guys, I did it yesterday. Anyway, I gotta get to town, so youse girls have a good day, okay?"

"Do we open it?" Sarah's mum, asked.

"Jules said to wait till she and Ange get here," Rod dipped his head in Sarah's direction as he made his way out.

"What do you think it is?" Sarah asked.

"Whatever it is, it's deceptively heavy. I don't think it's work boots," Alison moved the box around, looking at the label. "It's all taped up so we can't open it."

"Well we won't have long to wait if the ladies are coming for lunch, I guess," Sarah sopped up the last of the egg yolks with a piece of toast. "You want some help to make lunch?"

"I made it yesterday, just have to heat it up. You go and get dressed, I'll clean up here and set the table."

"Okie dokie," Sarah put her plate in the sink before heading off to get dressed. She was looking forward to meeting her mother's friends, she'd heard quite a bit about the women and their strange ways.

Alison was a great believer in the mystical and

spiritual. Sarah remembered her going to classes to learn how to read tarot cards and zodiac signs, something she found embarrassing at the time as the classes were held at her local school. She hated that her friends thought her mother to be a weirdo and a witch and she would get into fights to defend her mother's reputation.

Now though, people came to her to have their fortunes told or their crystals read, and her mother made a living out of providing these services to the locals. She even had a part time position in an alternative bookstore in Heathcote, reading the tarot and making little spells.

Sarah dressed in jeans and a t-shirt and pulled her thick hair into an elastic at the nape of her neck. The kitten didn't seem too impressed with the loss of her hiding place but found she could climb into the hair above the tie and curl up in a ball. Sarah found the sensation strange, she'd never had this much hair to deal with, the weight of the kitten making it even more unfamiliar.

Her phone had two texts from Michael, and she answered them with a selfie showing her kitten hair, and one of her old room. Michael answered straight away and Sarah smiled at his eagerness.

She made her bed then went back into the kitchen to help her mother prepare the table, but she was already finished and the kitchen was empty. Sarah walked out of the kitchen door, now open, only the screen door pushed over. She walked down the stone path that led around the house and down into the gardens, and Sarah could hear voices, very faintly, as she walked.

A grey whippet bounded up to her, followed by another, a fawn coloured one bringing up the rear. They were excited to see Sarah and jumped up and wagged their tails. Zac finally made his way over to her, his tail wagging with happiness and Sarah bent down to cuddle him, immediately regretting her decision as the three younger whippets showered her with their cold wet noses, their pink tongues licking her face and neck.

The kitten hissed in fear and the dogs reacted in surprise, barking and jumping, trying to grab the kitten out of her hair.

"Dogs! Come!" a woman with rows of rainbow-coloured braided dreadlocks called and the three young whippets immediately ran to her side. Zac stayed with Sarah as she approached the woman.

"Thanks, I was getting loved to death!" Sarah smiled and held out her hand. "I'm Alison's daughter, Sarah."

"Yes, I can see that, I'm Julia, or Jules, as everyone calls me, and this is Ange, my partner," a blonde-haired woman stepped forward and shook Sarah's hand.

"Nice to meet you," Ange smiled shyly, her Irish accent charming. "You're as beautiful as your mother said you were."

"Thank you!" Sarah felt her face grow red. "I'm sure all mothers think their kids are beautiful."

"In this case your mother was right," Jules looked at Sarah's hair with her brows knitted tight. "What on earth have you got in your hair?"

“That’s the kitten I told you about,” Alison drew up to the others, a basket filled with vegetables in her arms. “That’s little Lilly.”

“Cute name, what made you choose that?” Ange asked.

“I didn’t,” Sarah explained. “The checkout chick at IGA thought of it, and it just sorta fits, I guess.”

“Let’s get back up to the house, I can get these salad veggies washed and prepared,” Alison said, walking ahead with Ange.

Jules walked beside Sarah, her arm looped through a basket that was filled with carrots and potatoes. “Your mum loves her garden,” Julia commented. “She really seems to have a way with the earth.”

“She’s always loved to garden,” Sarah said. “I remember our house in Mill Park, people would stop and ask who our landscaper was. Mum did it all herself, the digging, the dirt, the planting. She says it’s what sold the house, that garden.”

Jules smiled but didn’t respond.

The kitchen was full of the scents of lunch as Alison had put the food in the oven before going outside. Sarah felt her mouth watering, even though she’d just eaten her breakfast. Her mother was a fantastic cook, and Sarah had sorely missed that home cooking.

The whippets all came inside but were very obedient, without being told they all made their way to the kitchen mat and laid down, a bundle of long legs and pointy snouts, all tangled up together.

“Let me see that little kitten of yours, Sarah,’

Jules held out her hand.

Sarah reached up to her ponytail so the kitten could step into her palm and she held it out to Julia.

"Oh my god, it's so tiny!" Jules clutched the little kitten to her breast, the bright blue eyes blinking as it looked at everyone.

"Let me have a cuddle!" Ange held out her arms.

"Okay, but give her straight back." Jules handed her over.

"Mum's worried that the dark man is using her to spy on me," Sarah explained. "She thinks maybe Lilly isn't safe."

"Nah, I can't feel anything but kitten and affection. And a little bit of hunger, too," Ange handed the kitten back to Jules' demanding hands.

"I agree, there's nothing malevolent there. She's just a sweet little kitten, aren't you, petal?" Lilly was subjected to multiple kisses from the rainbow haired woman. "Such a darling, she's so precious!"

The kitten looked over at Sarah and mewed.

"She wants her mamma back," Jules handed the brown fluff back to Sarah, and it immediately made its way back onto her shoulders, but this time didn't curl up in her hair, instead choosing to sit purring near her ear.

"This kitchen smells like what I imagine heaven smells like," Ange pulled out a chair to sit down. "Though I don't believe in heaven, per se. Maybe something heaven like, perhaps."

"You're rambling," Julia teased. "But she's right, you have to be one of the best cooks ever, even better than my mother. That's high praise, believe me."

"There's no dieting when my mother's around," Sarah agreed. "But it's all so good and healthy, I just wish it didn't taste so good so I could eat normal sized portions."

"Stop it, the lot of you, or my head will be too big to get it through the door," Alison opened the oven and pulled on her novelty brown cow oven mitts so she could lift out the cast iron casserole dish.

Sarah felt her mouth water again, the aroma was quite delectable. She opened the fridge and took out the brightly painted carafe of water.

"Sit down, everyone, and dig in," Alison invited, and no one needed to be told twice.

"I have to say Sarah, your hair is absolutely amazing," Jules smiled at her. "Your mum tells us you never had thick hair before."

"Mum told you about the plants as well?"

"Yes, she did, she told us everything you told her. I have to say, it's very alarming."

"You're not kidding! The people dying are the worst, I'm too scared to talk to my best friend and my brother. Just being here with mum is putting her in danger."

"We don't know that, sweetie," Ange said. "So far it seems only those that threaten you are attacked."

"Yeah, I get that, but what if I have a fight with her, or even just get pissed off? I mean, we're all human, not everyone gets along all of the time. What if you guys say something that I don't like, or if it upsets me and I dream about you? What happens then? I don't get any warning; I can't stop what I dream so I can save you." Sarah felt hurt, and angry tears started to fall. "I'm worried that if I even watch a movie that gets me thinking and my brain happens to add someone I love into my dream, what happens? What happens then?"

Alison leaned over and hugged Sarah. "Hey, baby, ssshh, don't cry. None of this is your fault, okay? We know that, no matter what, you'd never do anything to hurt anybody."

Sarah accepted a tissue from Ange and wiped her face. "It won't make things any better, though. I don't want to hurt any of you, I couldn't live with that, whether you blame me or not."

Julia was looking at her, but she had a bright expression across her face, her lips turned down in a wry smile. She continued to eat but seemed to be observing in an almost knowing manner.

"We knew the risks before we came here, Sarah, your mum told us all about the things you were worrying about," Ange lay a comforting hand on Sarah's arm. "We'll work together to fix this for you, for your family, okay? We promise you that."

"Believe her," Julia leaned forward. "Ange is powerful, and I'm no lightweight, either. I'm half Somali, half Aboriginal. Ange is Irish Gypsy, directly descended from the Fairy folk, I think. She has a very strong gift, we both do, and our links to the Earth and the Elements is beyond your comprehension. We *will* fix this for you, and we fully accept any risk."

Sarah smiled and took a breath to calm herself. "Thank you, thank you so much."

"Hey, we did make sure to protect ourselves first. We've made sure we have protection, and we've sent over a special box to contain the cards."

"They've already got a special box, a wooden one. Hasn't protected shit."

"This box is different," Julia served herself another bowlful. "We put spells and charms all through it, and we blessed it in the running water of a sacred waterfall. And then, just to keep extra careful, we had Rod make a lead lining for it so that nothing can get through it or out of it. We even gave him special items to put into the lead to give it extra charge. Nothing's getting in or out of that box."

Sarah pushed her plate away; she was so full she was feeling ill. "What then? What do I do after that?"

"Well, if it works, that's it. You can leave the box here and live your life as normal. That's it."

"Seriously? You think it's that easy? I mean, this magic, the magic on the cards, it must be pretty powerful. Those cards killed people. They made my freaking hair grow, and they created a kitten, a living thing!"

Julia nodded and swallowed her mouthful before speaking. "I understand that honey, I do. But between Ange and me, well, there really isn't very much we can't do."

"What if the cards are one of those things that you can't?"

"We have back up," Ange replied. "We've got

Julia's people, both sides of her family are super spiritual and powerful, and you've got my family. This blonde hair is dyed, I'm a black-eyed gypsy through and through, and in these days of technology my family are only a video call away."

Sarah nodded. "Okay, good. So when do we start?"

"Right now, I guess, if we're all finished?" Julia asked.

"I'll just do the dishes first, if nobody minds?" Alison stood up and began gathering the plates.

"We'll all help, that way we can get to the cards quicker. We also need the table," Ange stood and helped clean up.

"I think we can use the dining table, it's bigger than this kitchen table, and we can really lay things out on it," Alison advised. "I've cleansed the dining room as well, and it's full of fresh wildflowers and branches from the gums. I think the dining room is perfect."

"The dining room it is! Let's get this cleaned up." The whippets all stood when they saw their people on their feet and Julia waved the dogs back to their mat. "You all stay there, puppers. We don't need you right now."

Chapter Nineteen

"The sand worked, you think?" Ange asked as Alison opened up the freezer.

"Well, I didn't dream," Sarah shrugged. At least, not one of the scary, people die kind of dreams."

"What about the feeling of being watched by your 'dark man', have you felt that?" Julia asked.

"Not since I left Kilmore. I drove around the block a few times, I thought that might confuse him. I haven't felt him here at all."

"It's only been one night in the sand, so there's no way to know if it worked for the dreams," Alison cautioned. "You said you don't have those dreams every night, right?"

Sarah nodded. "I don't, that's right. And not every dream is a dying dream, either, that just happens when someone does something to hurt or upset me."

"There's the cooler," Alison said. "Who picks it up?"

"I should, I don't want anyone else infected," Sarah said.

"Interesting choice of words," Julia said. "But we're protected, remember? We have these." She reached under her shirt and pulled out a small leather bag tied to a thin cord around her neck. "They won't let any boogie-men or their weird magic touch us."

Sarah bit her bottom lip. "I think you're

underestimating the power in these cards. They're next level, I'm telling you. They're more powerful than you think."

Julia looked Sarah in the eyes, a very direct, unsettling stare, but didn't say anything. After a few seconds she nodded.

"I think you can bring the cards inside. Lead the way," she said.

"What made you change your mind?" Sarah asked as she pulled the cooler out of its sandy surroundings.

"You did. When you described the cards, I could actually feel their power. They're in you, and all around you, and the closer you get to them the stronger it is."

"I can feel it, and it's really rather unsettling," Ange added.

"Lead the way," Alison said, her face creased with worry.

The dogs tried to get inside and Julia moved them from the door. "You puppers can stay right out of this. It's better, you'll be safer outside. Go find yourself some rabbits to chase."

The dogs seemed unconvinced and turned their big brown eyes up to their master, pleading to go inside.

"Go, go on. Go play!" Julia commanded, and the dogs turned around and loped off, even old Zac followed, but at a much slower pace.

Sarah placed the cooler on the dining table and waited until everyone was in the room before she turned it around to open it.

"Not yet," Ange said. "We just want to do another cleanse or two, okay?"

"Well I'll make a pot of tea, then. Sarah, can you bring in the cups and saucers?" Alison asked her daughter. "There's some scones left from yesterday, too."

"I think everyone's full, Mum."

"Nonsense. There's always room for scones," Alison hurried off into the kitchen and Sarah followed as Ange lit a bundle of sage and Julia climbed up onto the dining table to sit cross legged. Sarah wanted to watch them, but she felt they wanted to be alone in their rituals, and that was why her mother had asked for help.

By the time the tea was made and cups and saucers, scones, jam and cream were all on the serving tray, the girls had finished and were waiting for Sarah and Alison's return. Sarah placed the tray on the table and sat down, Alison following close behind her. Julia no longer wore the wry smile, her black eyes seemed solemn now, serious, and Ange's expression was stern.

"Can you open the cooler box now, please, Sarah?" Julia asked.

Sarah touched the handle and she felt a strange tingle on her fingertips, like a very mild electric current running through it. She folded the handle down and opened the clasp, then lifted the lid off. The atmosphere in the room changed, a subtle, but definite change.

Sarah reached into the cooler, the sage and garlic surrounding the plastic wrapped cards. She had to wriggle the frozen sage around quite a bit until she could break them up enough to lift out the wooden box. Her mother grabbed a tea towel and spread it out on the table to catch the drippings from the melting ice and Sarah placed the package on that.

"Should I unwrap it?" she asked Julia, who nodded.

The plastic wrapping was hard to navigate, it was wet, very cold, and didn't want to show any ends. "This is like a roll of sticky tape when you lost the end," muttered Sarah as she picked and pulled, finally getting off the first few layers. As she continued, she could feel the charge in the atmosphere grow, there was a staticky, electric feel to the air. The hair on the back of her neck rose and she broke out in goosebumps, but didn't get the feeling that the dark man was near. No, this feeling was all about the cards and the power they held, the power that seemed to swirl about her, lifting her hair, making her cheeks flush and her stomach contract.

The kitten growled, rather than an angry sound it was filled with fear, and for the first time the little thing climbed off Sarah's shoulders and ran off.

Sarah dropped the box onto the table and moved to follow the little brown thing, but Julia held up her hand. "Let her go, every door is shut, she can't get out. I guess it just shows that Lilly isn't evil, at least."

Sarah looked into the eyes of the indigenous woman. "But it does show the cards are, is that what you are saying?"

"No, no, not at all. I don't think they're actually evil, Sarah," Julia explained. "I think they are very powerful, and they have no, how could you describe it? Filter, they have no filter. They pick up on emotions and act on that."

Sarah frowned. "So it's me that's killing people?"

"No, Julia's not saying that, honey," Ange said. "The cards are doing that, not you. They are taking any kind of emotion you have and escalating it. So if you get irritated, the cards decide that *they* will do something bad, it's not you, not you at all."

Sarah was unconvinced, it all sounded like they were just trying to make her feel better, but if what they were saying was true then it was absolutely her fault. If she hadn't been angry or upset no one would have died. The cards read what she silently wished, like the kitten, or her hair. She didn't ever think she wished anyone dead, but she did wish they'd go away and leave her alone. Dead was a pretty final way to make sure someone would never bother her again.

She picked up the cards and unwrapped another layer, pulling the plastic free. Another layer came off, and she finally hit a dry layer where the water had not seeped all the way through. She continued unwrapping, trying to think of nothing except the task at hand. She pulled the last few layers off as one, exposing the intricately carved box underneath.

It felt warm to her touch, something that she found very puzzling after it was stored in the ice and freezer for so long. She turned it around and then offered it to Julia who held up a hand.

"I think you should just place it on the table for now, away from the plastic and stuff."

Alison put the tea towel and plastic wrap in the cooler and took it into the kitchen. She came back with another cloth and placed this on the table for Sarah to sit the box on.

"What's this cloth? Is it a tarot reading cloth thingy?" Sarah asked.

"No baby, it's one I especially made for the cards," Alison said. "The symbols on it are protective runes that Ange showed me how to write, and Julia supplied the threads to embroider the cloth with. It won't hold the power in, or even out, but it will help."

Sarah opened the box, and everyone gasped. She didn't know what they did, she didn't see anything different, but Ange jumped up from the table and backed away, one hand out in front of her. Julia looked pale, her eyes huge and frightened, and her mother's mouth formed a perfect O.

"What is it?" Sarah asked as she slammed the box closed.

"Can't you feel that?" Julia whispered. "Can't you feel the evil, the malevolence coming from the box? Ange and I are shocked, as you can see. We didn't realise how evil the cards could be."

Sarah felt tears well up in her eyes, her distress rising. "No, I can't. I can feel something, but not evil. It feels, I don't know, maybe powerful. Sort of warm, and really strange, like they belong to me, like they're mine. I don't know if that makes sense or not, but it's the best way I can explain it."

"They don't feel bad?" her mother asked. "Not even a little bit?"

"No, Mum, if they did, I would never have touched them," Sarah wiped a tear from her cheek. "Does this mean I'm evil, because I can't feel the evil in them?"

Julia got up and took Ange by a hand to lead her back to the table. "Sit down, my girl, I've got you, you'll be okay."

Ange sucked her lips in, making her mouth a thin, determined strip, but she nodded and allowed herself to be led back. Julia sat her down then turned to Sarah. "You're not evil, you hear me? Ange and I would know if you were evil, we'd feel it just like we could feel the cat wasn't evil, and the way we can feel the cards are. Don't you dare start thinking you're anything other than good and pure and wonderful, understand?"

A short laugh broke from her. "Maybe not that pure," Sarah said. "Sorry Mum."

"I didn't mean virgin, that's not even relevant. I meant pure of heart. You're pure of heart, and I know this with all my being."

Sarah sighed, but let it go. She picked up the box and opened it again, and this time she took the cards out, the purple cloth still wrapping them tight. She moved the wooden box aside and put the cards on the table. She unwrapped them, slowly, one eye on everyone's reactions, the other on the cards. The cards were face down, and Sarah left them that way, lifting them gently to take the purple cloth away so the cards were now sitting on the special fabric her mother had made.

She lifted the first card and turned it over. It showed the garden, the plants growing lush and wild, the tiny cat at the bottom. Julia stood so she could see the card better, moving beside Sarah and Ange joined her other side, almost touching her shoulder. No one spoke, though Ange pointed to the image of the little cat.

Sarah turned the next card and it showed a tall man, fair of skin and hair, his back broad and strong. He was turned away from them, facing the other direction, and the plants covered him up to the small of his back. Sarah turned the next card, and this one showed great birds, cockatoos and lyrebirds, and many others that Sarah couldn't identify. She turned more, just slowly going through them, showing everyone the animals, the jewels, the stunning artistry and portraits of the cards.

“They're actually very beautiful,” Alison said. “I’ve never seen such wonderful illustrations in a card deck before.”

“That’s why I couldn't stop looking at them, they didn't just feel right, they’re also gorgeous to look at.” Sarah turned another and pointed to the woman. “That’s the hair I admired.”

“I can see why,” Ange said. “Your hair looks just like hers, only shorter.”

“It’s still growing, though,” Sarah said. “I noticed it this morning, it’s a couple of inches longer than last week.”

She turned the next card and everyone leaned in.

Sarah closed her eyes, then opened them again. Her arms were covered with goosebumps, as if a chill had touched the air, but the day was warm and there was no breeze. She let out a breath she'd forgotten to release and shook her head. It was the dark man, and he was turned away from her, but not all the way. He had moved again, moved a little, so the barest outline of his profile could be seen. The foliage was lower, but his buttocks were still, for the most part, covered up.

"That's him," Sarah said. "That's the dark man."

"He doesn't look so bad," her mother said. "He looks strong, and very tall, but that's about it. Maybe naked, it's hard to tell."

"He's naked. For a few days he turned almost the whole way around, and I could see most of his bum. It's a nice bum, by the way."

Alison laughed and reached out to pick the card up, but Julia grabbed her hand before she could make contact.

"I think it's wise that none of us touch the cards, no one but Sarah, at least for now."

Alison withdrew her hand. "Good thinking," she agreed.

"What do you feel when you look at him," Ange asked, her voice hushed.

"All my hair stands on end, quite literally," Sarah held out her arm to show the gooseflesh. "And I have this feeling in the pit of my stomach, it's like, um, you know when you think something bad is about to happen, or you're going to get into trouble?"

Everyone nodded.

"Well, it's like that, sort of, but not as bad. It's just this really weird feeling, and I can tell when he's watching me."

"How do you know it's him watching you, honey?" Alison asked. "How do you know it's not someone else, maybe someone connected with the cards, or drawn to their power?"

Sarah frowned. "I never thought of that. No, it has to be him, the guy I see is dark, and tall, and though I've only seen him from the back his hair is the same."

"Hey, all my Somali relatives look like that from behind," Julia said. "And not just the male ones."

"Shit, you think it's not him? But I can't get my head around that. I mean, seriously, whenever I get the weird feeling it's exactly the same as I get when I look at this card. You think some outside guy is tapping into the cards or something and using the power?"

"It's a theory," Ange nodded. "I think this guy hasn't actually shown himself to you yet, so why would he be hanging around spying on you?"

Sarah chewed her bottom lip as she thought about it. She picked up the card, noticing everyone drew back as she did that, and looked at it closely. They ladies were right, there was no way to tell if the man she was seeing everywhere in her periphery was this figure on the card or not. She held the card against her chest and closed her eyes, trying to feel if he was around, if he was the same man, if he was spying on her, following her everywhere.

She couldn't tell. She had no idea if what the ladies suggested was right, or if it was just a baseless theory. She sat the card back down with the others and turned the next card over. This one looked a little darker than the other cards, it held an image of the moon, with the silver beams of moonlight reflecting a distant view of gravestones, crosses, angels, and various other stone cemetery markings.

Sarah turned the next card, and this one held the picture of a sleeping baby, a very young infant, perhaps newborn.

"Don't," her mother said.

"Don't what?"

"Don't say you want a baby someday. I don't want some mysterious pregnancy and a grandbaby that I'll forever wonder if it's cursed or something."

"Good point," Sarah said as she turned the next card.

This card showed a sky of swirling purples, bright red roses scattered on dark green grass and in the distance loomed ominously dark mountains. In the foreground was a jewelled dagger, held by a hand that connected out of frame. The dagger had a wavy blade, and it dripped blood from the tip. Sarah shuddered and turned to the next card, this one showing dingos, many of them, scattered around a rocky den. Pups were playing on the ground as the adults lounged around.

The next card was dark, a midnight sky where the half-slip of the moon barely showed through heavy clouds. A spear of lightning was hitting a tree, the sparks and flame captured so lifelike it looked like a photograph. Sarah's mum leaned forward; her face scrunched in a frown.

"That tree, does it look familiar?" Alison stood up and walked to the dining room window. "Look, there in the middle of the yard. It's the same tree, I swear, it looks just like it."

The other three women stood and joined her at the large bay window and Sarah held the card up to the glass. The tree wasn't just similar to the one in her mother's garden, it was exactly the same.

"Alison, the rose garden you have there, see how the mountains behind them look like the card Sarah held up with the dagger?" Ange pointed to the red roses in the far corner of the house yard. "Sarah, grab the card, would you?"

Sarah turned back and grabbed the card, holding it up to the window. Ange was right, it was exactly the same.

"What was the card in between those two?" Julia asked.

"It was the dingos, all laying about."

Julia tapped the glass. "Like that?"

The whippets were lounging in her mother's unfinished rock garden, Zac up the top of a large rock, two of the whippets were playing in front of the rock while the other one slept nearby. Sarah gasped. "None of the other cards looked like this place, did they?"

They returned to the table and Sarah flicked back through the cards, her fear intensifying when everyone realised that the gardens were exact pictures of her mother's gardens, all laid out the same, down to the last stone and ornament. The cards embellished the existing gardens by adding extra colour and flowers, more swirling vines and wildlife, but the gardens were the same.

"What does it mean?" Alison asked, and Sarah noticed her voice was tight with fear.

"Just keep turning the cards, Sarah."

"Are you sure? What if they're warning us or something?" Sarah looked at Julia.

"Whatever they're telling us, we've already started the process. All we can do is see what they want to tell us." Julia reached over and took Ange's hand. "We're here to look after you and your mum. We'll keep you safe."

Sarah exhaled slowly, trying to calm her nerves. She didn't want the cards to pick up on her fear, she didn't want them to interpret that fear as a threat from any of these people at the table.

She turned the next card. This one showed three unicorns, and her mother stifled a cry.

"Mum?" Sarah queried.

"They're my horses, see? That's Raj, and Al, and Indy. Just, you know, my horses don't have horns or strut about wearing flowers in their hair."

"The buildings in the background are the same, though," Ange noted as she reached over and took Alison's hand. "The house is in the distance, it's like you're looking up from the creek."

The next card showed a house, and Sarah frowned. It was her mother's house exactly, even the daisies by the front porch were the same.

"There's something weird here," Sarah whispered.

Everyone was looking at her, waiting for her to continue.

"I've looked at these cards dozens of times, like, examined them and everything. This house wasn't here before. I mean, there was a cottage, but it was different."

"What are you saying?" Julia asked.

"I'm saying the cards have changed. I didn't notice it with the darker one," Sarah flicked the cards back and started to lay them out on the table so everyone could see them. "This card here, the one with the gardens, I thought it looked a little different, and it is. I'm sure of it. The horses, um, unicorns, there were four of them before, now there are only three, and one is black, like Mum's horse. There were four white unicorns before. And the hair girl, look at her. The girl is you, Julia, look at it."

They all leaned over, trying not to touch the cards, but Julia cried out. "It's true! That's me, that's my hair, only before I had it braided. It is, isn't it, Ange?"

Ange nodded. "Yeah, I actually thought that earlier, how much it looked like you, I just didn't want to say anything."

"The dogs have changed," Alison said, her voice now hoarse with her growing alarm. "Look at the dogs."

They were no longer dingos, they were now clearly whippets. There were no playing puppies, now all four dogs were asleep. They were still in the rock garden, but now all of them were together, curled up in a bundle of long legs and snouts, basking in the sun.

"This is not something I've ever seen before," Angela said.

"No shit," Sarah's hands were shaking. "I'm full on freaking out. I don't want to turn any more cards. Fuck it. If I don't turn them, they can't change."

"I think you have to continue," Alison said. "I don't think you leaving them unturned will stop anything."

"Fuck me," Ange pointed to the card of the blonde man. "That's me, it's changed and now it's me!"

She was right, the card now showed Ange from behind, her bleached hairdo clearly seen, the coiffed flip hanging down over one eye as she stood with her back to them, her face half turned so they could see her profile. There was an intricate tattoo on her lower back, and Julia's finger hovered over it, pointing it out to the others. "Definitely her."

"The baby hasn't changed," Alison said. "I don't know what it means."

"I do," Sarah stood and pointed to the wall. "It's you, Mum. That's the picture of you as a baby Grandma sent before she died."

They all looked at the large framed picture on the wall, and saw it was true. The baby on the sheepskin rug was the same as the baby in the cards. Sarah sat down, her hands on her forehead. "I can't do this. I can't."

Julia placed a hand on her shoulder. "You can, Sarah, you can. We need to get to the bottom of this, we need to figure out what's going on." She squeezed Ange's hand. "Let's all sit back down and go through the cards. So far, they're not telling us anything other than they know where they are. Maybe it's not ominous at all."

"Yeah, and that's not blood dripping from the dagger," Sarah muttered as she picked up the next card. She exhaled hard at the sight of it, then dropped it to the table.

"Fuck this. I'm over it. Burn the lot of them, fucking burn them. I can't do this anymore," she turned and ran from the house, her breath catching in her throat in a tight sob as she ran.

The card had landed face down on the table. Julia stood and picked up the corner of the cloths and used it to flick the card over. She grabbed her face in her hands as she fell back into her seat.

Alison stumbled backwards, knocking her chair over as Ange sunk to the floor.

The card showed the three of them, Julia, Ange, and the baby, lying dead, eviscerated, on the rocks in the unfinished garden. The dogs were dismembered, their limbs scattered around the rocks, and their blood made everything red. In the background stood a tall, dark man and his face was turned away from the scene.

Chapter Twenty

"We should go get her, maybe?" Ange folded the tea towel and placed it on top of the dishes she had dried. "She's been out there for over an hour now."

"I know, I just don't want to upset her, though," Alison looked pale and drawn, the cards had thrown her, and she was still on the verge of tears. "If we upset her, who knows what will happen? Will it make the scene in the cards come true?"

"We have no control over that, no matter what we want to think," Julia was leaning on the kitchen table, the kitten in her arms. "I think we need to sit down and really go through this, figure out what to do. We need her to come back inside, or we go out there, but we need to decide on a plan."

"I'll make some tea; we can go sit in the garden under the willow tree. It's beautiful out there," Alison said. "And it wasn't on any of the cards either. It'll feel safe, it's like a giant umbrella, and the fronds reach the ground."

"Good, let's do that. Ange, grab the cookies you made, they're over there in the basket. I'll get my cards and the notebook." Julia stood up and sat the kitten on the floor. "I feel so much better knowing we are going to do something positive."

Alison retrieved a large tray from atop the fridge and placed the silver teapot on it, then grabbed the cups and saucers. She filled a little jug with milk and Ange handed over the sugar and the plate she had filled with her homemade cookies. They didn't speak while they prepared things, the tension was palpable, they all felt frightened and overwhelmed, and needed to move forward to resolve the terror of the cards as quickly as they could.

Julia carried the tray outside, Ange following her with three whippets at her heels as Alison walked in the other direction, a little kitten and the last whippet in her trail as she thought to retrieve her daughter. Sarah had perched herself on top of the old wagon near the pond, she sat on the faded leather seat with her arms wrapped around her knees, her head on those knees, looking out over the hills in the distance.

She looked like a postcard up there on the wagon. Alison had planted various climbing roses and clematis, the soft pink and mauve blooms attracting copious amounts of brightly coloured butterflies that fluttered around the wagon, some landing on Sarah's shoulders and head. Alison took a breath, taking in the scene, her daughter, and the beautiful flowers. She breathed in deeply, hoping this wasn't her last day on her beautiful farm, wasn't her last day to talk to her daughter, to try and ease her fears.

"Hey baby, you okay?" she called gently, not wanting to startle her girl. She saw Sarah scrub a hand across her nose, but she didn't answer. Alison walked up to the wagon and reached up, her hand resting on Sarah's ankle.

"Sweetie, I've made some tea, and Ange has brought over her triple choc fudge cookies. They're better than crack, let me tell you. We're under the willow, come and sit with us, please?"

Sarah lifted her head and looked down at her mother. Her eyes were red and swollen, and her face was stained with tears. "I'm so sorry, Mum, I didn't mean to bring you this mess."

"Oh, honey, it's not your fault! You didn't plan on being cursed! You didn't do anything to deserve this, or trigger it, and you didn't bring anything to me that I didn't ask you to bring. Come down, my baby, and let's get this sorted. We can finish this, once and for all, and then we'll all be a lot happier."

Sarah nodded and held out her arm for her mother to grab as she leapt down from the wagon lightly. The kitten immediately climbed up on her shoulder and tucked itself under her hair. "Okay, then. But only for the cookies."

"They really are brilliant."

"How do you know if they're better than crack? What do you know about crack?"

Alison looped her arm through her daughter's and gave it a squeeze. "My lips are sealed, girl."

Sarah's phone beeped and she slipped it out of her pocket to look at it, then popped it back.

"Work?" Alison asked.

"No, actually. It's that guy from my building, the one that shifted across from me."

"Ooh, the handsome one?"

"Yeah, he's pretty cool. We've been messaging every day since he's been away in Sydney."

"You like him?"

"I think I do." Sarah held out an arm to sweep

the long trailing fronds from the willow, allowing them both to enter the tent of the large tree.

"This is super awesome!" Julia smiled brightly at them. "The whole tree is like a giant marquee, it's super quiet, and really pretty in here. I love it!"

"Yeah, me too," Alison pulled out a chair for Sarah to sit at the wrought iron setting. "Sarah brought home the willow branch from a school picnic and planted it here. It grew like an absolute weed, and I planted all the pansies and hellebores underneath it. It's just dreamy here. I have to keep the horses away from it as they love a good munch on willow leaves."

"Mum says these cookies are better than crack," Sarah took one from the plate Ange offered her.

"Well, she should know," Ange winked at Alison and Sarah laughed.

"My mother was quite wild when she was young!"

"That was a long time ago. Don't do drugs, drugs are bad," Alison scolded, but her eyes twinkled. She bit into a cookie and closed those eyes with delight. "I do love these cookies!"

"I'll pour the tea, but we need to talk about the cards. We need to work out a viable plan, and then get to action," Julia lifted the tea pot. "We didn't even get to tell you what we'd researched and found."

Sarah nodded; her smile gone. Alison took her hand and squeezed it reassuringly. "It'll be okay," she told her.

Sarah looked at her mother, and her expression

was so bleak it hurt Alison's soul. "You can't know that," she whispered as she turned back to Julia.

"We think the cards were made for someone as either a gift or a curse, and even though we can see images of Australiana on them, we don't think they're necessarily Australian," Julia explained.

"I'm actually sure of it," Ange added. "I took some pictures and sent them to my great Aunt, she lives in England. She said they are definitely an ancient design, and even though they look new they are most likely centuries old. She said they would have come here alone, without a person, because once they are anchored to a person, they can't leave that place. Like, it traps them in one country. I didn't ask her to explain that part, it's very early in the morning there and she was still in bed."

"Does she know who or where they would have come from?"

"Well, your brother called your mum while you were outside. The lady that had the stall where you got the cards emailed him. She said the boxes were sent to them by their grandmother who passed away, she lived in Latvia." Julia flipped over a page in her notebook. "They went to her sister as the stall lady was travelling at the time. She had no idea what was in the boxes, she just wanted to get rid of everything that belonged to her sister."

"Get rid of it? Did she say why?" Sarah asked.

"They didn't get along. It seems her sister passed away leaving a huge mess to clean up and a very large debt. She wasn't happy at all about her sister and her lifestyle, apparently."

"Helpful much?" Sarah shrugged.

"Actually, knowing they came from Latvia could help, I've let my great aunt, Mathilda, know." Ange took Julia's notebook. "She'll get back to me when she has more information, but she's basically told me what we know already. The cards are very powerful, and they're very cursed. Or under a spell, she used a Romani word that means both. Anyway, she said we need to bind them, she gave me a spell and the instructions, and we need to bury them in a sacred, hallowed site."

"What, like a churchyard?" Sarah asked.

"Maybe. Julia thinks they'd be better in the sacred grounds of her forefathers. There's some extremely sacred ground not too far from here, and there'll be people there that can help bind them and place protection in the hole with them."

"Why can't we just burn them?" Sarah asked hopefully.

"I think you had the idea that it might release the curse, or spirits, or whatever they are?" Julia asked and Sarah nodded. "Mathilda thinks the same thing, that the spirits are bound to the cards and if you burn them, you'll set them free. While that could see them disappear, it could also see them attack you and there would be no way to stop them, so she said not to try that. She also thinks what we saw earlier with the blood and dismemberment was a warning to us. The cards are worried that we are going to destroy them, or bind them, or whatever. Either way they're worried."

"Them being worried makes me breathe a little

easier," Alison nodded. "It means we might be onto the right track here."

"So why are we sitting around? Why aren't we binding the cards right now?" Sarah asked as she leaned forward.

"We're just waiting for my Uncle Wally to come. He'll lead us to the sacred place," Julia said.

"Okay then. I'll go pack those fucking things up and be ready." Sarah made to stand up, but Alison stopped her.

"We want Uncle Wally to look at them before we pack them up," Alison said. "And, well, we just don't want you to be around the cards too much anymore. Just keep away from them for now, and we can pack them up when he gets here."

"Okay, sure," Sarah rested back in the chair. "I'll have another one of those cookies, please."

"Knock yourself out," Ange lifted the plate but stopped as a crack of lighting gave them all a start.

"Lightning? There's not a cloud in the sky!" Alison explained and stood up. "I can smell the ozone, but where did that come from?"

They all walked to the edge of the willow as the thunder growled and cracked the air. The dogs started to howl, huddling close to their owners as they shook and cried with fear.

Julia held the thick curtain of willow leaves to one side and gasped. There was the blackest, heaviest storm front rolling in, it was arced with lighting and the thunder shook the ground. Wind swept up from nowhere and seemed to blow in every direction. Dust, leaves and twigs whipped around, and the willow groaned and swayed with the force of the onslaught.

"We need to get into the house," Alison yelled over the din. "I'll grab the tray; everyone make a run for it!"

Julia kept her hand on the fronds, allowing Alison to pass through with the tray before she hurried after her. As soon as everyone had cleared the safety of the willow the rain fell, it stung and bit in icy fury, coming at them from every direction, borne on the spiteful winds.

The ground quickly became a slippery mess and Sarah grabbed her mother's elbow to help steady her, the tray slopping and swaying, the dishes almost dropping as the four hurried across the yard.

The dogs had not followed, they all stayed in the relative safety of the willow, but as the winds pushed their way into the green sanctuary the four whippets made a break for the house, one crashing into Ange and bringing her to her knees on the wet gravel. Julia hauled her up as they ran, finally making the veranda as huge hailstones the size of chicken eggs hit the ground.

The sound of the hail hitting the tin roof of Alison's house was a cacophony of ear assaulting noise and they all hurried inside. The doors and windows were slamming open and shut throughout the house and Alison shouted for everyone to close the windows. They all ran to different rooms; the wind and rain was finding entry at every possible window.

Ange ran into the bathroom and pulled the sash

window closed, hooking the lock on top as the bathroom door slammed shut. She frowned and turned; the door had slammed after the window was closed so there should have been no wind to slam it so forcefully. She reached for the handle, oblivious to the dark skinned, tall figure that was reflected in the mirror.

Julia ran into Alison's bedroom and pulled the windows closed. Alison's room was on the front of the house and her large bedroom had four huge windows, each one protesting and resisting the tugging to close and lock them. As she finished the last window, the door slammed, a sound that cracked through the room like a rifle shot and made Julia cry out in surprise. She didn't think of how the door slammed shut after the window closed, she just walked to the door to open it, a reflection in the mirror catching the corner of her eye, and she turned.

Alison closed the kitchen window and turned to Sarah. "I'll do your bedroom and the laundry, can you close the windows in the dining room, please?" She had to yell over the noise of the wind and the hailstones on the roof, and Sarah nodded her reply, knowing her mother wouldn't be able to hear her if she spoke. Sarah hurried off and Alison ran down the hall, noticing that only Zac followed her mother, his worried face and hunched back an almost comical caricature of fear. Alison glanced into the laundry and noticed the window had not been opened, so she just closed the door then made her way into Sarah's room with Zac close behind her.

She shut the window and closed the hook as Zac started to back up, he was howling and screeching, his barks full of fear, and Alison looked at him and frowned. He wasn't looking at the window and barking as he often did in a storm. He'd never been scared of storms as a younger dog, but now, in his very advanced years, the storms brought on extreme anxiety and he would often stand in the main room, barking at the window as if he could scare the thunder away.

This time he was staring at the dressing table mirror, the whites of his eyes showing, his hackles raised and saliva flicking off his yellowed fangs as he barked and growled, all the time backing up and away from the mirror. Alison grabbed his collar to lead him out of the room when the door slammed so forcefully the porcelain doorknob split and shattered, half of it dropping to the floor and splintering into a thousand pieces. Alison looked at her dog, then looked at what he was barking at. She looked at the mirror and screamed.

Sarah could hear nothing except the thunder and rain, the hailstones clattering and slamming against the roof. It was so loud it sounded like rockets were being launched at the corrugated iron and she hurried to close the window, the curtains flailing in the wind like the sails of a ship, the rain coating the floor in front of the window. She slammed the windows shut and hooked the closures, grabbing the tea towel from the dining table to wipe some of the rain from the floor.

The hail stopped but the rain continued, a heavy,

out of season rain that was already flooding the yard and creating large puddles of yellow sand and clay.

She looked over at the other window though couldn’t see much, the heavy rain screening out all but the house yard, the rest of the property a wall of grey-white water. She flicked her hair, which was pretty soaked on the top, and felt the kitten shift a little to keep its position. She should probably put the hair dryer on it for a few minutes before Uncle Wally turned up. She pulled at her wet clothing. Maybe a dry top so she didn't look like some cheap pub wet t-shirt competition entrant wouldn’t be a bad idea either, she thought.

A howl from one of the dogs brought her attention back into the kitchen and she saw three of the dogs huddled together, Julia and Ange's dogs, and they were terrified. They howled and writhed and clung to each other as if in agony, Sarah had never seen animals so distressed. She tried to reach out to them, but they were snapping and yowling, she didn't want them to lash out in their fear and hurt her.

It was then she realised she was alone, the others were taking a very long time to close a few windows, and she felt the first iron band of fear tighten in her gut. She knew calling out to anyone in this storm would be useless, the sound of the rain and constant thunder rendered her ears and voice useless. She turned on the light in the hallway, the black clouds had turned day into night, and she made her way to the bathroom, the first room on her left.

She tried the knob, but the door was locked. She banged on the door, banged hard and shouted, but there was no reply. She couldn't remember who was going to close the bathroom window, and as she couldn't gain entry she turned and went to the laundry. The door wasn't locked, and the window was closed, so she turned back into the hall and checked the spare room. The door was unlocked but the room was dark and unused, so she closed the door and walked to her mother's room.

That door was locked, though she couldn't remember if there was even a lock on the door. She tried the knob again and pushed hard with her shoulder, trying to open the door, but it wouldn't budge. Sarah banged her fist on the door and called out, her voice lost in a massive crack of thunder, so she left the room and ran to her own bedroom, where her mother had said she was going.

This door was also locked, and it was dark inside, no light shone under the crack at the bottom of the door. She banged her hand against the door and called for her mum but couldn't hear a reply. The storm continued to rage and the lights flickered, Sarah was worried she would be plunged into darkness, all alone in this house, everyone else gone, and she banged on the door again as her panic rose.

She could hear something, very faintly, but there was something. She placed her ear to the door and thought she could hear barking, that she could hear Zac howling like the world was ending around him. She banged on the door again and scrambled out

"*MUM! MUM! Mum, can you hear me*?"

There was no answer except for the barely heard barking, so Sarah ran back into the kitchen. Beside the door were a set of key hooks. Her mother kept a spare set of keys to every lock in the entire property, so she looked through the bunches until she found one labelled *house*, then combed through that until she found *Sarah's room.* Clutching the bunch of keys, with the one for her room pointing straight out ahead of her, she raced back to her bedroom and tried to unlock the door. Adrenaline and fear had taken over her fine motor skills and she scrabbled the key several times, her hands shaking so badly she couldn't find the keyhole. Using her other hand to steady her shakes, she finally got the key in the lock and turned it. The door still did not want to budge so she put her shoulder against it and shoved it with all her might.

The door gave suddenly and she fell into the room.

She landed in a heap and spun on her arse before leaping to her feet. Zac was cowering against the wardrobe; he had peed all over the floor in fear and was scrambling on the wet floorboards. Arms grabbed her and Sarah screamed, but the hands on her face were warm and gentle. Turning her to see it was her mother that clutched her, Sarah clung to her and sobbed.

"Oh my god, I was so scared! Why did you lock yourself in?"

Alison shook her head. "I didn't, honey. It wasn't me. Quick, let's get out of here, hurry!"

Alison grabbed Zac's collar with one hand and her daughter with the other and pulled them from the room as the door slammed shut again.

Alison was yelling something that Sarah couldn't hear, so she leaned up close to her mother's mouth.

"Where are the girls?" her mother yelled.

Sarah shook her head and handed her mother the keys, then pulled her by the arm to her own room. She tried the doorknob again, but the door wouldn't open, so she stood back and pointed to the lock. Alison got the idea straight away and flicked through to find the right key, sliding it into the lock.

She was instantly thrown back, hitting the wall behind her as if she was hit by a bolt of lightning. Sarah grabbed her mother, checking for anything broken, any injuries, but Alison pushed her away. "I'm all right," she yelled, and Sarah helped her to her feet. The storm was too loud to allow her to explain what happened, so she just pointed to the door.

Sarah reached out to touch the key as the storm stopped suddenly like a switch had been flicked, and the silence was overwhelming after so much sound.

"What the fuck?" Alison breathed. "What the fuck is going on?"

Sarah shook her head; she had no answers.

"Should I try the door?"

"It was like electricity hit me when I tried it, it didn't really hurt, but it sure threw me around," Alison stepped closer to the door. "I'm ready to catch you if it does the same to you."

Sarah's heart was pounding so hard she thought it would break from her chest. Gingerly, she reached for the key, fully expecting to be thrown across the hallway, but the key was fine. It was just a key, and Sarah turned it in the lock and opened the door.

Julia sat in the corner of the room, her hands over her head, her knees drawn up close and her eyes closed. Sarah leaned down and touched her on her hand and Julia screamed, making Sarah fall back with surprise.

"Julia, it's us, it's Alison and Sarah," Alison grabbed Julia's hands. "Open your eyes, you're safe, it's just us."

Julia opened her eyes and burst into tears. "Oh my god I thought you were him, I thought you were him and you were going to kill me," she sobbed. "He was here, he was here in the room!"

Sarah and Alison helped the woman to her feet.

"Who was here, Julia?" Sarah asked.

"The man, the dark man. He was here. Well, no, he wasn't really here, he was in the mirror, I saw him."

"What do you mean, he was in the mirror?" Sarah asked.

"I could only see him in the mirror, just for a second. He was right there, in the room with me, I mean, he was in the reflection."

Sarah grabbed her arm. "We need to find Ange, let's get out of this room, hurry."

"Ange is missing?" Julia stumbled along with Sarah, desperate to try and keep up.

"The bathroom, have you checked the bathroom?" Alison suggested.

Sarah frantically searched through the keys until he found the right one, her hands no longer shaking. She stabbed the key into the lock and turned it, the door creaking open ever so slowly. Julia pushed through, her face pale and worried. "Ange? Ange, are you in here?"

The blonde woman lifted her head to see over the edge of the bathtub where she'd been hiding, the towels piled over her. Julia grabbed her and hugged her, and both women were sobbing.

"We should get into a room where we can't be locked in, maybe the sitting room, or dining room?" Sarah suggested.

"Yes, good, let's go," Alison pulled at the back of Julia's jeans. "Hurry, we don't want to get stuck in here. There's plenty of candles there if the power goes out, too."

The dining room was dark, the clouds had not parted to let the sun through, and as the women entered the winds came back, buffeting and assaulting the house. Along with the wind the torrential rain returned, and it hit the roof with a frightening force. The terrified dogs came running and jumped up onto the sofa, huddling together in a panicked bundle.

Alison opened a drawer on the buffet and pulled out several extra candles and a couple of boxes of matches. She lit all the candles in the room, then walked into the sitting room to do the same.

Sarah flicked on the light switch and the room

was flooded with bright illumination, making their fears seem distant in the reflected glow of electricity. It seemed unreal to be fearful in a room full of overstuffed cushions and brightly coloured wall hangings, and the women stood awkwardly, looking around themselves as if trying to reconcile what they had just experienced.

"What the fuck is happening?" Ange's voice was filled with fear and uncertainty. "What the actual fuck? I saw that dark man from the cards, he was in the mirror, in the fucking mirror!"

Julia hugged her close. "I saw him too; he was in Alison's dressing table mirror."

"Me too," Alison yelled above the storm. "And Zac saw him, too, he was absolutely terrified."

"I didn't see him," Sarah said. "I could feel him, though. He's somewhere around, but I don't know where. I'm scared, really scared."

"He could have hurt us when we were all alone, he could have killed us," Alison soothed. "He didn't, though. He just closed the doors, but he didn't hurt us."

"What, you think he's good? You think he was protecting us or something?" Sarah asked.

"No, no I don't. I felt so scared, and Zac went crazy. Zac doesn't do that unless there's something very, very wrong." Alison reached down and patted the frightened dog that was pushed against her leg. "I think he's *not* good, not even a little bit."

Thunder pounded and shook the house, sounding like bombs detonating. Sarah walked over to the dining room window. "Look at that lightning, it's insane!"

The others joined her and watched as multiple bolts of lightning hit the ground, sending water sparking and arcing up into the air.

"My horses!" Alison cried. "They're out in this, oh my god, I can't see them, I hope they're okay."

"You can't go out in that and check, Mum," Sarah pointed out the window. "You could be hit by lightning without walking five steps from the house."

A loud clap of thunder made them all jump, and a spear of white-blue lightning hit the tree outside the window, just as the cards had shown. Julia screamed and Angela cried out, holding onto the darker woman she pulled her back from the window. Alison stumbled away from the window, but Sarah just stood there, mesmerized by the sight of the tree burning. Even though the rain was falling so heavily that it was hard to see the shape of the tree, she could still see the red and orange flames.

"Sarah, come back from the window," her mother called.

"It's still burning," Sarah replied.

"What? I can't hear you," Alison yelled as she tugged at Sarah's top to pull her back.

"The tree, it's still burning. The rain is heavier than I've ever seen it before, but the tree is still burning!"

"I'm not even going to think about how weird that is," Alison pulled Sarah away from the window. "Too many weird things are happening now."

Another loud crack of thunder sounded, and the lights went out, plunging them into relative darkness, just for a second, as their eyes adjusted to the candlelight. The small flames flickered and moved, lending strange, moving shadows across the pale cream walls.

Sarah's kitten hissed, making her jump; she had forgotten the little thing was on her shoulder. She felt it stand up and hiss again, a growl issuing from its tiny throat.

"There's something there," Sarah said as she backed up, her hands reaching behind her to find her mother's grasp.

"Where?" Alison asked.

"There, where the shadows move," Sarah pushed back. "I can feel it, and the kitten is going nuts on my shoulder."

"I can't see anything," Alison said.

"What do you think you see?" Julia asked.

"The shadows are moving," Sarah said.

"Yeah, the candles are fluttering making the shadows move in a weird way, it's not anything supernatural," Ange explained.

"I know that," Sarah stepped back another couple of feet. She felt her stomach grow cold at the sight of the shadow on the wall. "Just watch the wall, watch it and see what I mean."

The rain continued to batter the roof as the wind howled, but the four women were silent, watching the wall Sarah pointed to. Zac started to bark at the wall, and the other three whippets joined in, howling and barking in fear and alarm.

"I see it," Ange yelled. "I see it, it's him!"

She pointed at the wall, her hand shaking.

They could all see it now, the waving, flickering outline of shadow. It was clearly a shadow of a man, a tall man, and it moved as if it were pacing the floor. It flickered and waved, the candlelight making the shadow dance grotesquely across the wall. The shadow seemed to emanate from around the corner in the sitting room, though no one wanted to turn the corner to see if anyone was there.

"It's not coming any closer, is it?" Alison asked, but she spoke too quietly for the others to hear above the storm. She repeated herself at a yell, and Sarah shook her head.

"Not yet, though the way the dogs are going mental, I'm not feeling safe."

"There's nowhere for us to go," Alison gripped Sarah's arm tightly. "We can't go out in the storm and we can't stay here."

"Can you grab the cards?" Julia spoke into Sarah's ear. "Bundle them up in the box, see if that helps?"

Sarah looked over at the dining table. She could easily grab the cards, though it did put her closer to the moving shadows. She didn't know if she'd be any safer than where she was, so she ran over and gathered them up before wrapping them in her mother's cloth, then the purple silk, before placing them into the wooden box, then slipped the whole thing into the lead lined box Rod had delivered earlier.

Alison ran over and grabbed the cooler and

offered it to Sarah, but she shook her head. “It doesn't make any difference,” Sarah yelled as she snapped the latch on the box closed.

The instant the latch clicked into place the rain abated and the wind swirled away from the house and died down.

“The shadows, they’ve stopped moving!” Julia exclaimed and she stepped to Sarah’s side. “The candles have stopped flickering; the shadows are just normal now.”

The power came back on, allowing the room to be flooded with light, and the dogs stopped barking. Sarah could hear the growl of the kitten in her ears but thought maybe the little thing was just a bit freaked out with the storm and the women’s heightened emotions.

Zac was still stuck to Alison’s side, and he, too, growled, just softly, his hackles raised as he continued to stare towards the sitting room.

“Is everyone okay in here?” a loud male voice spoke, and Alison screamed in alarm.

“Sorry, sorry, I didn't mean to frighten you. It's just me, Uncle Wally, Julia’s uncle.”

“Oh, Uncle Wally, oh my god, we didn't hear you come in,” Julia ran to the man and hugged him. “We didn't see your headlights in the storm.”

“There’s no storm, girls, it’s a bright sunny day. Well, it's bright everywhere but here. You have some strange dark clouds over the farmhouse.”

Alison frowned. “There’s no storm anywhere else?”

“Nah, all good everywhere, but I see it’s very

wet here. Did that cloud above you rain just on your house?"

The women looked at each other in surprise. "It didn't rain anywhere else? No storms, no lightning or thunder?" Alison asked.

"Lordy no, it's a beautiful day. Not a cloud in the sky! Well, there is now, but just here. I thought it was funny driving up because even your paddocks are clear, it's just around the house that's all stormy and wet." Uncle Wally looked at his cap and then looked up and smiled. "Who's the guy in the other room?"

Sarah felt her legs turn to jelly. "What did you say?"

"The man in the other room, why don't you introduce me?"

Sarah ran into the dining room, turning around to take in the whole room. "There's no one here," she cried. "There's no one here except me!"

Wally stepped forward and pointed to the corner of the room. "There was someone there when I walked in. I swear to you girls, there was someone there."

"We saw a shadow just before you came in, but it was strange because there was no light behind where he would be to leave a shadow," Alison stood in the archway between the two rooms. "How did you know there was someone there? There was no shadow."

"I felt them, felt their presence. They were very powerful."

"Were?" Sarah turned to face the man. "What do

you mean, *were*?"

"Well, clearly he is not here anymore," Wally smiled, his straight teeth a brilliant white against his dark skin. "This blackfella doesn't miss much, but I did miss where he went. There's something here, isn't there? More than his power, more than that. There's a reason there was a storm over your house, and I'm guessing it wasn't a good reason."

"I told you about the cards, Uncle," Julia said.

"Yes, you did, but the power here is stronger than a card could hold. It's the strongest I've felt in a very long time. There's something going on here, something that makes me feel very alarmed."

Sarah held out the box to Julia's uncle and he held a hand over it. Closing his eyes, he hummed a strange tuneless sound before withdrawing his hand.

"Where did you get these from?" Wally opened his eyes and looked at Sarah.

"They were in a box of stuff I got from the market."

"The last owner died, is that right?"

Sarah felt tears welling up in her eyes and she bit the inside of her cheek to stop crying. She nodded. "You can feel that?"

"I can. These cards hold a very powerful curse. We need to end its hold on you, or we will lose you as well. I feel they will take everyone you love and then take you."

"How can you know that, Uncle Wally?" Julia asked. "You haven't even seen the cards; you've only held your hand on them."

"The power is so strong that I don't need to see

them. They showed me already what they can do when I held my hand over them. They are dangerous, and we need to go now, straight away, and unbind them from your little friend before we bury them. We can't waste any time. We need to leave now."

"Okay, sure. We can take our car," Ange said. "It will fit everyone."

"We should take two cars, even three," Wally suggested. "These cards will try to stop us, so if we break down in one car they win. I'll take my car; you girls should go in the other four-wheel drive."

"That's my car," Alison said. "Let's go. I'm terrified for all of our safety; I just want this over with."

"Amen," Julia whispered as she followed everyone out to the cars.

Chapter Twenty-One

"He seems like a bit of a character," Alison glanced in her side mirror as she changed lanes to keep up with Wally's car. "Is he like an elder or something?"

Julia laughed and leaned forward in the back seat. "No, he's not. He's a bit of an outcast, truth be told. He married a Somali girl he met at Uni, and my mum married his wife's brother, that's how he's my uncle. An uncle by marriage."

"He's an amazing man," Ange added. "He's actually a doctor, he works in the local Aboriginal Health Clinic as well as volunteering at the Young People Skills workshop. He also drives the bus for the aged care unit on most weekends and works with drug affected youth."

"Wow, that's amazing!" Sarah turned as much as she could in the seat so she could see the women in the back of the four-wheel drive vehicle. "He just looks like your average guy you see at the pub on the weekends."

"That's what he wants to look like, it makes people, especially the local Aboriginal people, feel comfortable around him. He used to wear a suit, but it put the youths off," Jules smiled at Sarah. "It's also why he gets everyone to call him Uncle Wally. He's Dr Walter Milestone, and he has a couple of degrees and specialties. After his wife died all he did was work. He really doesn't do much else."

"She died, that's so sad! What happened?" Sarah asked, but Julia just held up a hand. Sarah nodded and turned back to face the front. If Julia wasn't willing to speak about the death of her Aunty, she wasn't going to push her. "How come he's so psychic?"

"He was always like that, apparently. He could talk to dead people when he was young, it used to freak out his family. He's fantastic at a party, he can guess what's in your pocket, or your handbag. Never gets it wrong. He also won the lottery about four times, he doesn't play anymore, though. And don't get him started about horse racing, he's super freaky, he never ever gets it wrong. He's not into gambling anymore, though."

"He won lotto four times? He must be a millionaire!" Alison gasped.

"He would be if he didn't donate almost all of it to the community, guy's too good to be true, I swear," Ange said. "He paid for our wedding, which was so lovely, and he sent us to Tahiti for our honeymoon. Such a great guy."

"I'm lucky he's helping me today," Sarah said. "Sounds like he is super busy."

"He loves helping people, Sarah. I didn't tell you this, but he rang me and said you'd be coming," Julia told her. "I didn't want to freak you out, but he said it wasn't good. He said you were coming, and you were in great danger."

"Are all of you in danger?" Sarah asked as she felt the cold fear creeping up from her belly. "Have I put you all in danger?"

"Sarah, when Uncle Wally rang me, he said we were already in danger, and we were to do everything we could to help you. It was inevitable, and we couldn't avoid it."

"Are we going to be able to stop the cards? I don't want anyone getting hurt," Sarah was breathing rapidly now, she could feel panic rising. "I'd kill myself before that happens."

"Don't say that!" Alison growled. "Don't ever say that! Promise me you won't even think about killing yourself, not ever!"

Sarah felt the hot tears she'd tried to hold back tumble down her face. "This is so fucked up."

"Where are we going?" Ange asked. "We've been driving for over an hour, I thought we were going to the back of the community to the Burnt Tree grounds."

"I don't know where we're going," Julia sounded concerned. "I'm thinking that Uncle Wally thought we perhaps needed somewhere stronger than the local sacred ground."

"I wonder where he's taking us," Alison said. "If it's too far I'm going to have to stop to get gas, and I'd rather get it somewhere before we head away from civilization."

"How can we tell him?" Sarah asked.

"You won't have to, trust me," Julia said. "He'll know, and he'll pull into a petrol station before you run out of LPG."

"Okay…" Sarah felt very doubtful. "I guess we'll see if he really does know what's going on."

Within minutes Uncle Wally turned off the

highway into a small town, then pulled into a petrol station. Julia laughed as the two women in the front expressed their surprise.

"What did I tell you?"

"I'm shutting up now," Sarah said. "I am convinced one hundred percent."

Uncle Wally filled up Alison's car for her, refusing to let her do it, then he paid for the gas. He came back from paying with a handful of soft drinks and bags of potato chips, and Sarah realised she was actually thirsty. She didn't know how Wally could know that, but apparently he did.

They were back on the road before too long, Sarah had the box of cards on the floor between her feet as she munched on her salt and vinegar chips.

"Did Uncle Wally get your flavours right?" Ange asked.

"Chicken for me, salt and vinegar for Sezzy, I'd say so," Alison said. "He even got me diet coke! He is beyond amazing."

"He never gets it wrong. When Julia's sister was pregnant, he would turn up with exactly what she was craving, without her even telling him. And if you think you really want to eat something, he'll bring it!" Ange sipped her drink. "He's amazing if you're in a restaurant, he can order for everyone and never get it wrong. I mean, not ever. Seriously."

"I'm feeling so much better, it's like he knew what we needed to cheer us up," Sarah put a chip into her mouth. "Turns out it was carbs. Man's a genius."

The women ate their snacks and listened to the

radio, but no one spoke much. Sarah was feeling that no one wanted to bring up anything that was even going to hint at turning the conversation towards the cards, and she was fine with that. She tried not to think about them, but the box was right there between her feet, bumping into them every time they turned a corner or hit a pothole.

Her phone buzzed and she grabbed it from her pocket, unable to help smiling when she saw a picture of Michael leaning against her door, a sad smile on his face. He had captioned the selfie *missing you*, and she realised she missed him, too.

"Is that the man across the hall?" Alison asked.

"Yeah. Oh my god, he's too sweet. He just sent me a picture of him at my door looking sad."

"Show me!" Ange demanded, so Sarah lifted the phone for the women in the back to see.

"Shit, Sarah, if I wasn't gay, I'd fight you for him," Julia teased. "He looks like a movie star!"

"I know, right?" Sarah looked at the picture. "I think maybe he's too pretty for me."

"Have you even looked in the mirror?" Ange asked. "If you were gay my poor wife would have a problem, because I'd go you."

Sarah laughed and Julia punched Ange in the arm.

"Seriously, he's a fine specimen of a human, but I worry he's too good looking. Women must be throwing themselves at him wherever he goes."

"You could always show his picture to Uncle Wally. He'll tell you if he's a good guy or not," Julia offered.

"He can do that? Like, he's not just limited to chips?"

Julia laughed. "I bet he already knows if this is a good guy or not. Once we get our other little problem cleared up, I wouldn't be surprised if he brings it up without you asking."

"That'd be nice," Sarah said. "It would be nice to be able to go on with my life in a normal way, not worrying that anything will happen to anyone if I don't like what they say or do."

Sarah flinched as the kitten stretched, the tiny claws digging into her shoulder.

"Are you okay?" Alison asked. "What was that, what you did there?"

"It's Lilly, Mum. I forgot she was on my shoulder."

"She's going to hate it when you go back to work and have to leave her at home," Ange said.

"I'm worried I'll forget she's on my shoulder and I turn up to work with her behind my hair." Sarah reached up and patted the kitten. "Though she's so good I don't think anyone will mind. Hey, do you think she'll disappear once the bond of the cards is broken? Or my hair, will it, I don't know, fall out, or something?"

"Who can tell?" Julia said. "My thoughts are *no*, but I'm not Uncle Wally. I've got nowhere near his talent, I only get hints and feelings, I can't tell what's going to happen. Well, not always."

"It doesn't matter, really," Sarah sighed. "I just want this all done with. I want it over, and that's it. Done."

“Hopefully this is it, and it will be over today,” Alison patted her daughter’s knee. “We can all go home and have a big meal and try to laugh about things.”

“I’m pretty sure there won't be much laughing.” Sarah looked out of the window as they drove. She didn't recognize any of the landscape, they had driven to somewhere she was completely unfamiliar with.

There were massive sandstone boulders out of her window, all balanced and piled up like some giant god had placed them there. They were a marvellous sight to see, and Sarah looked at them in awe. She would have loved to find a place like this when she was young, she could imagine the games she would have played amongst the massive boulders.

She smiled absentmindedly when she saw a herd of goats frolicking over and around the sandstones. They were about the only creature that could make use of that paddock, she supposed. Lilly mewed in her ear and she wondered if the kitten wanted to go to the toilet, but she just curled up and went back to sleep.

“We’ve been driving for nearly four hours,” Julia said. “I wonder how far he’s taking us.”

“We’ll never get back before dark,” Alison commented. “I have no idea where we are anymore.”

Julia’s phone rang. “It’s Uncle Wally,” she said as she answered it. “You’re on speaker, Uncle.”

“*Good, okay. I know you’re all wondering where*

we are going, aren't you?"

"That's right, we've been driving for ages," Julia answered.

"*I'm sorry, I didn't initially plan on going this far. It's just that I keep getting the feeling we need to move on, every sacred place I draw close to tells me it's not right, and we should keep going.*"

"Do you know where we're going?" Julia asked.

"*No, I don't, not really. I just know we're going in the right direction, and we need to keep going until we get there. We aren't close, I feel we won't get there for at least a day. Sorry about that.*"

"A day?" Alison was shocked. "We didn't bring a change of clothes or anything!"

"*I know, and I am truly sorry. But we need to keep going or this will never end. This curse will follow you until you are all dead. When I find somewhere we can stop for the night I'll pull over. Sorry girls, I really am.*"

"Don't apologise, Uncle. You are looking after us, you're doing the right thing for us. Thank you."

"*Catch,*" Uncle Wally hung up.

"Wow, this is going to be a marathon, by the sounds of it," Sarah twisted to see the women in the back. "I'm so sorry, everyone. I brought this trouble to you."

"That's the last I want to hear of that girly," Julia growled. "Uncle Wally said this was ours to fight, and that's all there is to it. We chose to be here."

"Amen," Ange added.

"I agree, Sezzy. We wouldn't be here if we didn't want to. God only knows how many people those cards hurt before they came to you. They need to be stopped, and stopped now," Alison took a breath and blew it out as a sigh. "I just wish it hadn't been you that got them."

"Me too, Mum. Me too."

They drove in silence for a while, always heading towards the setting sun. The day was nearly over, the shadows grew long, and the sky became a vivid display of reds and purples. Alison yawned, hiding the action behind one hand, but Sarah noticed. She didn't say anything, didn't offer to drive, but only because she wanted to see if Uncle Wally picked up on her thoughts. Not ten minutes went past before Uncle Wally's indicators showed he was pulling over. Alison followed suit, stopping at a large truck stop on the highway.

Sarah climbed out of the car, her legs stiff from sitting for so long, and she heard her mother groan a little as she unfolded herself from the car. It was harder on Alison, she was a very tall woman, just over six feet in height, and her legs needed to stretch after sitting behind the wheel for so long. Wally walked over to the car and smiled at the ladies. "I know you need a break," he said. "I also know the kitten needs to go pee pee."

Lilly mewed. "Where do I let her go? I'm frightened she may run off," Sarah looked around, but the kitten took the decision out of her hands, rushing down off her master and running into the small, pebbled garden bed by the roadside and squatting.

"What a good little thing," Alison smiled. "She's

such a sweetheart."

"She was born of magic, that little thing," Wally said. "But she's not connected to it anymore. Not that I can tell, anyway."

"I hope she's not, I really like her," Sarah watched the kitten try to cover her waste, before she ran back up onto Sarah's shoulder. "I think she likes me, too."

"I'm sure of it," Alison said. "You've always had a way with animals, but this connection is much stronger than that."

"I think we should all get something to eat and stretch our legs a little. This place should be cool to pick up some essentials, you know, toothpaste and toothbrushes, maybe some underwear," Uncle Wally scratched his stubbled cheek. "I don't think there'd be much else, no PJs or that kinda stuff."

"We should get the food to take away," Sarah said. "It's not safe here."

Everyone turned to look at her, and she knew they could see the worry on her face, she had probably turned white, or as white as her olive skin would allow. "We need to hurry."

"Is he here, Sezzy?" Alison asked.

"Something is here. Something not good," Uncle Wally spoke quietly.

"He's here. I can feel him."

"Do you want to wait here, and I'll grab some stuff?" Alison asked.

"You and I can go," Ange said. "The rest of you wait here. We'll be quick. Any requests?"

"See if there's something for Lilly to eat, if you

can. If they don't have cat food, then maybe a piece of chicken I can pull off the bone?"

"Will do. We'll get some water for her, too." Alison kissed Sarah on the forehead. "We'll be as quick as we can. Bear in mind they probably have to cook the food, so don't panic if it takes twenty minutes or so."

"We'll be here. I guess we should fill up the cars a bit more, doesn't hurt to have full tanks," Wally pulled his wallet out and handed a few bills to Ange. "Here, this is for the food."

"You don't have to do that, Uncle Wally," Ange tried to push the money away.

"No, I don't. But I do want to. I don't have much to spend my money on, and I do have quite a bit of it. Please, take this, and buy what we need. Don't forget the toothpaste."

Sarah drove her mother's car up to the pump and Wally filled it before he filled his own car, he then went in to pay. Sarah got out of the car to wait, knowing she'd be stuck inside it for quite some time to come.

"Can you still feel him?" Julia asked.

"Yeah, but it's not strong. It's like he's watching from a distance, you know?"

Julia nodded. "I think so. And maybe he is. Watching from a distance, that is. I hope the box we had made for the cards is restricting the cards' power somewhat."

"Maybe," Sarah said as she pulled her mobile out of her pocket to check the time. "I need to pee."

"Me too, but I thought we should wait until the

others come back."

"I'm back," Wally called. "The toilets are over there, in the other block. Go together and stay together, okay?"

"Okay, Uncle," Julia nodded.

"Anything goes sideways, just scream. I'll already be there."

"Thank you," Sarah hugged him, and Wally reeled back a little in surprise.

"You're welcome, young lady. Now hurry up, I need to go too."

Sarah was worried about going into the toilet block with only Julia beside her, and she got the feeling Julia was just as worried. The two women hurried and almost ran back to Wally when they were finished, just as Ange and Alison were walking back with a couple of large, brown paper bags and a few white plastic bags including one that seemed full of bottles. Alison also had a tray of coffees.

"Do you want to eat while we drive?"

Sarah frowned. The feeling of being watched had grown much stronger.

"Sarah?" Wally touched her arm. "Is it stronger, the feeling of his presence?"

Sarah nodded.

"Let's go." Wally accepted a bag and coffee from Alison. "I've called ahead and made reservations in a motel that's about three hours away."

"Do you want company?" Ange asked. "We don't think you should have to drive alone."

"No, I'm fine," Wally smiled at the offer. "If I'm alone I can listen to my own music, as loud as I want, and I can think. I need to think, to tune into the various whispers of what the elders of this land are trying to tell me."

"Okay then, but if you change your mind or get tired, just sing out," Ange took her bag of food and climbed into the car.

Sarah climbed behind the wheel, and while Alison raised an eyebrow, she accepted that, climbing into the passenger seat. As they drove, she handed Sarah a burger, and put some water into a plastic plate for Lilly.

"How're you feeling, Sarah?" Julia asked. "Is the watched sensation gone?"

Sarah swallowed before answering. "It's gone, well, it's sort of in the background. It's getting better the further we get from the truck stop."

"I don't understand that," Alison said as she sipped her coffee. "If the cards are here, how can we be leaving the dark man behind?"

"I don't know, but that's just the feeling I get. It's like he stalks me in certain places, whether the cards are with me or not." Sarah took another bite of her burger. "I mean, I felt him all over town and not once did I have the cards with me."

"Next time fill your mouth up some more before you speak," Alison teased. "Here, I got some chicken thigh for Lilly. Can I see if she'll come off your shoulder?"

"I'm sure she's starving. Just offer it to her, I'm sure she'll come running."

Alison pulled a piece of flesh from the bone and held it near Sarah's shoulder. The kitten didn't need to be asked twice, she crawled down off Sarah's shoulder and bounded onto Alison's lap where she purred as she ate the pieces of meat she was offered.

"That was a great burger," Julia wiped her mouth on a white paper napkin. "And I'm not saying that just because I was hungry."

"I agree," Sarah said. "It was like the burgers you used to make, Mum. It really hit the spot, I must say."

"Uncle Wally hits another home run!" Julia laughed, trying to keep the mood light. Despite her efforts, everyone fell silent and Sarah put on the headlights as the light left the day.

They drove for a while until Wally pulled into a motel, Sarah followed him but waited in the car while the man checked them in. He came out with three keys and handed two of them through the car window to Alison.

"I could only get three rooms, ladies. I hope you don't mind sharing with your daughter, Alison."

"Good heavens, no, I think I prefer it, with everything that's going on none of us want to sleep alone," Alison held up a hand in apology. "Oh, sorry, Wally, you'll be alone!"

"I will be fine, trust me. I have the good fortune to be forewarned if anything should threaten me, so I feel pretty safe. I also have a few little items of protection as well." Wally pointed behind him. "We have those three rooms that all are in a row, so we're really close to each other. I didn't mention the kitten, though."

"I didn't think to grab anything for her to use as a kitty litter!" Sarah slapped her forehead.

"No worries there, my girl, believe it or not I have a bag of kitty litter in my car. I use it for oil spills at the youth centre. Some of the old cars those kids drive leak like a holey bucket."

"Wow, thank you. She's a good little thing, never makes a mess outside of her box."

Wally slapped the roof of the four-wheel drive then returned to his car so he could park it in front of his motel room. Sarah followed suit and they all piled out, locking the cars behind them. Wally invited everyone into his room so they could chat before calling it a night, and everyone followed him inside.

"Where are the cards?" Wally asked.

"I left them in the car," Sarah answered. "I didn't want them in the room with us."

"I think you need to get them. Put them in the freezer if you want, but you don't want anyone breaking into the car and stealing them. Make sure you keep them safe until we can control them."

"If you think that's best. I don't want to go outside by myself, though."

"No, of course not, I'll come with you," Wally smiled at her, his kind face making her feel better. "No one messes with Uncle Wally, my dear."

Sarah stopped at the door, her hand on the knob. "I really don't want to go outside," Sarah said. "I can't. I can't walk out there."

Julia stood up. “Something’s out there, is that what you’re feeling?”

Sarah shook her head. “I don't know, it’s so strange, I actually *cannot* go outside!”

Julia pulled her away from the door. “It’s okay baby girl, me and Uncle Wally will go out to the car and get them for you. Give me that bag, I’ll scoop the box up with it, so I don't have to touch them.”

“Is that the first time they’ve controlled you like that?” Alison asked, her face lined with worry.

“Yeah, I think so,” Sarah climbed up onto the bed beside her mother. “The thing is, how do I know? Maybe when I thought I changed my mind about something, it was them controlling me?”

Alison wrapped her arms around her daughter and hugged her tight.

“Don't fret, little one. Tomorrow this should all be over.”

“God, I really hope so.”

“They’re taking a while, aren’t they?” Ange asked. “I mean, they only had to go out to the car which is right in front of the room.”

Sarah frowned. “Open the door and have a look?”

Ange nodded, but she didn’t move.

“It’s got you too?” Sarah looked at her mother. “Can you get to the door?”

Alison took her arms from Sarah and stood up. She walked to the door, opened it and glanced back at the two inside before stepping out, leaving the door wide open. Ange looked over at Sarah. “It's so weird, I don't feel like anything is stopping me from getting up, or that I can't physically move. It's more like I don't want to," Ange ran her hands through her hair in frustration. "I want to see if my wife is okay, but I just can't get up and check. I can't even look out the door."

"I can look out, I think," Sarah climbed off the bed, but the door slammed shut before she could reach it. "Fuck, Ange, what do we do?"

Ange shrugged. "We'll be okay."

Sarah shook her head. "You're way too calm, there's something very wrong. I need to open the door and see what's going on!"

Lilly started to hiss and growl, and Sarah felt her fear grow, knowing her mother and the other two could be in grave danger. She took a deep breath and closed her eyes.

"I can do this," she hissed. "I can open the door and walk outside. I can."

She turned and moved one leg. Then the other. Like a robot, she stiffly walked to the door, then grasped the handle.

"Good on you," Ange said, her voice way too calm for the situation. "Don't stop, I mean, I can't help you, but I know you can do it. Keep going."

Sarah took a deep breath, held it, and turned the door handle. Releasing the breath, she pulled the door open and saw her mother standing still, like a statue, beside the car. Julia and Wally were there too, and they all looked like they were in a trance. Sarah pushed herself to make it out of the room; the effort was tremendous, she felt she was fighting through a fierce void, but she pushed through. Once she was out of the motel, she felt released, and could move freely.

When she reached her mother, she grabbed her arm and Alison slowly looked down at the hand on her arm. Sarah shook her, shook her hard, and Alison seemed to wake up from her fugue.

"What?"

"Mum, you were frozen here. Can you move?"

Alison shook her head to clear it. "Oh my god, Sarah, I was a million miles away. It was like I was looking through a tunnel!" Alison stumbled backwards but Sarah's grip was tight, and she found her feet quickly.

Sarah let her go, grabbed Julia's arms and shook her, and Julia recovered quicker than her mother had. She helped Sarah rouse Wally, who looked shocked that he was controlled so easily. "Can you grab the cards, Sarah, now that you're out here?" he asked her, his voice husky and strained.

"Yeah, sure. I'll put them in that plastic bag so we can put them in the freezer," Sarah held her hand out to Julia.

"Where's Ange?" Julia asked as she gave Sarah the bag.

"She's in the room. She's sort of frozen, too. She can talk, but not get off the chair."

Julia hurried inside to check on her wife. Wally turned his gaze to Sarah as she exited the car, the box of cards in the flimsy plastic bag.

"I'm sorry, child. I didn't think that I could be at risk. I should have been more careful." Wally looked back at his car. "I just need to grab something; I won’t be long.”

Sarah handed the bag of cards to her mother. “I don't want anyone out here alone, Uncle Wally. I’ll come with you, if you don't mind.”

Wally nodded. “Probably a good idea. Come on, let’s hurry.”

“What do you need to grab?” Sarah asked him.

“I made some protective little bags, like dilly bags, and I think we should all wear them. I was saving them for when we were performing the banishing ritual, but I think we need them now.”

“I’ve got to agree with you there. Do you have enough for all of us?”

“Yes, I do, child,” he pulled out a duffle bag, slammed his door shut and locked it. “I think I even have enough supplies to make something for that little thing on your shoulder.”

“You think she needs protecting?”

“Maybe not protecting, as such, but if something got control of her, she could scratch your eyes out at night. Now, I’m not saying that’s something that could happen, but I don't want to find out if it’s possible, either.”

“Good thinking. Hey, Uncle Wally, could you feel anything different before you, um, froze?”

He looked at her and stopped outside the hotel door. “Why, girl? Did you?”

“No, I didn’t, but I do now,” she said. “I can feel him, and I think he’s near.”

“Hurry up, let’s get inside, and get ready. I think we don’t want to risk getting caught out here by anyone.”

"He's right here, Uncle Wally, like, *here*," Sarah whirled around to look but Wally just grabbed her arm and hustled her into the motel, slamming the door behind them.

Ange was sitting on the floor, Julia beside her, a hot cup of tea in their hands. Alison handed Sarah a cup and smiled at Wally. "Would you like tea or coffee?"

Wally smiled back at her; his kind face was a myriad of wrinkles. "I'll have white sweet tea, thank you ma'am. And while you get that I'll get started here."

Alison sat Wally's tea on the table he had cleared and pulled a chair up for herself, a mug of tea cradled in both hands. Sarah set about making a kitty litter tray out of a cardboard box her mother had found in the back of the car, and Ange and Julia pulled chairs out at the table and sat watching Wally.

The man had his five little dilly bags on the table, and was burning a handful of brush, the smoke strong and acrid. Julia leapt up and pulled the smoke alarm open, prizing the d-cell battery out and placing it on the small kitchenette counter. Alison smiled at her, but no one spoke.

Sarah placed a plate on the floor and pulled some more chicken from the bone for her kitten, then made sure she had water before placing Lilly into the litter box.

Leaving the kitten to eat and use the litter box, Sarah sat on the last chair at the table, then got up and pulled over the chair from the desk on the other side of the room so Wally would have a seat.

Alison had divided up the toiletries, and she also had a few snacks and chocolate bars from the bag which they munched on while they watched Wally. The room was quite thick with smoke and he sang a song in his own tongue. After a few minutes he indicated for Julia to stand up and she joined him, this time the song was different, and Julia was obviously familiar with it. She sang with a voice that was strong and clear, very melodious, while Wally's deep baritone complimented and balanced Julia's higher tones.

Sarah felt the power that these two were conjuring, the spirits of their people, perhaps, or of the land. She was embarrassed to think she knew so little of the indigenous lore of the first nation people, the indigenous people in the land she had been born into, loved, and respected. She decided that once this was all over, she would take the time to learn more about these people, and make sure she knew their stories and their history.

Wally threw a handful of tiny white shells on the table, and both he and Julia stopped singing. Wally picked up the little woven bags and swung them through the smoke a few times, then waved the smoking brush over the shells. He put a couple of shells into each bag, then pulled a small piece of string from his duffle bag and threaded it through a tiny hole in the last shell.

Wally handed the string out to Sarah. "This is for Lilly. It has been blessed but was sacred before that. She should be protected fine with this. And these bags," he waved a hand over the dilly bags, "they are for us. I want everyone to wear one, and I don't want you to take it off, not to shower, not for any reason, until this is over."

"Okay, I'm going to have a quick shower then I'll put it on," Sarah stood up. "I don't have PJs, but I can sleep in my t-shirt."

"I think we'll all be doing that, sweetheart," Alison said as she handed Sarah her dilly bag. "Be quick, I want this bag on you as soon as you get out of the shower."

Sarah hurried into the tiny ensuite bathroom. The kitten mewed at the door but before she could open it, she heard her mother speaking gently to the little thing, and surmised her mother was looking after it.

She stripped off her clothes and turned on the water, thinking that she no longer felt the influence of the dark man, not since Wally lit his sacred smoke. She showered quickly, not washing her hair, and dried off before dressing in her underwear and t-shirt. She carefully pulled the string over her head that held the dilly bag and felt it hit her chest. It had an earthy, gum tree aroma, and when Sarah touched it, she could feel a slight reverberation, realising the power from the bag felt almost as strong as the cards.

She opened the door to the bathroom and frowned.

There was no one there, no one at all.

Even the kitten was gone.

She looked at the table and was confused. There were four dilly bags there, no one had put theirs on.

Sarah reached over to the nightstand and picked up her mobile phone. There were a few messages from Michael that she hadn't read which she decided to ignore for now. She looked up her mother's number and rang.

Alison's mobile was on the other nightstand, surprising Sarah when the vibration went off.

She picked up her mother's phone and unlocked it, pleased that her mother used an older phone and that the passcode was her brother Sam's birthday. She flicked through the contacts until she found Julia's number and rang it. There was no vibration in the room, so Sarah hoped that Julia had it with her. She listened to the ring tone, and after a few moments it went to voicemail. The message gave Ange's number as an alternate contact, and Sarah dialled using her own phone.

Ange's phone vibrated on the floor and Sarah hung up. She tried Julia's again, and again, hanging up every time it went to voicemail. She was so worried, if they had gone without taking their phones or handbags, and most importantly, their dilly bags, Sarah was sure something bad had happened.

She didn't know what to do, she was starting to panic, the feeling of losing her mother, of losing the people that tried to help her was overwhelming. Sarah stood, her hands in her hair, trying to calm down enough to think of a plan. She decided to look out the front window, see if she could see them, thinking perhaps they were frozen again, and she'd know how to fix that.

She pulled a little bit of the heavy, mustard coloured curtain over and saw the four missing people standing out the front, but they weren't frozen. She pulled the curtain a little more and saw they were talking to a policeman, and the police car was a few parking spots away where another cop was talking to some other people.

Sarah tapped on the window and her mother turned around, giving her a wave of reassurance. Sarah saw Lilly poke her head out from her mother's hair and she released the breath she had been holding.

While she didn't know what the police wanted, she was relieved to see her people alive and well, and not under some strange spell wrought by the cards. She decided to pull her jeans on just in case the police came into the room; she didn't want to be caught standing there without pants.

She had just done the zip up when the motel door opened and everyone filed inside.

"What happened? You weren't wearing your dilly bags, and I panicked when I couldn't find anyone!" she exclaimed, and Alison grabbed her in a reassuring hug.

"We're fine, baby, we're okay. There's just something..." Alison looked at Wally.

"The motel manager called the police when he saw a very tall, very dark man lurking around our cars and trying to look in the window," Wally explained. "By the time the police arrived he was gone. They are going to hang around for a little while in case he comes back, the manager was very frightened. It seems there were a few crimes committed by a dark man recently and they've decided this man could be him. We were just telling the nice men in uniform that we have no idea who it could be and that we don't know a very tall, dark man."

Sarah sat down on the bed. "It was him, wasn't it? I could feel him before, especially right before you all froze," Sarah shook her head. "I haven't felt him since Uncle Wally did the cleansing smoke thing."

"That's probably about the same time he disappeared, I would guess," Julia said. "We just played dumb, well, it wasn't hard, really, because we really don't know who he is or what he wants."

"You know, you're right. We really don't know what he wants," Ange sat down next to Sarah and took her hand. "But we do seem to be safe for now. We should get some sleep while we have the cops guarding us and make an early start."

"Fantastic plan. What time are we setting the alarm for?" Julia asked.

"Dawn, what's that, five thirty?" Alison picked up her phone. "Is five thirty okay for everyone?"

"I don't know if I'll be able to sleep at all," Sarah said. "So yeah, fine by me."

"That's decided then. We can get breakfast on the way, if we want," Uncle Wally picked up his dilly bag and slung it around his neck. "Everyone please arm yourselves, and make sure those cards go into the freezer compartment of the little fridge. If I'm not up in the morning, please feel free to bang on my door."

"We will," Julia promised as Wally kissed her cheek. "Good night, Uncle."

"Good night, everyone. Try and sleep," Wally opened the door and let Julia and Ange out first. "And please, do not worry. It won't help anything, and it could make you dream."

Sarah tried to smile, but her lips just didn't want to make the expression. She nodded and watched the door close.

"I'll take the bed closest to the door," Alison said. "I'll just brush my teeth, then I think we should try to sleep."

"Sure thing, Mum," Sarah answered as she walked over to her double bed. She read through Michael's messages and looked at the pictures he sent her, and then finally smiled when Lilly climbed up onto her bed and snuggled into the pillow. She turned off her lamp and pulled the blankets up. She didn't want to sleep tonight; she was too scared of dreaming.

Chapter Twenty-Two

Alison's alarm went off all too soon. Sarah hadn't realised she'd fallen asleep, her last thought was lying in the too hard motel bed and staring at the ceiling, the kitten softly purring beside her ear. She stretched and yawned, then stretched again. The room was dark, and it looked like it was still dark outside, no lights bled under the thick curtains.

"Mum, turn off the alarm," she croaked, her voice not quite ready to wake up just yet.

Her mother didn't answer, so Sarah turned on her lamp. Her mother wasn't in her bed, in fact, the bed looked like it hadn't been slept in. Sarah frowned. Didn't her mother come to bed after brushing her teeth last night? Try as she might, Sarah just couldn't remember.

She pulled herself out of bed and turned off the alarm. There was no light under the bathroom door, but Sarah checked it anyway.

There was no one there.

She frowned. Where was her mother?

She looked at the table and gasped. There were three dilly bags there. Julia and Ange must have forgotten to put theirs on, and her mother's one was still sitting there too. Sarah remembered Wally putting his around his neck, and she was certain of that memory.

She pulled on her jeans and sneakers and ran a hand through her hair. She wasn't sure which room was Uncle Wally's, and which one was Julia and Ange's, but that didn't really matter. They were in the two rooms to her right, so she made sure she had the door key and her kitten on her shoulder, and she left her room.

She banged on the first door and waited.

There was no answer. She banged again, but still, silence.

Sarah tried the next room, feeling more hopeful when she saw the faint glimmer of light appear around the window. Someone was in that room, and they had turned on the light.

Uncle Wally opened the door, his salt and pepper hair sticking out at odd angles, and he had no pants on. Sarah was glad that his button-down shirt was long enough to cover his lower region. Around his neck hung the dilly bag, and Sarah's hand snuck up and touched her own.

"Sorry, child, I slept right through the alarm," Wally scratched his stomach. "I've never ever had trouble getting to sleep. Now, waking up, that's a whole other story."

"My mother's gone, her bed's made like she never slept in it, and Julia and Ange aren't answering the door." Sarah could hear the panic flitting around the edges of her voice.

Wally stared at her for a second then ushered her inside. "Let me just get on my trousers and shoes," he said, pulling his jeans from the back of a chair. "Over there on the desk are the spare keys for all of the rooms, I got two for each room, just in case. Grab them and we'll see what's going on in the girls' room."

"Oh, I found their dilly bags on the table, too. Three of them," Sarah told Wally as he buckled his leather belt then started to pull on his shoes. He stopped and looked up at her.

"Didn't they put them on last night? I thought I saw them put them on."

"I don't remember seeing that," Sarah wrung her hands together. "There's three bags on the table, right where you left them. You and me are the only ones wearing them. Oh, and Lilly has her shell still."

"This isn't good. I told them to put them on, and not take them off. This isn't good at all."

Wally finished doing up his shoelaces and took the keys Sarah offered him.

"Do you want to come with me or wait here?" Wally asked her. "Though really, I'd feel better if we didn't split up."

"I agree, I'm too freaked out to stay by myself anyway."

Lilly meowed as if she agreed, and Sarah followed Wally out into the predawn darkness. Wally walked up to the door and tried the key. The door opened, and Sarah peered around Wally into the darkness of the room.

"The light switch is on the right-hand side," Sarah said.

Wally flicked on the lights and gasped. Sarah felt her knees go weak and her head spin.

"No, no no no no no," she moaned. "Oh god, no, this can't be true, please, god, no."

Wally grabbed her around the waist and pulled her back as she tried to lunge into the room.

She couldn't breathe, couldn't think, couldn't do anything but moan.

The room was covered in blood. There were splashes and sprays of the thick red fluid everywhere, across the walls, the roof, and even the mustard coloured curtains. The beds were soaked, and the blood dripped onto the floor, the green and yellow carpet now splattered and splashed with viscous red.

On one of the beds there was a head. The tight cornrows that were braided with bright hues were now sitting in a heap beside the head, having been cut off and piled there like so much trash. Sarah couldn't see Julia's body, but she could see Ange's. She was hanging from the small light fitting in the middle of the ceiling, some kind of electrical cord was slung under her arms and tied behind her. The head was missing, and the stomach had been cut from pubic bone to breast, her intestines were hanging out, the great loops of blue-grey and red shining in the dull light.

The worst thing, the very worst thing, was Sarah's mum. She was sitting in a lounge chair, and was sort of slumped over to one side, like she was trying to see around the hanging body in the middle of the room. Someone had put an axe through her head. Someone had split her head right down to her neck, and then sat the axe on her lap. One side of Alison's head was lying flat on her shoulder, the other side just sort of tilted a little, with half of the tongue poking out in a strange, almost comical gesture.

Wally pulled Sarah back, but stopped, his face inches from hers, his eyes bulging. "Wally?" Sarah sobbed.

Wally grunted, his mouth open, and Sarah screamed as blood fell out of his mouth in a large dark glob.

"Ack," Wally grunted and looked down. Sarah continued to scream as she saw the pointed tip of a blade sticking from his chest, the dark red bloom of blood growing around the blade. She tried to pull free from Wally's grasp, but the man gripped her tight, his hands spasming in his death throes, his eyes wide and the blood now pouring from his mouth. Sarah screamed and screamed, and someone grabbed her from behind, their fingers digging into her shoulders as they shook her and called her name. She continued to scream as they shook...

... "Wake up baby!" Alison shook Sarah's shoulders as the scream died in her daughter's throat.

"Mum?"

"Yes honey, you were having a nightmare, you even started to scream!"

Sarah scrubbed her hand over her face and shook her head to try and clear it.

"What were you dreaming about?" Alison asked as she sat down on the bed.

Sarah looked at her mother and burst into tears. "It was terrible, just terrible."

Someone knocked on the door and Alison got up to look through the peephole before opening the door. Julia and Ange walked in, followed by Uncle Wally.

"I thought I would be the last up, but I surprised myself by actually waking up to the alarm," Wally smiled, but the expression froze when he saw Sarah. "What happened?"

"She had a dream, a bad one," Alison said. "I couldn't wake her, I shook her and slapped her face, it took forever to wake her up."

Sarah ran a hand through her hair and wiped her tears. "I'm okay, I'm okay. Just give me a minute to get dressed and wash my face, and I'll be ready."

No one spoke to her as she hurried to the bathroom, but as soon as she shut the door, she could hear them all talking in hushed tones. She couldn't hear what they were saying, but they all sounded very concerned. She splashed her face with water and brushed her teeth before pulling on her jeans. Grabbing her sneakers and socks, Sarah opened the door. Everyone stopped talking as she came out of the bathroom and she tried to smile.

"Awkward much?" Sarah joked.

Instead of playing along with her joke everyone shuffled their feet and looked around, no one could make eye contact with her.

"Lilly, time to get up," Sarah sat on the bed with the kitten and pulled on her socks. "I'd better take care of the kitty litter before we go."

Lilly ran to use the litter box as Sarah did up her laces, and the silence became even more awkward.

"Should we make some tea?" Sarah asked.

"I think we should just get a move on; we can grab something to eat on the way when we stop for fuel," Wally twisted his cap in his hands. "Do you want to tell us about the dream?"

Sarah picked up the cardboard kitty litter box. "No, I don't. And if we can just get away from this motel, like, yesterday, I'll be happy."

"Let's go then," Julia put her hand out for Alison's key. "I'll drop these off in the manager's key box."

Alison pulled the door shut behind them and Sarah shivered, her flimsy t-shirt no match for the predawn chill. Lilly snuggled right up under her hair; she was also feeling the cold. "Oh shit, I forgot the cards in the freezer," Sarah called out to Julia. "Can you bring back the keys?"

"That's a worry," Wally said. "It's like they are trying to distance themselves from you."

Julia opened the door and Sarah grabbed her parcel from the tiny bar fridge's freezer. She couldn't believe that she nearly left the cards behind, and not one of the others said anything. She tossed them in the footwell and climbed into Uncle Wally's car.

"Hey Uncle Wally, can I ask you something?"

"Sure Sarah, anything you want, just ask."

"Did you get two sets of keys for the rooms?"

Wally shook his head. "No, why?"

Sarah shrugged. "Doesn't matter. I'm freezing, let's go!"

"My turn to drive," Julia said. "If you don't

mind, Alison?"

"No, I can sit in the back, so Ange can ride up front with you."

"I may as well ride with Wally, give him some company," Sarah said. "Is that okay?"

"Fine by me," Wally said.

"Sure, honey, if you want to," Alison said. "See you soon."

Sarah kissed her mother and climbed into Wally's four-wheel drive. It wasn't what she expected, she just imagined the car to be rough and dusty, instead it was immaculately clean and tidy, and had a pleasant coconut scent. Wally glanced at her and chuckled.

"You were thinking bush man, animal bones and take away food wrappers, weren't you?"

Sarah ducked her head. "I'm embarrassed to admit that, but yeah."

Wally nodded. "I keep the car rugged, if you will, because I don't want to look pretentious. It's often hard to get kids, or even adults, to trust a figure in power. They don't want to deal with someone who's more educated, or more in an authoritative position, even if he is a fellow blackfella."

Sarah nodded. "Yeah, I get that. You must care about people a lot."

"I do, absolutely. I wish there'd been someone like me when I was growing up, someone who could listen, maybe help, but just be there. Very often there isn't anyone, especially in those times where you really need someone."

“I guess I’m very lucky then,” Sarah reached up and gently caressed the kitten on her shoulder. “I’ve got a mother who’d do anything for me, a massively supportive brother, and some really good friends. And now I have Julia and Ange, and you, Uncle Wally. You are all putting your lives at risk to help me, and not for anything. I mean, you don't want anything in return for helping me.”

“Oh dear, didn’t your mother tell you my fee for helping?”

Sarah frowned. “Fee?”

Wally laughed. “I’m no good at pulling people’s legs. You’re right, we’re doing this purely as a favour for your mother. Well, for you as well, now that we know you.”

“I can't tell you how grateful I am.”

“I get that, I do. Now, can I ask you a question?”

Sarah nodded, squinting at the headlights from a truck coming in their direction. “Yeah, sure, ask away.”

“What was your dream about last night?”

“Well, just for the record, I think I only dream in the morning.”

“Morning then, but you’re avoiding the question. What was your dream?”

Sarah breathed in but held her breath. She wasn't sure she should tell him what she dreamt, or even if she could live that moment again, that horrific image, that memory, that shock and horror. A tear found its way down her cheek, a tear that shone in the reflected light from a passing car and caught Uncle Wally’s eye.

"You can tell me, child. I know it's not going to be pretty. In fact, I'm fairly sure it's going to be something that I don't want to hear. But I think you need to tell me, I think you need to get it off your chest, and off your mind."

"Okay, okay, I'll tell you, but it's like you said, not pretty. In fact, I think it's something that's going to give me nightmares for the rest of my life."

Wally patted her knee but didn't speak.

Sarah took another breath, she breathed deeply to steady herself, then let it out slowly before starting her tale of madness.

Chapter Twenty-Three

"This looks like a good place to stop," Wally turned on his indicator. "Your mother needs to use the toilet, and I think that little dust ball on your shoulders is also needing to relieve herself."

"Can you always tell what people are thinking or needing?" Sarah asked him.

"Pretty much. It's not with everyone, but with most people, though I can turn it down sometimes."

"Really? That would be cool, like tune in when you need it."

"It's not always that cut and dry, sometimes things just reach out to me whether I want it to or not. Sometimes there is a power, or a need, that breaks through no matter what I do.'

"Bummer. But I have to ask, am I one of those things?"

Wally pulled up beside a pump. "You are not a thing, Sarah. You didn't call out to me, but the cards did. Well, the power of them. They didn't call, as such, but the ripple that the cards made was felt all over the place, and that includes me. I felt them, I bet I felt them the instant you opened the box. Now hang on to all of your questions, I have to go put some fuel into this thing and use the bathroom. If you need to go, don't worry about locking up. I'll grab some breakfast, as well."

"I'll take Lilly to the nature strip to have a pee, I think."

Wally gave her the thumbs up and walked around to the pump, so Sarah slipped out of the car. Her mother was hurrying over to the toilet block with Ange as Julia fuelled the car. Sarah stood on the sand that made up the nature strip and the kitten climbed down, her little claws scratching against Sarah's skin. She dug a tiny hole and emptied her bladder as Sarah watched on.

A strange prickle on her skin was all it took for her to know she was being watched, and she looked around to see if she could pinpoint the origin. Her concentration was broken when a dog barked, and a fat white Jack Russell terrier lunged at Lilly, who immediately ran and climbed up Sarah's jeans onto her shoulder.

The family walking the dog muttered begrudging apologies and moved on, and Sarah turned to see where her people were. She could see Wally had finished filling his car and was walking in to pay and order food, Julia was walking with him. Her mother and Ange were still in the toilet block, and Sarah knew for the first time since they left her mother's house that she was alone. She wanted to go to the toilet but didn't want to leave the cars alone. The cards were inside Wally's car. She didn't want to leave them unattended, but she also didn't want to be left alone. She frowned, unsure as to what to do, then Wally stopped and turned to look her. He spoke briefly to Julia and Sarah was relieved to see the woman walk towards her as Wally turned and continued into the cashier.

"Hey girl, sorry about that," Julia called to her as

she drew closer. “None of us should be alone right now.”

“Uncle Wally is alone,” Sarah said.

“I think he can handle himself for a few moments. As soon as your mum comes back, we can head off to the toilet, if you want.”

Sarah nodded and leaned on Wally’s car. “I don’t want anyone left alone, not even Uncle Wally.”

“Because of your last dream?”

Sarah didn't answer. She knew Julia was fishing for the details of her dream, and she wasn't willing to go through it all again. Telling Uncle Wally had been hard enough, and she was not wanting to relive the horror that the dream had shown her.

“There they are,” Julia announced as Alison and Ange left the toilet block. “They can wait here while we go pee. I’m about to burst, I tell you.”

“Is your uncle ordering food for us?” Sarah asked.

“Yep, he’s going to get enough for everyone. He’s exceptional at matching the right food to the right person, but I’m doubtful he'll have much to choose from in this little place. Doesn’t look like a very nutritious establishment, I think.”

Alison nodded to them as they passed. “The toilets aren’t particularly clean,” she said. “At least it’s better than squatting beside a bush.”

“Barely,” Ange added. “I suggest the hover method myself.”

Sarah laughed at the phrase and followed Julia. Her mother was right, the toilets left a lot to be desired, so the women did what they came to do and hurried back to the car. Wally wasn't back yet and Alison offered to go help him carry the food.

Lilly mewed and Sarah patted her, knowing she didn't have to remind Wally that the little kitten would need to eat. Julia leaned on the car beside Sarah as Ange stood in front of them.

"How far do you think we'll have to go?" Ange asked.

"I'm not real sure, but I think it will be quite a drive still. I wouldn't be surprised if he doesn't take us all the way to the border, maybe even over it."

"To South Australia?" Sarah was shocked. "We've been driving so long; I didn't realise we were coming up to the border."

"Yeah, I think it's because Uncle Wally is taking all the back roads," Julia yawned and scratched her stomach. "I don't know why, I'm sure it's a lot longer, but he'll be following some hunch or the elders or something."

"You don't believe in that?" Sarah asked.

"Yeah, I do believe, I just don't understand it all very much, and he doesn't really explain it."

"Explain what?" Uncle Wally placed a cardboard tray of disposable cups on the bonnet of his car. "The one with an 'A' is a hot tea, Alison," he added.

"I'm sure you know exactly what we were talking about," Julia laughed. "So, do you want Sarah to drive with you, or someone else now?"

"I don't mind who wants to come with me, anyone is welcome," Wally said as he handed a bag to Julia. "I think you and Ange are coming with me and Sarah is going with her mother. That's just a feeling I have."

"He got the food placed into the bags based on that," Alison said. "Okay, let's get going, I want this over and done with."

"Amen to that," Sarah said, and she climbed into the passenger seat of her mother's car. Everyone got into the cars and Wally turned his onto the road, with Alison following close behind.

"What did he get us to eat?" Sarah asked as she opened the bag. "I hope we have something for Lilly."

"Yeah, there's actually cat food in there, though not any good brand or specific kitten food," Alison said. "The other food was just what they had in the bain-marie, not a lot to choose from."

"Bacon and egg sandwiches, that's not so bad," Sarah handed a sandwich to her mother. "I'll feed Lilly on the floor, but I can't give her water while we're driving."

The cat food had a ring pull top and Sarah put the can on the floor and sat the kitten beside it. While the kitten ate, Sarah ate her own sandwich and sipped the hot but tasteless coffee. There was a comfortable silence between the two, and Sarah was grateful for that. She knew her mother would be desperate to ask about her dream and who died but held her tongue for now.

The radio was playing some obscure station, the music was bad and the DJ even worse, but neither of them moved to turn it off. Alison finished her sandwich and handed the wrapping to Sarah, who replaced it with the tea.

"Here you go, Mum," Sarah said as her mother sipped the hot beverage. "The coffee wasn't great but I guess it's the best we'll get for a while."

Alison screwed her nose up at her drink. "I hope we go home by the main highway, at least there'll be bigger places and towns and hopefully better food and drinks."

"Did Uncle Wally tell you where we were going?"

"No, and I didn't ask. I figured if he wanted us to know he would have told us already. And maybe he doesn't know himself, he just drives until he gets some sign that it's the right place or something."

"I hope we get there today, I'm sick of wearing the same clothes, and eating shit food. My week off has proved to be quite the disappointment."

"You won't say that once the cards are gone," Alison reassured her. "Hey, where are they, anyway?"

"I left them in Wally's car. I hope that's okay with him."

"I'm sure he'd say something if it wasn't. They'll still be in the plastic bag, yeah? No one has to touch them?"

"That's right," Sarah sighed. "I am absolutely over them, and this whole thing. Hey, is that your phone ringing?"

"Yeah, it's in my handbag there on the floor, in the back. You should be able to reach it."

Sarah twisted around and reached for the bag, hooking it on her first try. She found the phone and answered it.

"Alison's phone."

"*Hey Sezzy, it's Sam,*" her brother's deep voice answered.

"Hang on a tick, I'll put you on speaker," Sarah pushed the button and held the phone in between herself and Alison. "Okay, you're on, and it's just me and Mum in the car."

"*You haven't reached wherever you're going yet?*"

"No, and we don't even know where we're going," Alison said. "What's up?"

"*I spoke to that lady, the one where you got the cards, Sarah. She finally rang me back.*"

"Nice. What did she have to say?" Sarah asked.

"*I'm not sure you want to hear this or hear all of it. I can just talk to Mum later, if you want.*"

"Nah, you better tell me. You're right, I don't want to hear it, but I guess I'd better."

"*Well, I think you already know that the woman got the cards from a relative, right?*"

"Right," Sarah affirmed.

"*So the sister, the one that owned the cards, she started to go a little crazy. They didn't get along, so the one I spoke to said that she didn't know about what happened to her at first, it wasn't until the police called her looking for the sister that she realised something was wrong. Seems the police were hunting for her sister as there were a lot of unexplained deaths that were directly connected to her.*

"*And she went completely nuts, lost her job, her*

dogs were killed, strung up on the clothesline apparently, and their parents were murdered. Then her sister was found in the bathtub, the police said she'd killed herself. The boxes were given to the woman you met by the cleaners that she'd hired to clear up the place, and she only had a quick look through them. She didn't find anything that was worth much, so she took it all to the market to sell it."

"You have to book those stalls months in advance," Alison said. "How long ago did her sister die?"

"*She already had the stall booked, she was doing a clear out or some shit. Anyway, she took along the stuff and didn't sell much, that's why she gave it to you and Kelli.*"

"Thanks bro. Cool story, extremely disturbing. Hey, have you heard from Kelli at all?"

"*We've been keeping in touch, making sure we're still alive, I guess. She's fine. We went out to dinner last night, and we check in a couple of times a day.*"

"Thank you, Sam," Alison said. "I'll keep you updated on what we're doing and everything, and you stay safe, okay?"

"*Always. Love you two.*"

"Love you more," Sarah said.

"Same same," Alison nodded for Sarah to hang up.

"I'm going to ring Julia and tell those guys what Sam said," Sarah dialled the number in the phone. "I'll put it on speaker again so you can join in."

Chapter Twenty-Four

"I am getting very uncomfortable," Alison groaned. "I've been in the car way too long. And I am completely sick of eating things while we drive."

"It's been quite a trek, that's for sure. I wonder how far we are from the place now."

"Oh, hopefully this is it," Alison said as Wally's car pulled off the road, and slowly traversed a rough dirt track. "I can see why we needed the four-wheel drive cars."

"Mine would not have liked this road."

"It's not a road, it's a billy goat track," Alison complained.

"That's such an ancient expression, Mum. You're really showing your age."

Alison laughed, but then gritted her teeth as she negotiated the difficult road. They travelled on the road for another hour, and Sarah knew her mother's back would be aching. Just when she was about to suggest they pull over and change seats the road broke into a clearing and Wally pulled over, parking behind a large number of four-wheel drive cars. Alison parked behind him but didn't get out yet.

"Can you see those people?" Sarah asked. "See, there's heaps of people over there, at the other side of the clearing."

"Yes, I see them. Are they all Aboriginals?"

"I think so, no wait," Sarah leaned forward to try

and get a better look. “Those other people look more like Africans; I’m thinking they’re Julia’s other relatives.”

“This will be one very weird ceremony, all the different beliefs and lore from such different tribes of people. I wish I could film it.”

“I just wish it was all over already. Should we get out?”

Alison’s phone pinged with a message and she grabbed it from the dashboard. “It’s Ange, she said Wally wants us all to stay in the cars until he calls us out.”

“Sounds like a plan. I just hope it’s not a long time to wait. Now that we’re here I just want it to be over with.”

“Here’s a depressing thought,” Alison raised her eyebrows. “What if this isn't the place, it’s just a stop to get directions and supplies.”

“I think I hate you a little bit right now.” Sarah lifted the bag that their breakfast came in. “I’m hungry, I could lick the wrappers about now.”

“Gross, Sarah. Maybe we can get some food from these people,” Alison shifted in her seat. “That is, if they don't murder us and dump our bodies in the bush first.”

“Racist much, Mum?”

“Not being racist, I’m being realistic. There’s a bunch of men in the middle of nowhere that we’ve never met, we don't know, most have their faces covered in paint and stuff, sounds like a plot to a horror movie to me.”

Sarah chewed on her lower lip. She didn’t want

to say that they were in the middle of their own horror plot right now, and that is what brought them to this strange place.

"Looks like he's made progress with them at least," Alison pointed to where Wally was shaking hands with some of the men. He turned to the car and indicated for them to get out and come to him.

"Should I take the cards?" Sarah asked.

"I'd leave them where they are for now, Uncle Wally will tell you when he needs them," Alison answered as she opened her car door. They climbed out of the large vehicle and joined Julia and Ange at Wally's side. They were introduced all around, but Sarah was sure she forgot every single name as soon as they were uttered. Very few spoke to the four women in English, instead relying on Wally to interpret for them, both in Somali and Aboriginal. He seemed fluent in both languages, and Julia was able to speak to them as well.

"Good news, everyone, they will help us," Wally smiled at Sarah. "But they want to feed us first, they said we all look very tired and hungry, and no good work can happen unless we are rested and fed."

"Sounds fantastic," Ange said. "I hope we aren't eating something too weird, though. This Irish lass needs her carbs."

One of the men spoke and Wally translated. "We have a barbeque set up just behind the clearing. All good white man food available, and some nice spicy Somali food if you are daring."

"Perfect!" Ange's big grin made everyone smile, and they were led through the dusty area to a very comfortable camp site. There were several large tents and a caravan in a circle, with a gaggle of laughing children running around followed by a few dogs, and women and older men crowded around the barbeques, cooking food that made Sarah's mouth water instantly.

"Hey Uncle Wally, did you lock the car? The cards are in your car," Sarah asked the older man.

"Yes, child, and I made sure they were hidden under the front seat as well. We don't want anything to go wrong now. There're also some people there to watch over the vehicles. Don't worry, we are nearly at the end, this will all be over soon."

"Not soon enough for me," Sarah offered a smile to the man helping her. "This food smells amazing."

"It does, and I've been told there's plenty to go around. Let's eat and rest, because the day is going to get very busy after this."

Sarah nodded as Wally patted her back, and she accepted a plate from a young woman who smiled shyly at her.

"I like your cat," the woman spoke softly. "May I hold her?"

Sarah, relieved to meet someone who spoke English, reached up to her shoulder, surprised to find the kitten standing and peering out from her hairy shelter. She lifted the kitten and handed her to the girl. "Her name is Lilly, please be careful with her."

"Oh, I will, is it okay if I give her some fish? It's fresh, I caught it myself, and she seems hungry."

"Yes, go feed the kitten," Wally laughed. "This

is Melita, my cousin's child. She speaks to animals, and they seem to speak to her. She lives with more bush creatures than should be considered normal."

Melita giggled and hurried off with the brown kitten, leaving Sarah to fill her plate with food from the trestle tables before she sat down on one of the long, smooth logs that surrounded the barbeque area. Her mother and Ange sat with her, while Julia and Wally caught up with what Sarah assumed were their relatives and extended families and friends.

They ate quietly, watching the children play and the colourfully dressed women laugh and chat with each other. They were very friendly people and came over to chat as the woman ate, seeming to understand the strain that lined Sarah's face. No one mentioned why there were there or the plans for the rest of the day, and Sarah was pleased not to have to talk about the cards for a little while.

She finished eating and someone scooped her plate from her hands, then replaced it with an enamel mug of hot, milky sweet tea, and a piece of damper spread thickly with jam and butter. Sarah took a bite then froze, the piece of scone-like food in her mouth. She felt the hair on the back of her neck rise, and goosebumps break out on her flesh.

The kitten came running to her in a streak of brown and flew onto Sarah's shoulders. She realised everyone had stopped talking and were staring at her. She swallowed her mouthful and looked around as Wally held up a hand to quiet her.

"They know, girl, you need not tell them," he spoke gravely, quietly, but his voice could be heard by everybody. “We need to make a move now, as the threat is so much closer. Please finish your meals, make yourselves ready, we leave in half an hour.”

Sarah turned to her mother. “I can’t finish this; I can’t eat anything else.”

“Try to eat, Sarah, try to finish. They seem to know what you need and what you should be doing; they must feel you need these carbs or something. You’ve turned white, so I know there’s something happening.”

Sarah felt the presence of something powerful grow and her stomach contracted. The people all around started to murmur and shuffle their feet, they felt it too. There was a shout from behind them, then a scream, and people started to run to the clearing. Sarah sat her mug down and placed the damper on top of it before standing.

“Stay here, Sarah, please,” her mother grabbed her arm. “You need to stay safe.”

“I agree,” Julia ran to join them. “We need to make sure we’re ready now for whatever happens. If you need to toilet or anything, go now.”

Alison and Ange stood close to Sarah, their presence comforting in her clear distress. They could hear voices yelling, people agitated and angry, and Sarah took a step towards the clearing.

Alison tightened her grip on Sarah’s arm. “Please, Sarah, wait until they call you.”

“Sarah, you need to come and collect the cards,” Uncle Wally called from behind them, and Alison let her daughter’s arm go.

"We'll come with you," Julia said. "We'll be right by your side."

Sarah walked towards Uncle Wally, her feet feeling too heavy. She walked slowly, like she was moving through a dream and the air was as thick as jelly. Her head felt like it was foggy, unfocused, and she couldn't see properly. Wally seemed to sense this and strode forward to take her by the arm, one arm around her waist as he led her through the thick scrub to the clearing.

"I want to warn you all, this is very confronting. Please don't be too alarmed, and do *not* blame yourselves. These people wanted to be involved, and they asked us to come. They do this every day; they make it their life's work to fight the evils and curses in this world. Please, remember that, and don't blame yourself."

Sarah's stomach rolled and she stopped, trying to control herself. After a couple of deep breaths, she nodded and gripped Uncle Wally's arm tight, swallowing to stop from throwing up and taking a step forward.

Wally led them into the clearing and Sarah's mother gasped, both Julia and Ange groaned, and someone let a sob escape them. Sarah felt her knees grow weak, and if it weren't for Uncle Wally's strong hands she would have collapsed to the ground.

There were people everywhere, rushing around and trying to help others, to help the men that lay on the ground. There was blood, so much blood, splashed over the cars, over the ground, and over the men laying on that ground.

There were pieces of men, as well, at least three people had been dismembered, legs, heads, and arms were strewn about, covered with blood and gore. Chunks of flesh and bone were scattered around, and Wally moved Sarah around someone's intestines, the loops of glistening flesh thrown randomly around the clearing.

"Wait here," Julia grabbed Alison's hand. "Wait here on the edge with us."

"Oh my god…" Sarah heard her mother's despair as the two ladies hung onto her, and she knew that the horror that was before them was something that would haunt her mother forever. And not just her mother, she was sure.

"The car is open; you just need to reach in under the front passenger seat and grab the plastic bag. The cards are still inside it." Wally led her closer to the car. "Don't worry about anything else, just get the cards. Understand?"

She nodded. Her voice wasn't working, and her mind couldn't put enough thoughts together to give a coherent reply. The car door was open, and there were a couple of men standing next to it, guarding it. Sarah paused and turned to Uncle Wally. She cleared her throat and coughed, then cleared her throat again. "He's still here," she croaked.

"He? You mean your dark man?" Wally asked her.

"I think I can feel something, and it's powerful, just like the dark man. I can't be sure if it's him or something else."

"It's something else," one of the men, a very tall man with a heavy Somalian accent, told her. "There was no man here that did this."

"You saw what did this?" Sarah gasped.

"No one that survived saw what did this, not completely, but I can tell you that it was not a man. I saw but a glimpse, and it was not something I have seen before, nor do I wish to ever see it again."

Wally gently moved Sarah forward to the car and she took the last few steps herself, almost falling into the door. She reached under the seat and felt the edge of the plastic bag. Pulling it free she cried out as it came empty and she threw it away from her.

"They've fallen out of the bag," she called out to Uncle Wally as she lay her shoulders down on the floor of the car and twisted her arm further back under the seat. Her fingers brushed against the wooden box, but it slipped further back, away from her reach.

She climbed out of the car. "I can't reach it, I need to get in from the back seat," Sarah told Uncle Wally and he helped her move to the back, pulling the door open for her.

She lay across the floor and reached over, the box slipped back, but stopped when it jammed against the side of the seat. She wriggled around, got two fingers on the side of the box and maneuvered it until she could get her hand over it. She pulled it forward and got both hands on it before she yanked it out. Sarah shook the box to make sure the cards were inside, then opened it to be doubly sure. As soon as she opened it, she heard shouts and screams from behind her, and the dog that had followed them into the clearing began to bark so she slammed it shut.

"What happened?' she asked as she slipped out of the car.

"There was something, the people on the edge of the clearing saw something, but it seems to have fallen back for now." Uncle Wally took her elbow and helped her back to her mother.

"What are they saying?" Alison asked as she grabbed Sarah in a bear hug before releasing her. "What are all the men saying?"

Julia shook her head. "It doesn't make sense," she looked up to her uncle. "They're saying the shadows were moving, the shadows were coming back."

"The dogs chased the shadows, they seemed to be scared of the dogs," Uncle Wally told them. "We should maybe keep a dog or two around us from now on."

"What do we do now?" Sarah asked, the cards held tight to her stomach.

"I don't want to take the cards into the rest of the people," Uncle Wally replied. "I think we should move now and get this all taken care of."

"I agree, Sarah said. "But I don't think I want my mum and her friends to come."

"I'm coming," Alison said. "I have to be there to help you."

"No, Mum, I want you safe. You need to stay here with these people, you and Ange and Julia, and let them look after you. Promise me, Mum, please. Take Lilly, look after her until I get back." Sarah handed the kitten to her mother.

"She's right, Alison," Uncle Wally said. "Only those that need to go should come along. We need to be very careful now, and we can't be looking out for you. You'll be safe here; you will be protected."

"But you need me to help you," Julia protested.

"We have enough people who can do what needs to be done," Uncle Wally shook his head. "You look after Alison, and the families, make sure that everyone is safe. You can do that, right?"

Julia nodded. "I can. Be careful, look after yourselves, and get back here quickly,"

"We will." Uncle Wally kissed Julia on the top of her head and led Sarah away.

Chapter Twenty-Five

"How long have we been climbing?" Sarah asked.

"It has been two hours," Adigo, the Somalian man leading their troupe, answered. "We are nearly there. Do you thirst?"

"Yes, I do," Sarah answered. "I'm very thirsty."

"That is good. You need to be thirsty, to be uncomfortable. It will make your power stronger."

Sarah didn't ask what that meant, she just cleared her throat and continued to climb the narrow path on the dusty, hot cliff face. She was lucky that it was a fairly easy climb, she supposed, though the oppressive heat made it so much harder. Her thirst was making her lightheaded, and the card box, now safe inside her t-shirt that was tucked into her jeans, was sticking against her clammy skin.

"We draw close now, and the curse will try to stop you proceeding. You must use care," Adigo told her. "Be careful, but smart. We will help you."

"See the blue rocks there?" Uncle Wally pointed off to the left of the path, maybe a hundred feet ahead.

"Yeah," Sarah replied.

"That's where we're headed. Not too far now."

Adigo sent his dogs up ahead, and everyone paused when the dogs grew angry, barking and snarling. They all waited until the dogs quietened, then proceeded. Sarah looked around at the men walking with her, there were twelve of them, a fairly equal mix of Somali and Aboriginals, and they had at least as many dogs accompanying them. Sarah thought all of the dogs looked like dingos, but she was no expert. They could have been anything, but she decided she would think of them as dingos.

The dogs had given her a wide berth and would whine and growl if she got too close. She knew it was because of the cards, and the curse they felt, but she still felt saddened that she couldn't touch one of these magnificent creatures.

The blue boulders were at the start of a path that no longer climbed so steeply, instead it took them along a winding, twisting track that led through stumpy trees and windblown shrubs. There were many birds singing loudly in the bright sunlight, and Sarah caught glimpses of bush wallabies here and there, all darting off when they heard the dogs and walkers approach.

They came to a massive circle of sandstone boulders, they seemed impenetrable but Adigo led the way around and they came upon a clearing. This one didn't look like a natural phenomenon; the ground was neatly swept and clear of any detritus, the rocks were adorned with many paintings, some fairly new, some that looked ancient, and there were little offerings of twigs, flowers and branches poking out from seams and crevices in the boulders.

Sarah could feel the reverence and power of this site, and she moved to follow the others as they filed into the clearing.

She couldn’t enter the hollow in the boulders.

Her legs stopped and refused to go any further. The dogs started to bark and howl, and the bright sky, normally devoid of any clouds, grew suddenly dark and stormy. Uncle Wally looked at her and then called out to the others in a language Sarah could not understand. They barked something back to him, and she felt herself lifted roughly up and carried through the opening and placed into the middle of the clearing.

Three of the men placed sticks and branches in the entrance and lit them, with most of the dogs inside and only two or three left out to guard the sacred place.

Sarah stood still, unmoving, her body betraying her in its motionless stance. She couldn't even move an arm; her feet were planted firmly in the sand and her head was like a rock on her shoulders. Only her eyes moved, only her eyes did not betray her.

Two of the men lifted her from the centre of the clearing and placed her to the farthest position from the entrance, her back at the rocks, her front facing the opening. She watched as they lit another fire, this one in the centre where she had been standing, and they sang and danced around the fire, calling on their spirits, their forefathers, and whatever gods and deities they begged to help them in their quest. Sarah could do nothing but stand and watch, her armpits pricking with sticky fear, her arms covered in goosebumps.

The dogs started to bark, running around the clearing, agitated and angry, and Sarah could see a figure standing on the other side of the entrance. It was obscured by the fire, hard to see, but it was there. She had no doubt that it was the dark man, though he was tall and as dark skinned as Adigo. She couldn't call out to anyone to warn them, though Wally seemed to notice and spoke to the others, pointing to the entrance as he did so.

Someone threw something on the fire at the entrance and it sparked and hissed, crackling like gunpowder. Sarah couldn't see the figure again. She heard the dogs outside barking and growling, perhaps trying to keep the dark man away, but her goosebumps told her they were not successful.

After what seemed like hours, but was probably only minutes, Sarah felt the stiffness leaving her body and she slumped to the ground, sitting with the boulders against her back. The men continued to sing and dance, the baritone rhythms soothing, mesmerising, and she felt her eyes close.

She didn't realise she had fallen asleep until someone shook her, and she opened her eyes to peer into a pair of dark, unfamiliar orbs. She drew breath to scream but he placed a finger on her lips. It was the dark man. She knew it, she could feel it, and he knew her. He drew back and for the first time Sarah saw his face.

He had high cheekbones, a strong, firm jawline, and a rugged look about him. The dark eyes were not brown or black, they were the deepest blue, a dark, deep sea blue, strange, wild, and savage. He smiled at her, his perfectly white, even teeth revealed behind his full lips.

"Who are you?" Sarah asked him, her voice a husky whisper.

"I am you," he answered, his accent, while strong and thick, unrecognizable. "I am all that was, and all that will be. I am forever, Sarah, and I am yours. Come with me, come away from here, and do not let these people part us. Once we are apart, we both shall die, but together we can live forever."

"You killed people, you hurt people, I don't want to go with you."

"I hurt no one, my love. I did nothing except give you the power, and it was you that destroyed those enemies of yours. I exist only to love you and obey you and make your every wish come true. Come with me, my love, come with me."

Sarah felt his power and felt his love for her. He loved her, she could tell that with every fibre of her being, with her entire heart and soul. This strange dark man loved her, and he would love her forever.

It was the kind of love that would never die, that she had searched her whole life to find. People lived and died looking for this kind of love, and here it was, all hers, to take with just one word.

"Say yes to me, my love. Say you will come with me, and we will live together, we will love together, forever. No one can come between us. Just say yes, and all these men will disappear, everyone that ties to you will be gone, and there will be just us. Just you and I, forever. Just say yes."

Sarah started to breathe faster, harder. Her heart was racing, and she could feel a cold sweat break out all over her.

"Please, my love, my heart, my every desire, please just say yes, and we will be together forever."

"That's all I need to do?" Sarah asked. "I just say that, and we can leave here?"

"That is right, my love. Say yes and I will take you away from everyone and everything. You will have everything you ever desired, everything you could ever imagine." He smiled at her again, and Sarah felt her stomach flip, her face hot and flushed, her body aching for his touch.

He held his hand out to her. "Take my hand now and tell me yes."

"What is your name?" Sarah asked.

"My name will be whatever you want it to be. I will be yours, just take my hand, my love, tell me yes." His dark blue eyes looked into her very soul. "I love you, Sarah, I will always love you. Be mine, my child, be mine forever. Just tell me yes."

Sarah looked at him, feeling her body long for him, yearning for his touch.

"I can touch you again, my love. You know how wonderful our bodies are together, you know the magic we can make. Say yes to me, say yes and we can be together again."

"No," Sarah gasped at her reply, shocked at her own conviction. "No, I will never say anything other than no *to you. I love my family, and I want them safe. NO, you hear me? NO!"*

The hands that roughly shook her awake grabbed her into a hug, and a soft kiss on her forehead woke her completely. "You are very strong, child. You should be proud of yourself. We are ready for you now, let me help you up."

Sarah let Uncle Wally lift her up and hold onto her until she had the strength to stand on her own.

"It wasn't easy to reject him, was it?" he asked her.

"Actually, it was the only choice," she replied. "He would have killed everyone, all of you, my family, my friends, I could only ever say no to that."

"We have the fire ready, and we have made a great hole for you to bury the cards," Adigo told her.

"Why don't we burn them?" Sarah asked.

"That will release the cursed spirits into the earth, we don't want that to happen," he explained.

"We need you to hold out the cards now for us to bind them, child," Uncle Wally said. "Take them from the box and their wrappings and hold them out for us."

Sarah did as they asked, placing the boxes and the two cloth wrappings at her feet. The men chanted and splashed her with water, and then tied the cards with fibrous reeds, careful to not touch the cards as they twisted and wrapped the reeds around them. They then indicated for her to wrap them, each time a new binding went on, then she placed them in the wooden box, which also got a series of bindings, finally the lead lined box, and it, too, was bound and blessed.

The dogs started to bark and howl, screaming in

fear and anger, and Sarah could feel her hair stand on end, she felt like electricity was racing through her veins. The dogs turned towards her, barking and foaming at the mouth, but Sarah tried to ignore them. She held the box out in front of her as the sky went from grey to black, and lightning split the darkness. Thunder boomed and the wind lashed around them, sleeting rain beating down.

The storm was as shocking and powerful as the one that wracked her mother's property. The dogs became fearful and backed away, huddling to one side as the storm grew in intensity. The rain was harder now, soaking Sarah to the bone, flooding the clearing, but not putting out the fire. As Sarah tried to peer through her soaking eyelashes, she marvelled that the fire was still roaring, it seemed to grow in ferocity, in direct correlation with the fierceness of the storm.

A hand on her shoulder made her jump, and Adigo leaned in to speak in her ear so she could hear him over the thunder.

"Now, child, throw the cards into the hole, do it now."

Sarah stepped forward but another voice in her ear stilled her motion.

"*Do not abandon me, my love,*" the breathy, deep voice of the dark man resonated and reverberated through her skull.

She took a deep breath, sputtering at the rain that filled her mouth, but kept her resolve. "*Sarah do not abandon me. I am here, I am your willing slave in love. Please do not betray me, my love, do not abandon me*."

She was at the edge of the gaping hole, and even though the clearing was now at least ankle deep in yellow, muddy freezing water, none fell down the hole. Instead it swirled and spun around the edge, none spilling into the hole that waited for its burden.

Sarah released her breath and threw the box of cards into the hole, as she leaned forward, she could see them fall and was shocked how deep the hole seemed to go. Uncle Wally grabbed her arm and handed her a shovel, pointing to the hole.

He was shouting at her, but it was impossible to hear what he was saying so she just took a guess that she was to fill it in. Although the dirt surrounding the hole couldn't be seen under the water, Sarah scooped up a shovel full of wet, sloppy sand and threw it into the hole. She did this a few times before the men joined in, quickly shovelling the yellow sand in. As they filled in the hole the storm lessened, the fierceness subsided, until there was just rain and a very light wind. The thunder and lightning were gone, and the water drained quickly from the clearing. By the time the last shovel full of sandy dirt was patted on the top of the hole the sky had cleared, and a setting summer sun warmed the wet people with gentle rays of sunshine.

The men chanted and sang for a little longer, and as they did the dogs came up to Sarah, sniffing her, wagging their tails, and licking her hands.

She breathed a deep sigh of relief as the men stopped, and the fire died out on its own as if a switch was flicked. They walked over to the fire at the entrance and pulled the burning branches away, letting the fire die naturally.

"We can leave now, young lady," Uncle Wally was smiling at her, his face tired. "We can go back down the mountain, it is done. The cards are bound and buried in sacred land, they cannot get out, they no longer have any hold over you."

Sarah burst into tears as she fell into the man's arms. She sobbed uncontrollably for several minutes, and Wally let her, his arms around her shoulders in a comforting embrace. When she could control her sobs Uncle Wally helped her stand on her own, and he handed her a wad of tissues from his pocket. They were soaking wet, but Sarah still wiped her face and smiled at the man. "Is it really done?"

"It is done," Adigo called out to her. "We must thank you for allowing us to contain this evil, to rid the world of this curse."

"I was going to thank all of you, you sacrificed so much to help me!"

"That's what you think, but no, we have a duty to remove these things from this land. This is our sacred duty, and one we have chosen to pursue. You were very strong and very brave to find us and bring the curse to us to break."

"My mother found you, really."

"You may think that, but it was you that started the search, it was your latent powers that sought us out and found us."

"My latent powers?"

Uncle Wally laughed. "You didn't know you had

talent? Why, that's the reason the cards attached to you! If you were without powers you would not have survived, just like the previous owners. The cards sought out your power, trying to bind themselves to you to make them invincible. You proved too powerful for that. One day you should return to us and we can teach you how to use your powers, and how to do what we have done today. Maybe you'll even join us in the hunt to destroy all evil."

"Not so much," Sarah laughed. "I think I'd just like a normal life for a little while."

Uncle Wally ushered her out of the opening and Sarah looked around in shock. "It's dry out here!"

"It seems the rain only fell in the sacred place, same as it did on your mother's house," Uncle Wally remarked. "Well, that is the last of that. Let's get down the mountain and have something to eat. All this exercise has made me starve. Oh, I meant to tell you, that boy you like, Michael? He's a really great guy. He's perfect for you!"

Chapter Twenty-Six

Sarah threw her duffle bag into the boot of her car and turned to give her mother a crushing hug. "I can't tell you how much you mean to me," she told her. "And thank you for everything."

"I'm so glad you came to me and let me help. And that we got a couple of days together without the worry of all of the, well, you know."

"Yeah, yeah, I do. I'm also happy my hair stayed, it's nice to have a decent head of hair! I know there's no guarantee it will stay forever, but I'll take it for now."

"Nice that your little kitten stayed as well. You back at work on Monday?" Alison asked as Sarah climbed into the car.

"Yeah, I have one day at home then back on Monday. I'm actually looking forward to it, now I know Paul looked after things fairly okay. And he's desperate for me to get back, he's run off his feet."

"Well drive safe baby, and ring me when you get home."

"I will!" Sarah started the car and Alison reached in to give Lilly a pat, before waving as Sarah drove away.

The drive home was fairly quick, the traffic light and the roads clear. She stopped at a supermarket for supplies, the kitten still under her hair, and she was pleased that there were no figures following her, no shadows that moved, no half-seen dark man from the corner of her eye.

She parked out the back of her apartment building and pulled her duffle bag out of the boot, along with her shopping, and struggled to get the door open to the foyer. As the elevator door opened, she sighed, now she'd have to drag the heavy bag and balance her shopping bags all along her corridor to her apartment.

"I've been waiting for you," Michael smiled at her from the elevator. "Let me take some of that, please."

Sarah felt her face grow warm. "Oh my god yes, thank you. It's all too heavy."

"I was so happy when I saw your car pull in, I was just getting ready to go and get something to eat. If you want, we can go and get something together?"

Sarah nodded. "I think I'd like that a lot," she stopped at her door and put the key in the lock. "If you can give me ten minutes to clean up, I'll be right there."

Michael hadn't stopped smiling, and Sarah was over the moon that he looked so happy to see her. "I'll wait in my apartment, with the door open, so just yell when you're ready."

She opened her door and beamed when she saw her plants were still lush and green, and Lilly meowed and jumped from her shoulder. Sarah fed the kitten and quickly showered and changed, not bothering with makeup. Lilly found her place on

Sarah's pillow, happy, it seemed, to be home and just wanting to sleep.

Sarah checked herself in the mirror before going out, and what she saw made her pause. Somehow Sarah looked different. There was something in her eyes that wasn't there before, some of the youthful carelessness was gone, and, she feared, gone forever. No one could come through what she had and not be changed, she supposed, and she would have to find a way to live with what happened.

A way to live in spite of what happened.

She wasn't going to let the cards win, she was going to be happy, and tonight was the first step in making that happen.

She opened her door and Michael was standing there, leaning against his own door, a single red rose in his hands.

"You look beautiful," he said.

Sarah blushed and smiled back at him. Yes, she was going to be happy.

Acknowledgements:

With thanks, as always, to my children. You are my inspiration.

I am so grateful to my publisher and editor Peter Blakey-Novis and his wonderful partner in crime Leanne, without whom this book would never have eventuated.

Thank you to my wonderful friends, Helen, Joan, Alison, Julia, and Vikki. Sorry I killed off some of you, nothing personal.

Thank you to Mary for being my practice reader, your feedback was beyond useful.

Thank you to Todd, for your invaluable support and letting me bounce some plot ideas and possible titles off you.

Thank you to all the wonderful readers who have left a review, you have no idea how special and inspirational they truly are. Please leave a review if you can, if it's not too much trouble and you enjoyed this book. Know always that I am inspired and sustained by them and wouldn't be able to continue without them.

Also from Red Cape Publishing

Anthologies:

Elements of Horror Book One: Earth
Elements of Horror Book Two: Air
Elements of Horror Book Three: Fire
Elements of Horror Book Four: Water
A is for Aliens: A to Z of Horror Book One
B is for Beasts: A to Z of Horror Book Two
C is for Cannibals: A to Z of Horror Book Three
D is for Demons: A to Z of Horror Book Four
E is for Exorcism: A to Z of Horror Book Five
F is for Fear: A to Z of Horror Book Six
G is for Genies: A to Z of Horror Book Seven
H is for Hell: A to Z of Horror Book Eight
It Came From The Darkness: A Charity Anthology

Short Story Collections:

Embrace the Darkness by P.J. Blakey-Novis
Tunnels by P.J. Blakey-Novis
The Artist by P.J. Blakey-Novis
Karma by P.J. Blakey-Novis
The Place Between Worlds by P.J. Blakey-Novis
Short Horror Stories by P.J. Blakey-Novis
Keep It Inside & Other Weird Tales by Mark Anthony Smith

Children's Books:

Grace & Bobo: The Trip to the Future by Peter Blakey-Novis
The Little Bat That Could by Gemma Paul
The Mummy Walks At Midnight by Gemma Paul
A Very Zombie Christmas by Gemma Paul

Novelettes:

The Ivory Tower by Antoinette Corvo

Novellas:

Four by P.J. Blakey-Novis
Dirges in the Dark by Antoinette Corvo
The Cat That Caught The Canary by Antoinette Corvo

Novels:

Madman Across the Water by Caroline Angel
The Curse Awakens by Caroline Angel
Less by Caroline Angel
Where Shadows Move by Caroline Angel
The Broken Doll by P.J. Blakey-Novis
The Broken Doll: Shattered Pieces by P.J. Blakey-Novis
The Vegas Rift by David F. Gray

Follow Red Cape Publishing

www.redcapepublishing.com
www.facebook.com/redcapepublishing
www.twitter.com/redcapepublish
www.instagram.com/redcapepublishing
www.pinterest.co.uk/redcapepublishing
www.patreon.com/redcapepublishing

Printed in Great Britain
by Amazon

42341803R00175